D0270600

A BLOODY HOT Summer

Trevor D'Silva

Withdrawn from Stock
Dublin City Public Libraries

Black Rose Writing | Texas

© 2019 by Trevor D'Silva
All rights reserved. No part of this book may be reproduced, stored in a retrieval system or transmitted in any form or by any means without the prior written permission of the publishers, except by a reviewer who may quote brief passages in a review to be printed in a newspaper, magazine or journal.

The author grants the final approval for this literary material.

First printing

This is a work of fiction. Names, characters, businesses, places, events, and incidents are either the products of the author's imagination or used in a fictitious manner. Any resemblance to actual persons, living or dead, or actual events is purely coincidental.

ISBN: 978-1-68433-371-4
PUBLISHED BY BLACK ROSE WRITING
www.blackrosewriting.com

Printed in the United States of America
Suggested Retail Price (SRP) $18.95

A Bloody Hot Summer is printed in Chaparral Pro

I take the opportunity to thank Reagan Rothe and the staff at Black Rose Writing for publishing this book.

I thank my editor, Dr. Angela Stokes, for editing this novel to make it suitable for publication and for also giving the characters their authentic British accents, which gives this book the aura of a proper British mystery.

I would also like to thank Prepare to Publish Ltd for proofreading the book. Lastly, I would like to acknowledge Dame Agatha Christie and Sir Arthur Conan Doyle, whose books gave me countless hours of pleasure, an understanding of British crime fiction, and the inspiration to write my own detective story.

I dedicate this book to my late grandmother, Maisie Saldanha, who was the first to recognise my love for writing and gifted me with a dictionary to encourage me to pursue my writing endeavours. She also gave me the confidence to start reading books at a very young age, and being with her was like being in the time period the book is set in.

To the Reader:

There is nothing more British than a good murder mystery set in the beautiful English countryside during the 1920s and 30s. That is why I decided to set my first murder mystery in England during the 1920s. Since this book is set primarily in Britain, I thought it appropriate to write it in British English. The editing of this novel was also done by a British editor to give the characters their authentic upper class, Cockney, and Scottish accents. Some of the dialogue may seem grammatically incorrect, but it reflects the authentic way the working class spoke in England.

For the convenience of American readers and/or those not familiar with British English slang or phrases, a glossary has been added after the Epilogue. It is my intention that the glossary will help the reader with any unfamiliar terms and, at the same time, enable the reader to learn a little more about British English and the history of the British Empire and its colonies.

Revenge is an act of passion; vengeance of justice.
Injuries are revenged; crimes are avenged.
— Samuel Johnson (1709–1784)

Pembroke Branch Tel. 6689575

Prologue

Argyle Castle Grounds, Scottish Highlands – January, 1903
It was a cold foggy night and the only sound was of the snow crunching under the feet of the couple walking up the path towards a small and isolated cottage. Wearing a long woollen coat and a flat cap, and tightly clutching a basket, the man towered over the woman walking beside him who, despite also being dressed in heavy clothing, visibly shook with the cold. The man knocked on the cottage door and it was quickly opened by a smiling middle-aged woman who pulled nervously at her bedraggled clothes when she recognised her visitors.

"Here y'are, finally..." she said. She looked at the shivering woman. "Ye poor wee hen, you're shivering, aren't ye? Come in an' get yourself warm."

The warmth from the roaring fire enveloped them as the couple entered the cottage and they felt their bodies finally relax. The shaking woman stood by the large fireplace, palms to the flames. A large cooking pot was bubbling and hissing over the fire and the comforting smell of stew wafted through the air, causing the couple's empty stomachs to grumble in anticipation. The man walked towards the large wooden table that filled the room and placed the basket down on the floor next to one of the chairs. The blanket in the basket seemed to move and the middle-aged woman bent down and slowly removed it.

"Ach! She's a bonnie wee bairn. How old is she?"

"A few months old, Mrs. Blair," said the man. "You have always been faithful to Lady Argyle's family and she trusts you with this. As agreed, we need to keep this a secret; not a word to anyone. We will send the money for the child. All you have to do is raise her as your own and make sure that she knows nothing until we say so. Is that understood?" he said, staring at her intensely.

Mrs. Blair's smile slowly vanished. "I understand, sir. Her Ladyship has already spoken tae me... Tae avoid any questions, I've already told folk here that she's my nephew's daughter an' her parents were killed in a carriage accident in London. My husband, Ewan, an' I will bring her up as our own."

"That's good. I am placing the money on the table. We'll send you more and our address in case you need to get in touch with us."

"Very good, sir. Thank ye for the money; I will wait for yer letter. When will ye be back tae see her?"

"Not sure, but if we do she must never know who we are... We have to leave now. We'll say goodbye to the child."

The man and the woman kissed the baby, took one last look, and went out of the door into the foggy night.

"I hope we're doing the right thing," said the woman with tears in her eyes.

"Yes, we are. We must do it for her. She's the only thing that matters now. Tomorrow we go to England and, no matter how long it takes, we'll accomplish what we came to do."

The woman smiled sadly as they walked down the snowy garden path towards a horse-drawn carriage that was waiting for them.

Chapter 1: A Delightful Gathering

Meadowford Village – June, 1927

"We will be arriving at Meadowford shortly, ladies and gentleman," the guard called as he passed through the carriage, pulling Arthur reluctantly out of his thoughts. Fond memories had come flooding back as the familiar views of the town nestled in cattle-filled meadows had come into view; it felt like a lifetime ago. Arthur gulped down the remaining liquor in his hipflask and made his way to the end of the carriage to alight from the train.

Despite the bustle of people on the platform, Arthur stood still for a moment. He lifted his fedora and wiped at his brow with a handkerchief. "Thought I'd left the heat behind in India," he muttered under his breath. He glanced around to get his bearings. The heady scent of the meadows surrounding the town mixed with the heavy coal smoke of the train as it left the station behind, slowly revealing the settlement behind it.

"Welcome to Meadowford Village, sir. Can I help you with your cases?" a porter asked, walking towards him.

"Thank you. I'll be needing a taxi too."

"Yes, sir," the porter replied as he picked up Arthur's suitcases. "Right this way."

As the two men exited the station, Arthur was taken aback by how much the village had changed since he was last here. "I reckon you've not been 'ere in a while," the porter said as he hailed a taxi.

"You are right. I was last here before the war, when I brought my bride to meet my family."

"Blimey, well a lot has changed in Meadowford since then, sir. We lost a lot of men, made it hard for a while. Things lookin' up now though; Meadowford's more of a town than village. Even got two inns now, you know. Of course, the Fitzhughs still own all the land abouts and plenty of farmers rent from them. That Lady Fitzhugh is celebrating her eightieth this week…"

"Which one?" the taxi driver asked as he pulled up in front of them. "The Meadowford Inn or the Carlton Inn?"

"Fitzhugh Manor... please," Arthur replied, smiling wryly as the porter and the driver looked at each other in surprise.

The taxi bounced as the car crossed the route of the long-gone ford for which the village was named. Arthur stopped paying attention to the scenery, closed his eyes and let his head fall back. He was glad that this long journey was coming to an end.

— — —

The residents of Fitzhugh Manor, a stately pile built during the reign of King Henry VII, were also feeling the effects of the heat. Inside the manor, preparations were hurriedly being finished for the eightieth birthday party of Lady Doris Fitzhugh. She was a spinster who had inherited the manor and its surrounding farmland when her father, Lord William Fitzhugh, had died of septicaemia some years before. A no-nonsense woman, Lady Fitzhugh didn't tolerate any unruly behaviour and she single-handedly oversaw the workings of the entire estate. She was held in high esteem by her family, the villagers, and the manor staff alike.

The kitchen downstairs was a bustle of activity. Slattery, the elderly butler, entered the servants' dining room where the food for the birthday dinner was laid out on the dining table, a wine bottle in each of his hands. He saw Alice – a slim, blonde, and attractive maid – sitting on the table next to the food, smoking a cigarette.

"Get off the table. Not near the food, for heaven's sake, child," he yelled at her.

She got up slowly and looked at him. "I'm on me break. You asked me t'look after the food and keep the flies away. I'm doin' just that!"

"But no smoking near the food. We wouldn't want cigarette ash or smoke on her Ladyship's celebration dinner, would we?"

Alice rolled her eyes. "I'm goin' outside t'finish me smoke."

"The guests will be arriving soon. Don't stay out too long." He placed the two wine bottles on a side table and smiled. "Her Ladyship has given us these because it's her birthday. We can have our own celebration here tonight."

Alice sighed. "Not likely with Miss Carter around. She'll pour the wine herself – you know how she hates us having a drink. I miss when your wife was housekeeper. She always let us 'ave some fun."

"Come now. Miss Carter only means well. She takes her duties seriously. Now, hurry up and finish that cigarette before Miss Carter sees you."

— — —

As the clock in the main hall struck six, the first of the evening's guests began to arrive. Slattery opened the door and greeted Reverend Joseph Howard of nearby St. Andrew's Church and his wife, Henrietta.

"Reverend, Mrs. Howard, how lovely you could come," said Pippa Fitzhugh enthusiastically as she rushed towards them. "Please come in and join the family in the drawing room while we wait for the birthday girl!" Pippa ushered them away from the front door and into the drawing room where she handed them both a glass of champagne from the table.

Pippa heard Slattery greeting the next guest and, recognising Richard Seymour's voice, she excused herself and almost ran out of the drawing room, smoothing her short bob-styled hair as she went. Her face lit up when she saw him and she held out her hands.

"Darling, how nice to see you; I am so glad that you came."

Richard, his dazzling smile returning her own, took hold of her hands as he stepped towards her. "Actually, I am quite surprised that I was invited a few hours before, considering that your aunts don't like me."

"My aunts seem to be warming to you, especially Aunt Flora. She's the nice one. Even Aunt Doris is beginning to like you. It was she who said that you could come," Pippa explained. "Please give Aunt Lilian some time."

"I will, my dear," he said as they walked into the drawing room together.

The next guests to arrive were Major Percival Havelock and his wife, Gerda. Slattery showed them into the drawing room and they were greeted by members of the family. Major Havelock walked with a limp; an old war wound in his right leg. He had served with Lord William Fitzhugh in South Africa during the Boer War, and Lady Doris Fitzhugh regarded him as a close friend and a member of the family.

The final guest to arrive at the manor was the family solicitor, Mr. Bertram Kerr. Lady Fitzhugh trusted him just as much as her father had. Tonight though, he looked less than his usual dapper self.

"Sorry for my dishevelment," he muttered to Slattery as he passed over his coat and hat. "It has been a very trying day." Mr. Kerr turned to the mirror to the left of the door, ran a hand over his balding head and adjusted his collar. "Don't just stand there, man," he snapped at Slattery. "Tell her Ladyship I have arrived… And bring me a brandy immediately."

— — —

Lady Doris Fitzhugh looked in the mirror and was pleased with her reflection. Her mother's emerald necklace complemented the emerald earrings she wore. She placed the diamond earrings which she had initially intended to wear back into the box and reached for the perfume bottle. As she dabbed the fragrance behind her ears, she heard a knock on the door.

"Enter," she answered, and the door opened. She saw the reflection of the person in the mirror. "Ahh! I've been waiting for you. Please come in. You will like what I've got to tell you."

After the person left, Lady Fitzhugh looked one last time in the mirror. Satisfied with her appearance, she got up and went out of her bedroom. She walked slowly down the staircase, holding on to the banister. She liked being independent. It was what her father had liked most about her, besides her sharp intelligence and resourcefulness.

Lady Fitzhugh's family and guests greeted her as she entered the drawing room. She was glad that everyone whom she cared about had come for her party. The last time she had celebrated her birthday was when she had turned seventy-five.

"Delightful gathering for your birthday, Aunt Doris," said Pippa.

"Yes, Pippa. After all, it is not very often that one turns eighty. Although I do wish your father were here to celebrate with us."

She saw Bertram Kerr, whom she fondly called Bertie, and he smiled at her. He came over and wished her a happy birthday and then bent forward a little and quickly whispered to her. She nodded. He went and sat down as Alice came towards him with a tray of champagne glasses.

Lady Fitzhugh spied her two sisters, Flora and Lilian, sitting together and walked towards them. Flora Ainsworth was three years younger than Doris and was the most amiable of the sisters. Her face exuded kindness, but at the same time commanded respect from anyone who met her. At seventy-five, Lilian Endecott was the youngest of the three sisters; however, she appeared to be older due to her morose and feisty nature and her habit of brazenly complaining all of the time. She was sometimes referred to as 'the battleaxe' by people who were unfortunate enough to be at the receiving end of her wrath.

"Delightful gathering but would be a lot better if we did not have this heatwave," said Flora. "I hope it ends soon; a few days is plenty."

"Hope it doesn't portend that something bad is about to happen. Reminds me of the heat back in India," said Lady Fitzhugh.

"I think Pippa going out with that Richard is an outrage," said Lilian, adjusting the pearls around her neck as she nodded towards the couple at the far end of the room. "Fancy a young girl like her, not long turned twenty-two, going out with some man twenty-five years her senior."

"Come now, Lilian, you and Edward were fifteen years apart. That didn't stop you from marrying him," said Flora.

"That was different. Edward knew Father and Father approved of him. God knows where Pippa met that man. We know nothing about him."

"Pippa said that she met him in London, at an art gallery. He's a painter – landscapes and portraits," said Lady Fitzhugh as she sat down next to Flora.

"He's even painted a portrait of Pippa, which hangs on her bedroom wall. She showed it to me, and I must say that he does have talent... and he is very handsome," added Flora.

"Good looks don't make up for poor breeding... It would've been good if she'd told us why she wanted to live in London. Cora should've put a stop to it. I wish Father or Allan were alive," said Lilian wistfully. "They would not have allowed it."

At that moment, a sickly boy – aged about thirteen – came into the room. He was chatting animatedly to a woman who was around fifty years old but looked older than that. She came towards her three elderly sisters-in-law, while the boy went towards the table.

"Ah, Cora, how's Hector doing?" asked Lady Fitzhugh.

"His fever has gone, but otherwise he is still the same." She frowned lovingly at the boy. "He refuses to take his tonic. He claims that he feels better when he doesn't take it."

"Dr. Fielding should probably take a look at him again."

"He did. He said that Hector needs to take his tonic and I'm trying to make sure that he does."

Lilian looked up as her son, an ashen-faced man in his late forties, came last into the room, wiping the sweat from his forehead with the sleeve of his expensively tailored suit. Without speaking to the others, he grabbed a glass of champagne and drank it, the colour returning to his cheeks. Lilian shook her head with disapproval. She and Arthur didn't get along because of his bad habits, but she still loved him. Arthur Endecott had recently returned from India, where he lived with his wife and three children. He claimed that he had come back for his aunt's birthday celebration, but everyone knew that wasn't true.

Lilian glanced back at Doris. "What was he talking to you about two days ago? He didn't look happy when he came out of your bedroom."

"It's between Arthur and me, Lilian. Once this party is over and when I've done what needs to be done, I will let you know in good time."

Lilian was annoyed. Even though they were adults, Doris still treated her sisters like children. They knew that she loved them, but they resented her air of superiority. Doris didn't notice Lilian's annoyance though because she waved her hand to get the attention of Mr. Kerr. When he looked at her, she beckoned him to come to her. She lowered her voice and asked him to wait in the library. A few minutes after he left, Doris got up and followed him.

Half an hour later, Bertram Kerr left the library and told Miss Carter and Slattery that Lady Fitzhugh wanted to speak to them. They both went into the library and she asked them to close the door. Ten minutes later, Lady Fitzhugh entered the drawing room. Her family and guests noticed that she looked happier than before. They wondered what had transpired between Bertram Kerr and her, but knew better than to ask.

Shortly after, Slattery came in and announced that dinner was served. Arthur insisted on leading his aunt, Lady Fitzhugh, to the dining table and the guests followed them. Lady Fitzhugh sat at the head of the table with her sisters on either side.

Arthur, who sat at the foot of the table, stood up and toasted his aunt. He wished her good health and happiness for many more years to come and made it a point to say that she was his favourite aunt. Some of the family and guests rolled their eyes as he said this. After the toast, they all clinked their glasses together and drank their wine.

After dinner, the family and guests retired to the drawing room where Slattery, followed by the staff, brought out the birthday cake. They all sang 'Happy Birthday' to Lady Fitzhugh and she blew out the candles. She thanked everyone for coming and stated that she was the first in the family to live to that ripe old age, and she looked forward to many more years and possibly a hundredth birthday.

When the last guest had left, Doris wished her family a good night and went upstairs to her bedroom.

— — —

The next morning, Alice went to Lady Fitzhugh's room, taking with her a tray of tea and a slice of toast. When she entered the bedroom, she noticed something was amiss. She went closer to the bed and looked. The next moment, her screams reverberated throughout the mansion as the tray fell, scattering its contents on the bedroom floor.

Chapter 2: Revolt in Kamalpore

British Cantonment, Kamalpore, Northern India – June, 1857
The whole country was in a state of tension about the impending rebellion by the sepoys and the native population. Rumours were spreading like wildfire that the cartridges for the newly issued Enfield rifle were greased with the fat of cows and pigs when manufactured at the English munitions factories. These rumours hurt the religious sentiments of the native Hindu and Moslem sepoys and sparked rebellion in many sepoy companies. The European population in India, especially the English, knew that they would be targeted by the natives for extermination. Even the Anglo-Indians were not immune from the wrath of the natives.

The scouts presented themselves to the two senior officers. The Indian summer was now in full swing and the heat inside the commander's room had them all sweating.

"Well, Chindi and Ram, what have you found out?" asked William Fitzhugh, wiping at his brow.

"Sahib, the rumours are true. The sepoys and people all over India are revolting against the British. You are not safe here," said Chindi.

"Damn it," Theo Fitzhugh shouted, leaning back in his chair and running his hand through his hair. "A single rumour – one which has no basis – and it has spread like a canker through the country. I have even had sepoys defect from the garrison. It will take a long time before this whole business will die down."

"What about the Maharaja?" William asked the scouts calmly. "Is he still loyal to the British?"

"Forgive us, Sahib, but we heard that he has joined the rebels. Since he is a Hindu and the cow is sacred to him, like the sepoys he is also very offended that the British might taint the cartridges with their fat. He has asked the Moslems in Kamalpore to join him in kicking the firangi out of India," said Ram.

"That swine!" said William, banging his fist loudly on the table. "He should honour his treaty to protect us. We would side with him if his enemies attacked Kamalpore."

"Calm down, William," said Theo firmly. "We need to think what to do next. The Maharaja isn't going to help us even though he welcomed us three years earlier and occasionally played polo with us and the garrison soldiers. These absurd rumours have made him distrust the British completely. Our position puts Kamalpore and the rebel threat to the front of us, so our only hope is escaping through the jungle behind, but the next British garrison is more than two days journey from here."

"Yes, but we need to think of our families. I've heard rumours that the natives have violated European women and murdered them along with their children. We must do something," said William.

"Let's send the scouts back to Kamalpore again to see if they can find out if an attack on the garrison is imminent. We have many soldiers and we can withstand an attack if it comes, but we cannot chance sending our families unprotected through the jungle."

"Good idea, Theo," said William. He reached into his pocket, took out four gold coins and placed them on the table. "Shabash! You have done well. Now, after a nice meal and some rest, disguise yourselves and go back into Kamalpore. If you find out anything about an attack on the garrison, let us know. You will be well rewarded for your loyalty."

"Thank you, Sahibs," the two scouts said in unison. They took the gold coins and smiled to each other as they went out of the door.

Theo then went out of his office and ordered his soldiers to be on high alert. The gates were to be locked at all times and nobody was to leave the garrison.

— — —

Clara Fitzhugh called her three daughters – Doris, Flora, and Lilian – aside and warned them not to go out of the garrison's gates.

"We just want to go to the pond," said seven-year-old Flora.

"No, children, it's not safe. These walls will protect us." From the corner of her eyes, Clara spied Sitara Bai, the ayah, who took care of the children. She beckoned her to come towards them. "Sitara, make sure that they do not leave the compound."

"Yes, Memsahib."

"Now, children, ask Sitara to tell you the story of how she got her name."

The children ran towards the Indian woman, who was dressed in a green sari with her head covered. Sitara loved the three British children like they were her own and in turn they were fascinated by her stories of her youth, especially the tale of how she got her name. She explained again how at the moment she was born a star had flown across the sky. Her father, thinking it a good omen, had added Tara, which meant star, to the name Sita. Despite her lucky name, life had not been kind to Sitara. Years of marriage had not gifted her with the children that she craved; instead she was labelled with the shame of being barren. As a result, her husband, Manu Lal, shunned her and had taken another wife with whom he ran a brothel providing entertainment, alcohol, music, and nautch girls for the men from the city and the English and native soldiers from the garrison. Despite her sadness, Sitara had found contentedness with her English charges.

Clara spotted her husband, William Fitzhugh, sitting on the veranda of the house, drinking whisky. He was a tall man with red hair and a mutton chop moustache. Clara sighed and thought back to the day they first met. Her father, a British general, had hosted a party at his bungalow in Calcutta. William was a soldier in the Hussar Regiment in Calcutta, and she had been smitten by his good looks and charm, and he by her innocence. They got married shortly afterwards, when they were both only twenty years old. She had been warned that he was a philanderer, but she thought she could change him. When she couldn't conceive again after their third daughter, Lilian, was born, he lost interest in her and started carrying on with other women. She knew he loved their daughters, but he'd wanted a son and she couldn't give him one. Clara, however, was raised with the belief that marriage was a sacred union until death and that is why she stayed with William, even though she knew that he was a frequent visitor to Manu Lal's brothel.

Clara walked across the compound towards her husband. As she sat beside him, William nodded towards his older brother and his family.

"There's Theo, with his annoying sanctimonious wife and their brats."

Theo was William's older brother and the garrison commander, and whilst William was immoral, ill-mannered, and a philanderer, Theo was the exact opposite. Theo was married to Rosalyn, a religious Welsh woman and the daughter of a clergyman. Because of a promise he had made to their mother, Theo always looked out for William and helped him when he got into trouble. Theo had even made William his deputy so that he could keep an eye on him. Rosalyn and William didn't get along because she disapproved of William and his ill-mannered ways, which put Theo in embarrassing situations. She sympathised with Clara and, whenever she could, she would quote scripture and urge William to mend his ways. Rosalyn would share her misgivings about her brother-in-law with her husband, but Theo wouldn't listen and made excuses on his brother's behalf.

Rosalyn saw Sitara with the three girls and told her children, Teddy and Eliza, to go to them. After the children left, Theo and Rosalyn went towards William and Clara. Like Clara, Theo and Rosalyn were anxious about the possibility of a sudden attack by the rebels. Their only means of finding out about any impending attacks was through William's two trusted native scouts, who would disguise themselves as fakirs, hawkers, or merchants and go into Kamalpore and mingle with the native population.

"Any news from Chindi and Ram about the revolt?" asked Theo.

William shrugged his shoulders. "My scouts have tried to gather information from the natives who visit Manu Lal's brothel and also the hawkers and vendors in the bazaar. They have reported that it's mostly just whispers. Some of the natives say that there are messages being sent with food, instructing when everyone should rise and attack the garrison. But they wouldn't dare. It's just those silly rumours about the tainted cartridges and also the prophecy about British rule coming to an end on the hundredth anniversary of the Battle of Plassey. I'm sure that the trouble will soon die down," said William, as he calmly sipped his whisky.

The two women were not comforted by that piece of news. If the reports of the natives killing Europeans were true, then they too were at risk. They had the children to consider and they feared for their safety.

A few months earlier, Theo had learnt that he had inherited Fitzhugh Manor and all its land on the death of his childless uncle. He was now lord of the manor and a very wealthy man. He had wanted to move back to England, but the possibility of an uprising had put an end to his plan for now. Rosalyn, however, was adamant that an attack was imminent and once again urged Theo that the children, at least, should be sent back to England where their grandmother would take care of them. She reminded him that even the Maharaja of Kamalpore was no longer their ally. However, Theo, who always put duty and honour before himself, said that, for the sake of the morale of the troops, they all needed to remain at the garrison, to which William also agreed. William also reminded them that the garrison had a well for water, was well stocked with food and other provisions and would be able to withstand a long siege. Theo promised the women to have the soldiers on alert until the threat of any attacks had passed.

— — —

The siege started five days later. The garrison was prepared, based on the intelligence gathered by the two scouts. Theo stood on the walls of the garrison, looking out over at the hordes of rebels gathering on the scorched earth outside. Whilst some were clearly well trained and experienced, preparing cannons and carrying guns, others looked like they had simply grabbed a knife, wooden club or meat cleaver on their way.

"The women and children are hidden as requested, sir," an officer shouted as he approached and saluted.

Theo struggled to hear the man over the rebels yelling for the blood of the firangi and those within the garrison, but the pit of his stomach relaxed and he turned to look behind him. He could just make out the tip of the gun in the window where he knew that his wife, Rosalyn, was now keeping watch. He hoped that the shooting lessons he had given her to increase her confidence would help Rosalyn to defend herself and the others hidden with her, if it came to that. The rebels wanted them out of India so that their own leaders could take over, but Theo had a duty to perform and a family to protect. "I'm not going to make this easy for you," he muttered under his breath.

The attack began with a thunderous roar from the rebels, which fell away just as their first round of cannonballs came hurtling towards the garrison.

"Take cover," screamed Theo to his men as he ducked behind a palisade just before they hit. Rock and splinters from the damaged walls rained down over him and his men. He looked down into the compound just as another cannonball tore through a line of soldiers with a wet thud and a cloud of red, the noise of battle sharpened by the screams of the newly ruined men. The once brown earth was now red, littered with entrails and body parts and meandering rivulets of blood.

Theo forced himself up and returned to the edge of the wall to assess the situation. As he peered over, he could see the rebels and defected sepoys were now running parallel to the garrison. He looked along their path and was horrified to see that the wall had been compromised.

"Fire at will. Hold them back. The wall is breached around the gate," he ordered. His heart hammered in his chest as he flew down the steps and towards the soldiers flooding to defend the newly weakened wall. "Barricade it in. Get some timbers over there. Don't let them…" The ground shook as the garrison's cannons barraged in unison. The smoke grabbed at the back of his dry throat causing him to falter.

As Theo took a moment to compose himself, his attention was caught by a shout from William on the other wall. "Push them back, men. Use bayonets." Theo looked up towards William and saw that peppered amongst the uniforms of the British soldiers and loyal sepoys fighting alongside his brother were rebels who had scaled the walls and were now fighting hand to hand. Theo looked back to the window of the house; his heart filled with pride when he saw shots coming from the window, repelling the rebels. Theo drew his sword and threw himself into the fray.

—   —   —

As the sun set on the hot and bloody day, Theo stood next to his wife and surveyed the damage to the garrison. Debris crunched underfoot and soldiers were attending the wounded or clearing the bodies of the fallen. Theo looked at Rosalyn proudly; her brave actions had helped to repel the rebels.

"I'm sorry, I should have sent you and the children home as soon as there was mention of a potential rebellion," he apologised. "I have put you all at risk. It will not happen again."

"Sssshhh," Rosalyn soothed him, grabbing hold of his arm. "You did what you thought best. You did your duty and you saw off the rebels."

"It was costly on both sides," he replied, shaking his head. "They will be back again, though, with reinforcements. I am not sure the garrison can take another attack like that right now. I will stay to oversee the repairs and to protect the barracks, but you will go to safety as soon as I can make arrangements."

"No, my love, my place is here with you," she said. "In good times and in bad; that's what I promised you before God when we took our wedding vows."

—   —   —

A week after the initial attack, before dawn broke, a caravan consisting of three horse-drawn carriages left the garrison to the next British fortifications run by a larger army unit. In the caravan were William Fitzhugh and his family, Theo's two children, two young British soldiers, and Sitara, Chindi, and Ram.

William was to take the women and children to safety at the next British fortification and then come back with reinforcements. They left that day because, based on the scouts' reports, the rebels were planning on attacking the garrison two days later. Theo told Teddy that if he did not make it back to England, then Teddy would be the next Lord of Fitzhugh Manor. Rosalyn gave Eliza her emerald necklace as a parting gift. Clara and William assured Theo and Rosalyn that if anything happened to them, they would take care of their children and bring them up as their own. Rosalyn cried on her husband's shoulders as they saw the caravan disappear from their view into the thick jungle.

Two hours after the caravan left, as Theo was overseeing the repairs of the garrison walls, they heard a loud cry. He and the soldiers looked in the direction of Kamalpore and saw rebels streaming out of the city with weapons in hand and some rolling cannons.

"Impossible!" said one of the British soldiers in surprise. "The scouts told us that the rebels would not be attacking for two days."

Theo did not answer but ran in the direction of the house. He found Rosalyn inside taking care of wounded soldiers in the hall, which had been made into a temporary hospital.

"Rosalyn, get into the bedroom. We're being attacked again." He looked at the wounded soldiers. "Men, come on, do your duty; this may be the last battle with the rebels. If we have to, we will all die like heroes defending Her Majesty's empire. Do it for the glory of England." The wounded soldiers, stirred by Theo's patriotic speech, got up and grabbed their weapons. Theo proudly smiled at the soldiers. He then saw to it that Rosalyn climbed the staircase and he yelled at her to shoot at the rebels if she had to. In the worst case she was to save the last bullet for herself; he did not want her being violated by the rebels since she was the only woman in the garrison.

Theo then dashed out and ordered his men to line up in three ranks facing the wooden gates, just as they heard the gates being hit by a battering ram. After four or five hits, the locking beam burst, and the wooden gates were thrown back. Rebels started pouring into the compound like water gushing out from a failed dam. At the same time, the weakened walls were breached once more allowing more, rebels to enter.

"This is it men, fight for queen and country and die like heroes," yelled Theo as he removed his sword from his sheath. The garrison's soldiers moved forward and the sounds of gun shots and swords clashing, along with the screams of men, filled the air. Soon, bodies from both sides littered the garrison's compound.

When Theo knew it was hopeless, he retreated to the house. Wounded and breathless, he staggered into the bedroom. He wanted to be with her as they met their fate. Rosalyn was praying; the pistol with which she had killed some of the rebels was lying next to her. He was glad that she had not yet shot herself. She looked up and gasped when she saw the large bloodied gash where a sword had glanced off his forehead. She ran into his arms and he kissed her. He comforted her, saying that at least their children were safe.

Suddenly, a bugle sounded and the fighting outside the house ceased. Theo and Rosalyn went over to the window. The remaining loyal soldiers had surrendered; the rebels were holding them as prisoners. Theo's blood ran cold when he saw the rebel leader enter the compound – he now knew who had betrayed them and why the rebels had attacked without any warning. Theo knew that his end would not be long now; his only remaining fear was for the safety of his children.

— — —

The caravan moved at a steady pace until it came to a lake and William commanded the caravan to stop. Clara urged William to move on because she felt unsafe. However, William curtly said that the horses needed to be watered and that this was the only opportunity where they could collect water because there was no other water source for miles. He reminded her again that his scouts had assured him the rebels would only attack two days later.

Clara was upset but didn't want to antagonise her husband. As they got out of the carriages to walk around, they heard the sound of galloping horses approaching. In a few minutes, three rebels rode up to them.

"It's my husband," said Sitara.

Manu Lal came forward, while the other two rebels pointed their guns at them. "We only want the two children of Theo Sahib. Give them to us and you will not be harmed."

Teddy and Eliza were standing on either side of Sitara and holding on to her. They looked scared when they realised that Manu Lal wanted them, and they began crying and buried their faces in Sitara's side.

Sitara pleaded with her husband to spare the children because they were innocent. He accused her of betraying her people by going with the firangi. Courageously, she reminded him that he had betrayed her by taking another wife because she was barren, but that the British had treated her kindly and she was like a second mother to their children.

"Then you will die along with your beloved firangi. Come with us," roared Manu Lal. Seething with rage, he pointed the gun at Sitara and ordered her to bring the two children to him.

Sitara complied and was forced to sit behind Manu Lal on his horse. Teddy and Eliza sat on the other two horses. They rode away, leaving the others bewildered at what had just happened.

Clara looked at William. "We have to do something. Theo entrusted his children to our care."

William knew she was right. He went to one of the carriages and picked up his sword and revolver. He commanded his two scouts to join him and they rode in pursuit of the rebels.

Chapter 3: The Bloody Murder Scene

Meadowford Village – 1927

Inspector Lester Enderby was a middle-aged man, almost six feet tall, with a thick reddish-brown moustache. He arrived at Fitzhugh Manor, along with two constables, and ordered all of the family members into the living room and the staff into the kitchen. When he saw the murder scene, Inspector Enderby knew that he was not dealing with an ordinary murder. He might have been in the police force for many years, but he had little experience when dealing with murders. So he told Constable Beckett to take pictures of the murder scene and went downstairs to find the telephone. Inspector Enderby asked the operator to connect him to the Metropolitan Police in London.

The telephone rang in the house of Mr. and Mrs. Edmund Carlyle. Edna Carlyle, a middle-aged woman, picked up the phone and then listened to the voice at the other end.

"Yes, he's here," she replied and then turned to look across the room. "Dermot, it's your boss."

Dermot Lucian Carlyle was almost twenty-four years old, six feet tall with sandy coloured hair, and a prominent aquiline nose. When he heard that the call was from his boss, his face fell. He reluctantly took the receiver and placed it to his ear.

"But, Detective Lloyd, I'm on holiday. I am off for two weeks. You promised that I could spend it with my family. I last saw them at Christmas."

"I understand, Dermot, but this is very important," his boss replied. "A gruesome murder has been committed and the police in Meadowford are not equipped to solve the case. I knew that you were holidaying nearby and, as you know, they only have a small police station and seven constables working there. Nothing much usually happens in Meadowford besides petty theft or a pub brawl."

"What happened?" asked Dermot, suddenly intrigued.

"I believe you know the Fitzhugh family from Fitzhugh Manor? They own most of the land about the village."

"Yes, they've been the land owners since Tudor times. My family were their tenants until a few decades ago."

"Lady Doris Fitzhugh was found murdered in her bed by her maid when she went to wake her up this morning. Inspector Enderby needs help to solve the case. You're the only one there who's been trained to investigate a murder and I think that your experience under me will serve you well. Oh, and one more thing, don't let Inspector Enderby's brashness get to you. With your patience, I think that the two of you would complement one another."

Dermot rolled his eyes. "All right, Detective Lloyd, I'll do my best but this will be my first case without your expert guidance."

"Thank you. I knew I could count on you. Now, remember to listen to everything, however insignificant and frivolous it may be, since it could be important. Interview the necessary witnesses and don't give out too many details to anyone... Good luck!"

Dermot placed the phone in its cradle and then explained to his parents. In less than half an hour, he was out of the house and driving his 1923 Bentley. He was proud of his car; it was his prized possession.

Fifteen minutes later, Dermot was in front of the gates of Fitzhugh Manor. He stopped the car and looked at the building in front of him. The Tudor building was situated on top of a small hill, with well-manicured lawns and flowering plants in front of it. As he drove on up the gravel driveway, he noticed that on the right side of the manor house the hill tapered off and there was a smaller building that looked like a stable. Next to that was a path that led to the meadow away from the woods. As a child, he'd always wondered if he would ever get to see the inside of the manor house and, now, he was about to do so. He parked his car and walked up the steps. Inspector Enderby was waiting for him at the front door. Dermot greeted him and introduced himself.

"Thank you for coming. Detective Lloyd speaks very highly of you and he assures me that you are the best man to solve this case."

"I'll try my best," Dermot replied with a smile. He walked inside with Inspector Enderby. Dermot was unsure of what to do; he still considered himself a novice where murders were concerned.

As the two men passed by the living room to climb the staircase, Dermot glanced at the people in there. They looked upset, but a young lady looked at him and smiled. He smiled back and then went up the stairs.

—   —   —

As they entered the bedroom, Dermot immediately got the smell of blood. He could see the broken teacup, along with the tray and toast where they had fallen. Except for the mess on the floor, the room was immaculate. He went closer to the bed and forced himself to swallow the vomit that came close to his oesophagus.

The murdered woman lay in her bed, bound and gagged. Her throat had been slit from ear to ear. Dermot was astonished to see the amount of blood that had come out of the frail body, bathing her skin and soaking the bed.

Dr. Fielding, the family doctor, was standing next to the bed. Slattery had telephoned him after the body was discovered. He had come immediately and was appalled at the scene. Just a few days earlier, he had examined Lady Fitzhugh and told her that she was healthy for her age and could live to be a hundred. Now, he was staring at her bloody corpse.

Inspector Enderby introduced the two men and Dermot nodded, still trying to stifle his attack of nausea.

"Nasty business, eh?" said Dr. Fielding, amused by Dermot's sickened face.

"Time of death, Dr. Fielding?" asked Dermot as he tried to hide his embarrassment.

"The heat in this room could put me off by an hour or two, but judging by the rigor mortis I would say around two a.m."

Dermot turned to Inspector Enderby. "Does anyone know who could've wanted her dead? She seemed like a harmless old lady. I remember her coming to the church fair every year and pulling out the winning Tombola ticket. I was the lucky winner one year."

"The family thinks a maid whom she fired a few weeks ago may've wanted her dead. That's all they can tell us," said Inspector Enderby.

"We'll have to talk to this maid. Does the manor have a housekeeper?"

"Yes, her name is Miss Esmey Carter. From what the family tells me, she was very devoted to her Ladyship."

"She may know why the maid was fired. Housekeepers usually do the firing of the servants under them." Dermot went to the open jewellery box on the table in front of the mirror and looked inside. "Is anything missing?"

"Yes, the emerald necklace that she wore for her party yesterday. It's supposed to be a family heirloom."

"I can see that being a motive for killing her, but to bind and gag her and then slit her throat in such a gruesome way seems too much for just a piece of jewellery. Besides, there are other jewels in here that look valuable, why not take them too?" said Dermot, still looking at the jewellery.

"Maybe she woke up during the robbery," said Inspector Enderby.

"Possibly, but the savagery of the crime seems like there's a lot more than meets the eye. Any sign of the murder weapon?"

Inspector Enderby shook his head. "No, but there is a curious impression of something on the carpet under the bed. Probably the handle of the knife that killed her."

"You could be right," Dermot said as they looked at the impression. "Was there a struggle?"

"There's bruising around her mouth and cheek. It seems like the killer put their hand on her mouth to prevent her from shouting for help. Of course, there's also bruising on the hands and legs because of the ropes," said Dr. Fielding.

Dermot went to the window and looked outside. He could see a blood stain on the window sill.

"Looks like the killer came in or left through the window. But the question is how could they jump from this height to the ground below? Even if the killer had a rope, the rope would still be tied to something in the room to enable the killer to climb down the wall. Unless, the killer had an accomplice who is someone from the household. The accomplice could've taken the rope after the killer escaped. I think perhaps this blood was planted later, to make it look like the killer or killers left through the window."

"How can you tell?" asked Inspector Enderby.

"The window sill does not show any sign of wear. If there had been a rope on any part of the sill, there would have been some wear as the killer climbed up or down."

"Hmm, you're right. So, there must be at least two of them," said Inspector Enderby.

Dr. Fielding wiped the sweat from his brow with a handkerchief. "I'll have Dr. Talbot examine the body at the hospital. The body shan't last long in this heat and humidity."

"Constable Beckett has taken pictures of the crime scene, so the body can be shifted to the morgue in the hospital," said Inspector Enderby.

Dr. Fielding nodded. As Inspector Enderby and Dermot walked out of the room, two men with a stretcher entered the bedroom behind them.

"How is the family doing?" asked Dermot.

"In shock, obviously. They just can't believe that yesterday she celebrated her eightieth birthday and then, a few hours later, she was murdered in such a gruesome manner."

They walked down the staircase and went into the living room. It was a beautifully decorated room with a giant chandelier hanging from the ceiling. Oil paintings of family members from past centuries hung on the walls. Everyone looked at the two men with curiosity, except for the young lady who once again smiled at Dermot.

Dermot stood in front of the family and introduced himself. He expressed his sympathies to them and said that he would need to interview all of them. He urged them to tell him everything related to the night before, however insignificant it may seem.

"Who put you in charge? You seem too wet behind the ears to handle my sister's murder," said one of the elderly women, clearly annoyed.

"Now, Lilian, I'm sure he knows what he's doing. Inspector Enderby wouldn't have him here if he didn't think so," said the other elderly woman who was sitting near the first.

Dermot opened his mouth to speak, but Inspector Enderby said sternly, "I know he's young, but he comes highly recommended by his superior, Detective Lloyd, who's an esteemed detective in his own right in London. Together, they have helped Scotland Yard solve some difficult cases. He grew up in Meadowford and has given up his holiday to help me with this case."

Dermot smiled at Inspector Enderby, thanking him silently.

"Thank you for coming, Detective Carlyle. I am Arthur Endecott, Lady Fitzhugh's nephew. Please forgive my mother; she's in shock."

Dermot nodded, took a deep breath, and tried not to bother with the many pairs of eyes staring at him. Usually it was his superior, Detective Lloyd, who did the talking and Dermot would be silent, waiting for his instructions. Now, standing in front of all of these people, his nerves were getting the better of him, so he inwardly sighed with relief when Inspector Enderby began to speak.

"We'll have to take your statements. I need to know where all of you were when the murder took place. Dr. Fielding estimates that the murder took place at around two a.m., give or take an hour or two. I understand that Lady Fitzhugh went to bed at ten-thirty p.m. – am I right?" asked Inspector Enderby.

"Yes," said the young lady who had smiled at Dermot. "She had her last glass of sherry and, after the guests left, she wished us all good night and went straight to her bedroom."

"Are you certain?"

"Yes, I am. Aunt Doris looked at the clock on the wall and stated the time," she answered, pointing to the clock.

"Now, can someone please give me a description of the emerald necklace that was stolen?" asked Dermot.

There were a few murmurs and then one of the elderly ladies said, "Look behind you, Detective. It's around the woman's neck in the painting."

Dermot and Inspector Enderby turned around and saw a portrait of a family of four hanging on the wall behind them. The woman had an emerald necklace around her neck. Dermot was impressed with the intricate details of the necklace that the painter had managed to capture. The emeralds were inlaid in a gold base and were surrounded by tiny diamonds.

"Okay. We'll be in the library. If you could all come in one at a time and answer a few questions, we can take it from there," said Inspector Enderby.

Chapter 4: A Time for Questions

Two hours later, Dermot and Inspector Enderby had finished interviewing the family and, after the last person left, they began comparing notes.

"Crikey, none of them have strong alibis. It could be any of them. Their bedrooms were close to the victim's and anyone could've let the accomplice in, gone into her Ladyship's bedroom, tied her up, and killed her," said Inspector Enderby.

"I assume that one of the family could be involved," said Dermot.

"Why would they do that?"

"Because, as stated by Dr. Fielding, she was in perfect health. Perhaps someone wanted to hasten her demise; after all, being unmarried, she might leave the property to her next of kin and that would be to her nieces and nephews. They could all get a good chunk of the estate."

"I see what you mean. So, any one of them could be guilty," said Inspector Enderby.

"Maybe I'm wrong. Let's go downstairs to the kitchen area. We have to interview the maid who discovered the body. The rest of the staff, I suppose, will probably tell us the same thing as the family – that they were nowhere near the murder scene and were asleep in their rooms. Do you have the guest list for the party?" asked Dermot.

"Yes, and we can interview them once we're done with the staff," said Inspector Enderby.

"One thing that surprises me is that the family doesn't seem particularly upset at what has happened. They seem unusually calm..."

"Dermot, you have to remember that they belong to the upper class. They have been taught to keep a stiff upper lip, even in trying times."

Dermot grimaced with amusement. "Well, my upper lip will only stiffen when I'm stone dead."

They laughed as they entered the kitchen and an elderly woman in her seventies wearing a pair of silver pince-nez came to them. She glared at the two of them and they stopped laughing. Inspector Enderby introduced her as Miss Carter, the housekeeper. She looked younger and stronger than most women of her age. Inspector Enderby asked her if they could talk to the staff in private and she suggested that they could use the servants' dining room. Inspector Enderby then requested her to send Alice in and, before she left, Miss Carter asked if they would like some tea, to which he replied that they would.

They entered the servants' dining room and sat down. Shortly after, Alice opened the door and walked in. She still seemed very upset and distraught. She greeted the men and they asked her to sit down.

"You must be Alice Hall?" asked Dermot. She nodded. "Please tell us how you discovered her Ladyship's body?"

Alice told them that she took Lady Fitzhugh her morning tea with some toast at seven, like she did every morning. She knocked on the door and when there was no response, she went in and discovered the terrible scene. She dropped the tray and started screaming, until Slattery and Miss Carter came in.

"Did you see anything else odd in the room?" asked Inspector Enderby.

"Nothin'. I was so upset, sir..."

"Understandable. What happened after Mr. Slattery and Miss Carter came in?"

"Mr. Slattery froze for a few seconds when he saw her Ladyship, and he then tried to calm me down. Miss Carter came in and I 'eard Mr. Slattery shout to her. They brought me out of there. The family started comin' out of their rooms and Mr. Slattery stopped 'em from goin' into the room. Mr. Endecott pushed his way in, then he came back out after a few minutes and closed the door. He looked white as a sheet, he did. Miss Carter and Mr. Slattery calmed me down and then brought me back down 'ere to the kitchen."

"Did Mr. Endecott say anything?"

Alice thought for a second. "Yes... he said he couldn't believe it as he never heard anythin' in the night."

"If that's all, then I thank you for your time. If you do remember anything, please contact me. Here's my card," said Inspector Enderby. "Would you send Mr. Slattery in please."

Alice nodded, took the card, and left the room. A few minutes later, Slattery entered the room and greeted the two men. He sat on the chair previously occupied by Alice.

"Ahh, Mr. Slattery, Mrs. Endecott told us that you have the habit of walking around in the middle of the night checking the doors and windows. Is that so?"

"Yes, Inspector. It helps me go back to sleep. It's an old habit I picked up whilst in South Africa with the late Lord Fitzhugh."

"Interesting. How did the habit come about?" asked Dermot, curiously.

"An English settler, known to his Lordship in South Africa, and his family were massacred either by the natives or by the Boers during the war. One of the windows was unlocked and that's how they entered and killed everyone in the house. Ever since then, I've had the habit of checking the doors and windows when I wake up during the night. I also do it before I go to bed."

"Now, did you see anything last night?" asked Dermot.

Slattery suddenly smiled. "Nothing at all. It was like a graveyard."

"What time did you sleep and wake up last night?" asked Inspector Enderby.

"Her Ladyship graciously gave us two bottles of wine for dinner. After everyone went to bed, we quickly ate dinner, toasted her Ladyship, and went to bed. That was close to midnight. I woke up around two a.m. and it was very quiet. I heard nothing."

"Ahh, I see," said Dermot smiling. "Now, tell us what happened this morning?"

Slattery explained that he was in the dining room setting the table for breakfast when he heard Alice scream. He ran to her Ladyship's bedroom and found Alice hysterical. He tried to calm her down and then Miss Carter entered and was transfixed when she looked at the dressing table. He called out to her and she broke off from her stupor, and they both took Alice out of the bedroom. The family had gathered by the door. Arthur pushed his way into the room and came out a few minutes later, closing the door.

"Could you see what he did inside?"

"No, the door was almost closed when he went inside, and I was trying to prevent the rest of the family from entering the bedroom."

"How long was he inside the bedroom?"

"Maybe two minutes... He came out and said to us that he couldn't believe that her Ladyship was dead because he hadn't heard anything during the night. That's all I remember. Then Miss Carter and I brought Alice to the kitchen."

"If there's nothing else, then I suppose there is no point in detaining you further from your duties. Please send Miss Carter in," said Inspector Enderby.

"Very good, sir." Slattery got up and, as he was about to leave, Dermot asked him why he and Miss Carter were summoned to the library after Mr. Kerr spoke to Lady Fitzhugh. He replied that Lady Fitzhugh wanted to talk to them about serving the wine during dinner.

After Slattery left, Miss Carter came in with a tray of tea. She poured for them; Dermot had his tea with milk and sugar, while Inspector Enderby had his with a slice of lemon.

"Wonderful tea, Miss Carter. I must say, this is the best tea I've ever had," said Inspector Enderby.

"Indian tea. We also have tea from Ceylon and China, but the family likes the Indian tea. The family was in India at one point in time."

"How long have you worked here?"

"For about five years. Lady Fitzhugh hired me when the former housekeeper, the late Mrs. Slattery, passed away."

"Did you see anything unusual last night?"

"No, I was sound asleep. I got to know of the murder when Alice screamed. It seemed the whole manor could hear it. That girl can really scream!"

"Why did you stare at the dressing table in the bedroom?"

"I saw the body and then I noticed the open jewellery box. The emerald necklace, which she wore last night, was missing. I remember thinking that she was probably killed for the necklace. Then I heard Slattery calling me and we took Alice out. The poor girl was in a state of shock."

"So, you were the last person to see her alive?" asked Inspector Enderby.

"Yes, besides the murderer, Inspector," she said haughtily.

Inspector Enderby smiled. "Of course, Miss Carter."

"Did you see Mr. Endecott go into the bedroom and come out?"

"Yes, but I couldn't see anything as I was comforting Alice and the door was almost closed. Mr. Slattery was preventing the family members from going in. Her Ladyship's sisters were adamant that they should go in."

"Did you hear him say anything when he came out?"

"Yes, something like he couldn't believe that her Ladyship was dead... I think."

"Why did her Ladyship dismiss a maid recently?" asked Inspector Enderby.

"Yes, Irene Shaw. Strangely, the emerald necklace, which is now missing, was found in her room. She denied taking it, obviously, but she wasn't a good worker anyway, so she was given a choice to either leave willingly without a reference or we report her to the police. She chose the former. Until the moment she left, she was adamant that she didn't steal the necklace."

"Ahh, so now we're getting somewhere. Somebody did have a motive to kill her Ladyship," said Dermot. "Did you notice anything else missing?"

"No, I did not." Miss Carter then straightened herself. "Can I tell you something?" she asked in a low voice.

"Yes, please go ahead," said Inspector Enderby.

"I think I know who you should be looking at. It's that nephew of hers, Mr. Endecott; the one who came from India. I tell you, he probably wanted her dead."

"Why do you say that?"

"I heard them arguing many times."

"About what?" asked Inspector Enderby.

"I cannot say. They spoke in low tones. Her Ladyship didn't like her nephew. They never got along. I heard from her Ladyship that he collects antiques; you know, knives and guns. She told me that he had brought an antique knife with him from India."

"You and her Ladyship were close?" asked Dermot.

"Yes, but I know my place. Ever since Irene was dismissed, I did her duties including tending to her Ladyship's needs. She trusted me and used to ask my opinions. I only gave them if I was asked."

"Do you know where we could find this... Irene Shaw?" asked Inspector Enderby.

"I don't, no. You could ask the agency in St. Crispin's Village that sent her here. They may know where she is now."

Dermot thanked Miss Carter and asked her to send in the cook.

A few minutes after Miss Carter left, a stout middle-aged lady walked in. Mrs. Withers greeted the two men with a high-pitched voice and they asked her to sit down. Dermot asked her if she had heard or seen anything unusual during the night. She replied that she hadn't, as she had taken a sleeping draught along with a strong cup of Miss Carter's chamomile tea.

"Do you always take a sleeping draught before bed?" asked Dermot.

"Yes, I've always been a light sleeper so I take the sleeping powder to get me a good night's rest."

"When did you hear about the murder?"

"When Miss Carter brought Alice to the kitchen. I just couldn't believe it... Poor Lady Fitzhugh! What a sad end!"

"How long have you worked here?"

"For nearly seven years. Mind you, everyone likes my cooking. I was a poor girl from London's East End and now I cook for the upper classes."

"Thank you, Mrs. Withers. Please send Abigail in," said Dermot, looking at Inspector Enderby with relief.

Abigail entered a few minutes later. She was the same age as Alice and her dark hair was tied back. She wore spectacles and looked a bit nervous. She greeted the two men before sitting down. Inspector Enderby asked her if she had heard anything unusual at the party or during the night, and she told them that she and Alice were busy serving the guests and also helping in the kitchen. She slept soundly at night because she was very tired and she never heard anything.

Dermot asked Abigail when she heard about the murder. She replied that she was in the laundry room and she heard people running upstairs. Then she heard Alice crying as she and Miss Carter passed by the laundry room on the way to the kitchen. She followed them and when Mrs. Withers enquired, Alice slowly told them that Lady Fitzhugh had been murdered.

"Do you always do the laundry?"

"Yes. First thing in the morning an' sometimes in the afternoon. I help with other chores too."

Suddenly, a cat came through the open door and stood next to Abigail.

"Does the cat belong to the manor?" asked Dermot.

"Not really, sir, but me an' Alice feed it when we can an' it stays on the property. Miss Carter doesn't like her much. I told her that the cat will sort out the rats, but she said we 'ave poison for that."

Miss Carter came into the room. "Abigail, I told you to get rid of that cat," she said sternly. "Now go and put her outside."

Abigail picked up the cat and held it close to her. She looked at the two men and they told her that she could leave. Abigail got up and left with the cat.

"If you shan't be needing us any longer, we've got to get back to work," said Miss Carter.

"Yes, Miss Carter. We're finished here and we'll show ourselves out," said Inspector Enderby.

— — —

The two men went upstairs and found Arthur Endecott in the library, sitting near an open window, drinking whisky, and reading the newspaper. He looked up and saw the two men approaching him.

"Is there anything else, gentlemen?"

"Mr. Endecott, you never heard anything last night?" asked Inspector Enderby.

"That's right, Inspector. Like I told you earlier, I was sound asleep. I had a cup of Miss Carter's chamomile tea and I only woke up when that silly girl was screaming like a banshee. Is there a problem?"

"Not that we know of, but you told us that you returned to England to attend your aunt's birthday party."

"Yes, that's true."

"Is there another reason why you came to England? You were overheard arguing with her Ladyship several times."

"Yes, but that's a private matter. It's of nobody's concern."

"Well, it is for the police. I urge you to be honest with us. It'll be in your best interest," said Inspector Enderby impatiently.

Arthur sighed. "All right. I was arguing with Aunt Doris about taking those guns with me back to India." He pointed to the collection of guns in a glass case.

The two men turned and looked at them and Dermot said, "Why do you want them?"

"They were gifted by the Maharaja of Kamalpore to my Granduncle Theo when he became the commander of the Kamalpore Garrison. I want them for my antique collection. Aunt Doris did not want to part with them, as Uncle Theo wanted them here. Once she's dead, who better to give them to but me? Nobody else is interested in them. Grandpa William once told me that I could have them."

"Did she finally say that you could have them?"

"Yes, Aunt Doris, stubborn as she was, saw sense in my argument. It took some convincing, but she finally agreed. She called me to her bedroom before the party and told me so." He smiled and took a sip from his glass. "Hot day. Would you two like a spot of whisky as well? I need a stiff one now that breakfast's been delayed."

Dermot ignored him. "Did you bring back any antiques; like a knife perhaps?"

"A knife?" asked Arthur, surprised.

"Yes, or possibly a dagger?"

"No. Who told you I did?" Arthur asked with his eyes widened.

"Are you sure?" asked Inspector Enderby sternly.

"Inspector, whoever told you this must be mistaken. I would never bring any of my antiques here. I am established in Delhi, and I only wanted to take those guns to add to my collection."

"All right. We'll take your word for it. Good day, Mr. Endecott," said Dermot.

"Not at all. I just hope you catch the killer. Aunt Doris was my favourite aunt," said Arthur and he took another sip of whisky.

The two men bid Arthur goodbye and left.

— — —

Inspector Enderby leaned over to Dermot and whispered, "Antique guns? My eye! I think he just spun us a yarn."

"You can be sure of that," replied Dermot, trying not to smile.

As they were walking out of the front door, Hector came towards them and asked if he could help collect clues. Dermot patted his shoulder, thanked him, and said that murder was not for children and that his mother and aunts wouldn't approve of him getting involved.

Hector sighed with disappointment. "What else can I do here? Mother never lets me do anything when I'm home. I wish I was back in Harrow." He turned and walked away with a sad look on his face.

"Murder must be exciting for a thirteen-year-old. Not a lot of things to do in these parts for a boy of his age," said Inspector Enderby, smiling.

Dermot nodded. "Especially for a boy who only has older women for companionship."

As they walked down the steps, a car came down the driveway. It stopped in front of them and Richard Seymour got out. He greeted the two men. "What the dickens is going on? Why are the police here?"

"Now, just who might you be?" asked Inspector Enderby.

At that moment, Pippa came running out of the front door and straight into Richard's arms.

"Darling, Aunt Doris is dead," she said sadly. "She's been murdered."

Richard was dumbstruck and hugged Pippa tightly. He slowly looked up and she turned and faced the two men. "This is Richard Seymour. He attended the party last night and left around..." She looked back up at him.

"...around ten-thirty p.m.," he finished for her. "I live in London and I had a long drive. So, I said my goodbyes and left."

"Why are you here? Impossible that the news has reached London so soon," said Dermot.

"Before I left last night, Lady Fitzhugh asked me to come back today. She said that she had something very important to tell Pippa and me."

"Poor Aunt Doris may've wanted to give us her blessing. She was beginning to like you."

Chapter 5: The Game is Afoot

Irene Shaw told the two men to wait outside for her. She had to finish serving drinks to the customers in the pub. She whispered to them and made it clear that she didn't want anyone hearing what she had to tell the police.

"On the house, gentlemen," she said as she handed them each a pint of ale. The two men went outside and sat at a table.

Irene Shaw was back in St. Crispin's Village where she lived with her mother. Due to the lack of a reference letter from Lady Fitzhugh, she'd had a difficult time finding a job as a domestic and, to make ends meet, was now working as a barmaid at the Boar's Head.

Presently, she came out, wiping her hands on her apron and adjusting her dark auburn hair. She sat opposite the two men, reminding them to keep their voices low. Nobody needed to hear what they discussed, because no one knew she had been dismissed from Fitzhugh Manor.

Dermot asked her why she had stolen the necklace, which she strongly denied. She also couldn't believe that Miss Carter told them about it, because they had agreed that she would leave without a reference and the police wouldn't be notified.

"So, how come the necklace was found in your room if you didn't steal it?" asked Inspector Enderby.

"I really don't know. It was found under my mattress by Miss Carter when Lady Fitzhugh gave her permission to search our rooms. I obviously denied stealing it, but they didn't believe me."

Dermot asked if she had seen the necklace before and Irene said that she had once been present with Miss Carter when Lady Fitzhugh had taken it out of her safe. It looked more impressive in person than in the painting and Irene recalled that Miss Carter had been awestruck and had asked Lady Fitzhugh about its history. She had told them that the necklace belonged to her mother, but it was actually her Aunt Rosalyn's necklace. The next time that Irene had seen the necklace was when it was discovered in her room.

"All right, now where were you last night at about two a.m.?" asked Inspector Enderby.

"I left work at one. When the pub closed at eleven, we had a lock-in so I worked late." She glanced sheepishly at the two officers, who both shrugged. "I walked home then and went to bed. I only heard about the murder an hour or two ago. My boss can confirm that."

"Do you own a car?"

"Not on my salary. I'd have to take the bus to go to Meadowford and they stop running at five. It's nearly fifteen miles from here."

"Thank you, Miss Shaw. You may go back to work," said Dermot.

She looked at them for a second. "Lady Fitzhugh was kind to me until that necklace disappeared. I would never have harmed her and I'm sorry she's dead, but I have nothing to do with any of this."

As they drove back to Meadowford in Dermot's car, Inspector Enderby asked Dermot whether he thought Irene Shaw was involved.

"I'm not sure. Certainly, it would be impossible for her to walk fifteen miles at that time of the night, murder Lady Fitzhugh, and then return. She seemed sincere about not stealing that necklace."

"Only time will tell... but did you notice the way she speaks? Not like a lady's maid, but like someone with good breeding."

"I did notice that. Very strange indeed!"

"I agree," said Inspector Enderby. "We have to meet Dr. Talbot who is conducting the autopsy of Lady Fitzhugh." He looked at his watch. "He must be done by now."

—   —   —

Meadowford's hospital buildings had been financed by Lord Fitzhugh after he had returned from South Africa and had been completed a few months after his death. There was a plaque at the entrance stating that fact. Dermot and Inspector Enderby entered the morgue and were immediately struck by the strong smell of formalin. Dermot hated hospitals; they reminded him of the time when he had been treated as a boy to remove his appendix.

They saw Dr. Talbot standing next to a sheet-covered body and reading from a clipboard. Talbot looked up and smiled at them.

"Dr. Talbot, this is Detective Dermot Carlyle. He's helping me with the Fitzhugh murder," said Inspector Enderby.

"Nice to meet you, Detective Carlyle. Don't worry, my hand's clean." He held out his hand and Dermot reluctantly shook it.

Dr. Talbot took them to another side of the room where they could see another body on a slab covered with a sheet. He slowly uncovered the face and carefully showed them the hands and feet by removing the portion of the sheet covering them. They could see the ligature marks where they had been bound.

"As you can see, the ropes were tied so tightly that they cut into her skin; it was the same with the gag." He then pointed to the neck where they could clearly see the cut mark on the throat. "The wound was made with a thin blade, although a bit blunt. It took some force to cut the throat and the carotid artery."

"How barbaric," said Inspector Enderby.

"It looks like it was done with such hatred. Whoever killed her must've hated her Ladyship very much," said Dermot.

"Yes, and Dr. Fielding's estimate that she probably died after two a.m. seems correct. The stomach contents showed that her dinner was partly digested. She had roast beef, vegetables, mushroom soup, and some cake. The blood analysis showed that she had alcohol – I guess sherry and wine."

"Yes, that's what they had for dinner," said Inspector Enderby, looking at his notes.

Dermot asked Dr. Fielding if he found anything curious about the body or the ropes and he replied that he had examined the ropes and noticed that the knots were similar to the ones used in the military. He was in the army in his youth, so he was certain that one of the killers was or had been a soldier.

— — —

After they left the morgue, Dermot and Inspector Enderby drove to the vicarage. Reverend Howard and Henrietta sat in the shade of a large oak tree, drinking tea. The Anglican Church and the vicarage were in the background.

Inspector Enderby greeted them and introduced Dermot to them. Henrietta offered them tea.

"Tea, in this heat?" asked Dermot.

"Remember, we're British... we can never go without our tea. It's what we used to say to one another when we were in Ceylon as missionaries. Even in the heat of the tropics, we never gave it up," said the Vicar.

"I am assuming that you are here to talk about the murder?" asked Henrietta. The two men nodded. "So ask away, Inspector."

"Did you see or hear anything unusual at Lady Fitzhugh's party last night?"

"Nothing unusual," Henrietta replied as she poured the tea. "She was happy she had made it to eighty." She held up a plate and offered them a garibaldi. The two men took one each and began sipping their tea. "It'll be sad not seeing her Ladyship at Sunday services any more. She was my school teacher before she became Lady of the Manor. She had a head for maths… Oh! She did say something about making changes to her will," said Henrietta.

"Did she say what sort of changes?"

"No, but she said that she had learnt that someone at the party wasn't honest. She also said that she had dodged a bullet a few weeks earlier when she couldn't add someone to her will. The wills had disappeared and then miraculously reappeared in the solicitor's briefcase."

"Wills?" asked Dermot.

"Yes, that struck me as rather odd… but before she could tell me any more, we were called for dinner. She was just like her father – always putting family first."

"That reminds me," said Reverend Howard. "She spoke privately to that solicitor of hers in the library."

"Yes, now I remember. After the solicitor left the library, the housekeeper and the butler went in and spoke to her for a few minutes. She was in a very good mood when she came out of the library," said Henrietta.

"At what time did you leave?" asked Dermot.

"We left around ten," said Henrietta. "She was in such a cheerful mood and that's the way I'd like to remember her."

The two men finished drinking their tea. "If you think of anything, you can call my home. I presume you have my parent's number?" asked Dermot.

"Yes, you are Edmund's son?"

"Yes, they come here for Sunday services."

"I haven't seen you for Sunday services in a long time. No wonder I didn't recognise you," said the vicar, eyeing Dermot to make him feel guilty.

"I live in London, and the last time I was at church here was for Christmas service. I'm here on holiday for two weeks," said Dermot, trying not to sound annoyed.

Reverend Howard seemed satisfied as he settled back in his chair.

"You poor thing. Investigating a dreadful murder while on your holiday and, to top it all off, this heat! You must wish that you'd never come back to Meadowford," said Henrietta, laughing at her own joke.

Dermot nodded as he and Inspector Enderby got up. He thanked them for the tea and wished them goodbye.

— — —

It was getting late and so Inspector Enderby decided to head to the police station. Dermot wanted to talk to Bertram Kerr and telephoned him from a public phone to let him know that he would be coming to meet him. He then telephoned Major Havelock, but Gerda, who answered the phone, told Dermot that the major's leg was giving him trouble and he had been prescribed bed rest by the doctor.

Dermot drove to the Meadowford Inn where Bertram Kerr was staying. On hearing about the murder, Kerr had extended his stay for two more days in order to attend the funeral and to read the will. Kerr was waiting for Dermot in the dining room. The head waiter showed Dermot to the table where Kerr was eating his supper. They greeted each other and shook hands.

"Please join me for dinner. The steak and kidney pie's delicious," said Kerr. He then beckoned to the waiter, a timid-looking man with drooping shoulders.

"What can I do for you, Detective Carlyle?" asked Kerr after the waiter left having taken the order.

"You drew up the will for Lady Fitzhugh, am I right?" asked Dermot as he sipped his wine.

"Yes, it was drawn soon after her brother, Allan, died."

"Can you tell me the contents of the will?"

Kerr agreed, but insisted that Dermot was not to reveal it to anyone before the will was read. Dermot nodded. In the meantime, the waiter returned with the food.

Kerr told Dermot that after Lady Fitzhugh's death, Hector inherits everything since he's the male heir of her deceased brother. There were also provisions for Pippa, Lady Fitzhugh's two sisters, Cora, Arthur, and Flora's two daughters in America and Canada. There were some legacies bequeathed to the manor staff and some monies left to various local charities. The will further stated that if anything were to happen to Hector, that Pippa will inherit everything and after that Arthur, since he was the oldest of the sisters' children.

Dermot then asked Kerr why he went to the manor with the wills a few weeks earlier, and Kerr told him it was because Lady Fitzhugh wanted to add someone to her will. When he asked why she had two wills, Kerr said that one of the wills was the late Lord Fitzhugh's will.

"Did she mention anyone in particular she wanted to add to her will?"

"No, she never told me."

"So, why didn't she add the person into the will?"

"Well, a strange thing happened. I thought that I had the wills in my leather briefcase, but when I opened it in front of Lady Fitzhugh they had disappeared."

Dermot looked puzzled and Kerr explained that when he had arrived at the manor, he went to the living room because he was supposed to meet her Ladyship there. She took some time arriving, so he left his briefcase on the table and went to the bathroom down the hall. When he went back to the living room, Lady Fitzhugh was waiting for him. He opened his briefcase and found that both the wills had disappeared. He checked his briefcase many times and removed its contents. He excused himself and went to his car, but they weren't there either.

"What was her Ladyship's reaction?"

"She was livid and sternly reprimanded me for my carelessness when I came back after searching my car. Miss Carter can confirm this, she was pouring some tea. Fortunately, I had made copies of the wills and kept them in my office safe. She told me to bring them the next time I came to the manor."

"The originals are still missing?"

"The strange thing is that when I returned to my office in London, I was emptying the contents from my briefcase and the wills were in another compartment. I just couldn't understand it as I had searched the whole briefcase, including the compartment where I found the wills later."

Dermot looked perplexed. "Did you leave the briefcase when you went to search your car?"

"I did, but I thought Lady Fitzhugh had her eye on it all the time. She had even mobilised the entire staff, including the chauffeur, to search the living room and the main hall for the wills."

"Wouldn't make sense if she had anything to do with it," said Dermot. "Maybe someone didn't want that will changed. Now the mystery is, who was she planning on adding to her will?"

Kerr nodded as he finished his meal and drank the last sip of wine.

"Did she ask you to come back with the wills when you told her you found them?" Dermot asked.

"When I telephoned her about finding the wills, she said to bring them when I came for her birthday party. At the party, we spoke briefly in the library and she said that she would like me to return with them the next day. She was thinking about making those changes and would finalise her decision that very night. Actually, today would've been the day, but..."

Dermot nodded, indicating he knew what Kerr meant. He then asked if any of the family members would have had access to the briefcase that day.

Kerr replied that the family had been picnicking near the stream behind the meadow and that's why Lady Fitzhugh asked him to come then to make changes to her will. As far as he knew, nobody left the picnic and came to the manor unexpectedly.

Finally, Dermot asked Kerr where he had travelled to on the day of the party, but he refused to answer, saying that it had nothing to do with the murder and he had to keep the confidentiality of his other clients' cases.

Dermot thanked him and said that he would see him at the funeral two days later. He gestured to the waiter to bring the bill and, while he waited, he said, "The family must be eager for the reading of the will."

"Yes, and in my experience there are some who will be happy at what they've inherited and others who won't be happy. I'm sure that will be the case here too."

The waiter came and placed the bill in front of Dermot.

"This man is a guest of mine," Kerr said angrily to the waiter, his voice raised. "I will pay for his meal... add it to my tab."

The waiter meekly apologised and hurried away, while some of the guests stared.

Dermot and the guests were perplexed at Kerr's outburst. He quickly thanked Kerr for supper and went away.

Chapter 6: Night-time Rounds

Slattery woke up in the middle of the night and lit a candle. He took the candlestick and went out of his room. He checked the windows and doors in the kitchen and climbed the staircase to the main floor. He was always haunted by the memory of the murdered British family in South Africa. Those had been dangerous times – the war was going on and the British were not popular. It was said that the killers were natives that got in through an unlocked window and maybe the Boers were involved too. People thought he was stark raving mad for doing this every night, but like he always said, better safe than sorry.

He walked into the library and towards the cupboard where he expected the money to be. What someone had said after the murder had made him suspicious of who might be involved. Nobody would've guessed anything because they had cleverly fooled everybody, but not him. He had decided to confront one of them. The look in that person's eyes had confirmed what he suspected, and the person readily agreed to buy his silence.

His loyalties were first to Lord Fitzhugh and then to Lady Doris Fitzhugh, but now both of them were dead and her funeral was only a few hours away. He would leave after he got what was bequeathed to him in Lady Fitzhugh's will, but extra money always helped. He liked his job, but he wanted more money so he could retire early and buy a small cottage near Dover, close to his daughter, and live comfortably for the rest of his life.

He had decided that he would publish his memoirs about his time in South Africa. People always read memoirs based on war experiences and he had an interesting story to tell. He had started writing it when he was in South Africa and wrote intermittently during the Boer War, but then he had stopped. A few months back, he had decided to finish the work and now he was almost done.

Slattery placed the candlestick on the table next to the cupboard and opened the cupboard's door. Rising up on his toes, he placed his hand on the top-most shelf and his fingers touched an envelope. This was the second envelope he was receiving. The first was the previous night after he confronted and made a deal with the killer. He smiled at his good fortune. If he could bleed that person for more money, even after he left, he would have more than enough.

"Good it's all here," he said as he counted the money inside the envelope.

Slattery heard a noise behind him and turned. He saw a face he never really liked, and then he saw the glint of metal in the candlelight and suddenly felt a sharp pain in his chest. As he fell backwards into the cupboard, his grip on the envelope loosened and he closed his eyes forever.

His killer took the envelope, blew out the candle and put it inside the cupboard next to Slattery's body, and closed the cupboard's door.

— — —

Fitzhugh Manor – The next morning
Lilian Endecott was upset that Slattery was not available and ordered the staff to search for him. The maids scurried around the manor to find Slattery. Miss Carter assured Flora and Lilian that she would make sure everything was organised in time for the funeral repast.

It was time for the funeral and they would soon be leaving for St. Andrew's Church. Lilian spied Pippa walking about and commented to Flora that Pippa's legs were showing and that she had no respect for the dead. Flora reminded her that the styles had changed since the war and that Doris only viewed death as an entry into the afterlife, like they were taught in church.

"Flora, traditions must be followed. Being a mere chit of a girl, Pippa only wants to defy... Oh and where has that butler gone to? He decides to disappear at the most inopportune moment."

"Maybe he doesn't want to attend the funeral because he is upset. He was devoted to Doris, like he was to Father," said Flora. She glimpsed Arthur coming down the staircase and asked him if the staff had located Slattery, to which Arthur replied in the negative but Miss Carter had also assured him that she would get everything organised. "Thank God for Miss Carter," said Flora. "She is ever so reliable. She even does the work of that thieving Irene with a smile."

"Here come Cora and Hector. At least Cora knows how to dress for a funeral, unlike her daughter," said Lilian.

Cora came towards them with Hector, and the two elderly sisters got up and walked with them out of the manor. They climbed into the waiting car chauffeured by Charles, a muscular man of medium height with blond hair, who also worked as a stable hand. After the whole family was in the car, Charles drove them to the church.

The funeral was well attended, packed with local villagers and members of some English aristocratic families who had all held Lady Fitzhugh in high regard. After the burial, the family and other mourners came back to Fitzhugh Manor. Flora went up to Major Havelock and Gerda.

"Thank you so much for the moving eulogy," Flora said, taking the major's hand. "Doris would've been so pleased about the wonderful things you said about her."

"You're welcome, Flora. Doris was very special to us. It was the least we could do," said Major Havelock, as he tried not to show the pain in his leg.

Gerda gave Flora a hug and condoled with her. The rest of the people who gathered there started helping themselves to the tea, sandwiches, and cakes that were laid out on the table.

After the meal, the guests departed and the family and staff gathered in the living room. Mr. Kerr came in with his leather briefcase and stood in front of the family, who were all seated around the table.

"Still no sign of Slattery?" he asked to a silent chorus of shaking heads and a tut from Lilian. "Well, we had better get on. We have gathered here today to read the last will and testament of Lady Doris Agnes Fitzhugh. She signed and dated this will on the thirteenth of July, 1917. In her previous will, her brother, Allan Phillip Fitzhugh, was her heir, but after his untimely death, she changed it to her current will."

Mr. Kerr began reading the will. As he had told Dermot, two days earlier, Hector inherited the lion's share of the estate with Cora as his legal guardian until he turned twenty-one. There were also some legacies bequeathed to the rest of the family and some to the staff.

Arthur was upset. After the staff left, he spoke up without bothering to hide his disappointment. "What about the changes to my inheritance Aunt Doris said she would make in favour of me? I saw you go into the library with her."

"She never confirmed anything. Lady Fitzhugh planned to finalise her changes the next day after thinking about it, but she never got the opportunity to do so," Kerr said, expressionless.

"You mean that she wanted to change some portions of the will and not just what Arthur could inherit? Just what did you and Doris discuss in the library during the party?" asked Lilian.

"I can't answer anything more. What we discussed was confidential."

"Where's Slattery? I am sure he'll be glad to know that he will get five hundred pounds," said Flora with a smile.

"Yes, good heavens! It's high time Slattery showed up. I will take him to task for disappearing without a word," said Lilian.

Suddenly, Alice came running into the room, stammering, "He... He... He's... in the cupboard."

"Who?" asked Lilian, impatiently.

"Mr. Slattery. He's dead. In the library."

Cora gasped, placing her hand over her mouth.

"What are you saying, you stupid girl?" asked Lilian, exasperated. "You seem to be finding dead bodies all the time."

"Are you sure?" asked Flora.

"Yes," said Alice, who crouched down on the floor as if she had no strength left.

Arthur got up and ran to the library. He went to the open cupboard door and peeped inside. As his eyes got used to the darkness, he could make out the outline of a body and the greying hair, and then he recognised the face. Slattery's white nightshirt had a bloody stain around the handle of a knife sticking out from his chest.

Arthur froze at the sight, and then gradually composed himself. He left the library and telephoned the police. A few minutes later, the residents of the manor heard the sirens of police cars approaching.

—   —   —

Dermot was at home having tea when he heard the phone ring. He had attended the funeral but, like Inspector Enderby, had decided not to go to the wake. His father answered the phone and called out to Dermot that it was Inspector Enderby. Dermot immediately went to the phone and listened. In the next few minutes, he was on his way to Fitzhugh Manor. He pulled up next to the two police cars and an ambulance parked at the front of the manor. He went in and saw Inspector Enderby interviewing Arthur. Dr. Fielding was just coming down the stairs, followed by Flora.

He went to Inspector Enderby and was briefed about what had happened.

"That girl, Alice, does have a knack for finding murdered people," said Dermot wryly.

"Well, she was searching for him like the staff were told to do and happened to chance upon the body. I suppose nobody else thought about looking in the library. After all, what would a butler do in the library?" said Inspector Enderby, almost laughing at his own joke.

They went downstairs into the kitchen and saw Alice sitting at the dining table being comforted by Abigail. Miss Carter was standing next to her, pouring a hot cup of tea. Alice appeared to be flushed, but was calmer this time.

"May we talk to her alone?"

"Yes, you may," said Miss Carter and she motioned Abigail to come with her.

After the door was closed, Inspector Enderby and Dermot sat down and Alice looked at them slowly.

"I know it's hard for you finding two bodies within days of each other, but do tell us how you discovered the body of Mr. Slattery."

Alice took a sip from her cup. She then took a deep breath and told them how nobody had seen Slattery since the previous night and that Mrs. Endecott was very upset as he had not served the tea or helped with breakfast. He was also responsible for the funeral repast. Mrs. Endecott had demanded that he be found at once and they had searched but couldn't find him.

"We thought maybe he couldn't 'andle her Ladyship's death and he wanted to be on his own instead of going to the funeral."

"Yes, I can see that. Were her Ladyship and Slattery close?" asked Inspector Enderby.

"Yes he was, and also to her father."

"So what made you go into the library?" asked Dermot.

"I didn't think anyone would have searched for him in there, so I thought I'd have a look. I thought he might be catchin' some shut-eye on one of them armchairs as he did walk about checking the locks at night."

"Why did you look in the cupboard?"

"There was candle wax on the floor next to the cupboard door. I wondered why and so I opened the door, sir. Poor Mr. Slattery, stabbed in the heart and stuffed into a cupboard like an old coat nobody could be bothered to hang."

"Did you hear him leave his room last night?" asked Inspector Enderby.

"I saw the light go by from under me bedroom door. Everyone knew about him checking the locks at night, so I thought nothin' of it."

Dermot looked at Inspector Enderby and asked him if he had any more questions. He had none. They interviewed Miss Carter and the other staff, but nobody saw anything suspicious.

Chapter 7: The Boer War Years

Dermot and Inspector Enderby went into Slattery's room. The room was immaculate, with everything in order. There was a small window that overlooked the woods and the stables behind the manor. On the table was a picture of his late wife and another of his daughter and her family. There were also some papers.

"Wonder why anyone would want to murder a man like Slattery? There's nothing to indicate he could be involved with the murder," said Inspector Enderby.

"Things may not be what they seem. He could've had some knowledge about who killed Lady Fitzhugh."

Dermot went to the table and saw a writing pad marked with indentations on the paper. He turned on the table lamp and held the pad towards the light. He could just make out a few words.

"...know what you did... Please meet..." Dermot read aloud. He then turned to Inspector Enderby. "So he was blackmailing someone."

"He didn't have any money in his pockets when his body was found. If he did get a payment the night after the murder, then it should be here," said Inspector Enderby.

They started searching the room and Inspector Enderby found some money in-between the pages of a notebook filled with Slattery's handwriting.

"Ten pounds. That's a lot of money," said Inspector Enderby.

"It is... Is that his diary?" asked Dermot.

Inspector Enderby turned to the first page and read, "The Memoirs of James Slattery During the Boer War."

"So he was writing his memoirs about his experiences in South Africa," said Dermot.

"He may've wanted to publish his memoirs. A lot of people write their memoirs, especially if they have experienced war."

"Let me keep the book," said Dermot. "Possibly the person he was blackmailing is mentioned in it."

"Maybe, but who? The only person who was in South Africa during the Boer War with Slattery was Lord Fitzhugh, and he's dead."

"Major Havelock was in the same regiment. We can ask him…" Dermot stopped and thought for a second, then said, "I'll say… you know those military knots used to tie Lady Fitzhugh… Slattery was probably involved in the murder and someone in the manor got wind of it and wrote that note on his writing pad."

"Yes, that's possible. However, everyone says that he was devoted to her Ladyship. Seems very unlikely," said Inspector Enderby.

As they left the room and climbed the stairs to the main floor, Dermot looked through the notebook and came to a page with some scribbling and drawings. When they were on the landing, he showed the page to Inspector Enderby.

"Look at these drawings of men with and without facial hair."

Inspector Enderby chuckled. "I heard that writers sometimes draw when they cannot write."

"Inspector, a thought just occurred to me. What if Cora is involved in the murders?…"

"Why do you think that?"

"Because Hector inherits everything when he comes of age and, until then, Cora is his guardian and gets a say in the property. Now, maybe Slattery saw her coming out of Lady Fitzhugh's room or maybe he figured it out and was blackmailing her. Then there is the other possibility that both Cora and Arthur may be involved. They both murder her Ladyship and then Cora gets control of Hector's inheritance and Arthur of his." Dermot paused before asking, "What do we know of Cora Fitzhugh?"

"Only that she's from Canada and she came to Fitzhugh Manor with Allan and Pippa after Lord Fitzhugh died. She mostly keeps to herself and is focused on Hector's education and upbringing. Oh, and she used to teach at the village school," said Inspector Enderby.

"I will ask Flora Ainsworth for more information. She seems willing to talk, unlike her sister," said Dermot. Inspector Enderby smiled and nodded his head as they climbed the stairs and reached the main floor.

— — —

Inspector Enderby and Dermot met with Flora in the living room. She seemed calm and composed. Dr. Fielding had given Lilian a sedative and she was now asleep. Inspector Enderby promised Flora that he would bring two constables, who would be replaced every twelve hours, so that they would have round-the-clock protection.

"Thank you, Inspector. It's all too much to take in. Poor Lilian is so upset. You know how high strung she can be."

Inspector Enderby smiled, wished Flora goodbye, and left. Dermot sat next to her and asked her to tell him about Lord Fitzhugh's life in South Africa during the Boer War.

Flora told him that her father spent most of his money gambling and living a lavish lifestyle after he retired from the army as a general in 1880. He had read in the newspapers that diamonds were being discovered in the Northern Cape Province close to Kimberley in South Africa. So he had decided to go there in 1898 and invest in a diamond mine. He thought it would make him rich very quickly. He also missed the colonial lifestyle and wanted a taste of it again. He invested in a diamond mine in Kimberley owned by a Boer farmer named Christiaan De Villiers. When the war broke out, Lord Fitzhugh volunteered for the British Army even though he was too old to fight. Because of his command experiences in India and England, he was given a small unit and Slattery, who went there as his butler, became his batman.

Lord Fitzhugh became the sole owner of the mine when Christiaan and his family were killed in the war. There was a clause in the partnership agreement that stated that if there were no direct living descendants to inherit the mine from the primary partner, then the surviving partner or his direct heir becomes the owner. On the day of the inauguration, the mine mysteriously exploded and it was deemed unsafe for further excavation.

The insurance company filed a lawsuit against Lord Fitzhugh because they suspected that he had deliberately sabotaged the mine to collect the insurance money because the mine did not have a huge diamond deposit. When it was proved otherwise, he won the case and returned to England a rich man.

"Why is all this important?" Flora asked curiously.

Dermot showed her Slattery's memoirs. "Slattery was writing his memoirs about his time in South Africa. Dr. Talbot, who performed the autopsy on her Ladyship, identified the knots used to tie her as ones that are used in the military. The only person in the manor that was in the military was Slattery."

"Major Havelock was in Father's unit during the Boer War."

"Ahh, that reminds me that I need to talk to him too... Now, did Slattery recently have a disagreement with Lady Fitzhugh?"

"Not that I know of. They got along like a house on fire. He would never do anything to harm Doris. He was just as devoted to her as he was to Father."

"Then probably he saw something he shouldn't have when he went on his nightly rounds and was killed for that. But he told us that he didn't see anything."

Flora shrugged her shoulders. "I don't know why he would deny ever seeing anything. Wouldn't make sense..."

"Where is Cora from?" asked Dermot.

Flora told him that Cora was from Toronto, Canada, and that she worked as a school teacher there. Allan had left England at the age of eighteen and met her in Toronto. Allan came back with Cora and Pippa in 1906, after Lord Fitzhugh died from septicaemia following gall bladder surgery. He didn't get along with his father, whom he nicknamed Henry VIII, because he blamed him for their mother's death when he was three. Clara had died of a broken heart due to Lord Fitzhugh's philandering, even though she had finally given him a son. Doris brought up Allan and she was like a mother to him. Cora now schooled Hector at the manor, as they had taken him out of Harrow.

When Dermot enquired why, Flora told him that Allan was suspected of being a spy because he was found dead from a gunshot wound in his London office where he worked for the War Office Intelligence Service in 1916. Doris had persuaded him to join the War Office as she didn't want him to be killed in action. The intelligence service thought that Allan would be an asset, since he had lived in Germany and other countries during his itinerant years. His knowledge of German was used to decode messages the intelligence service had intercepted from Germany. The two people he worked with were given chase by the police and they perished in a car crash. The papers labelled Allan as a spy. When Hector went to Harrow, some of the boys bullied him about his father being a traitor.

"Children can be so cruel, Detective. Hector is the spitting image of Allan and he felt the loss of his father even though he was only two years old and barely out of his nappies when Allan died. He tried to defend Allan's name by fighting with the boys who tormented him. They even defaced a plaque with Allan's name on it for winning a rugby tournament."

"He's a bright young lad. He wanted to help us in the murder investigation," said Dermot, smiling.

"The cheeky devil! If Cora or Lilian get wind of this, they will box his ears."

Dermot looked at the wall and saw the portrait of Theo Fitzhugh and his family. He asked Flora what had happened to them and Flora recounted the events that took place in India during the mutiny. Lord Fitzhugh pursued the rebels, with his two Indian scouts, when they took Sitara and Theo's two children as hostages. He was wounded in the pursuit, but he was the only one who returned alive – everybody else was killed. Lord Fitzhugh then inherited the estate, since Theo and his children were killed.

The emerald necklace was gifted to Rosalyn by one of Theo's Indian soldiers, because Theo saved the woman that the soldier loved from becoming a suttee. The woman was wearing the necklace when her relatives were taking her to be burnt with her dead husband. When Eliza was killed by the rebels, Clara got the necklace.

Dermot looked perplexed. "I wonder why the rebels didn't take all of you as prisoners if they wanted hostages to exchange for fellow rebels."

Flora shrugged. "Father told us that when he caught up with the rebels, they told him that our ayah, who was the estranged wife of the rebel leader, had betrayed us by sending messages to her husband detailing when to attack the garrison and also planned the kidnappings. They had attacked the garrison a few hours after the caravan left and burnt it to the ground after killing everyone in it. Lilian's demeanour changed after the ordeal because she was the ayah's favourite."

"So Mrs. Endecott was not always so... sharp?"

"Not at all... When we were at finishing school in Kent, we heard from classmates how their ayahs had sacrificed their lives to protect them. Some of them literally crawled from under the dead bodies of their ayahs, who had stood between them and the rebels' swords. One ayah had used opium to put a classmate's infant brother to sleep and she hid them with their mother in a cupboard and told the rebels that there was no one at home. After the rebels left, she took the three of them to safety. These stories distressed Lilian, because our ayah had betrayed us."

"So the events of the mutiny still have a hold on Mrs. Endecott, even after all these years?"

"Yes, Detective. She never had a good marriage because she couldn't trust her husband. Mother had told us about Father's infidelities. Lilian was also too strict with Arthur and that's why he is the way he is."

"You don't say!" said Dermot with a smile.

"Detective, I just remembered something. It may not be important. While Father was dying in agony, he received a note that contained a single sentence. If I remember correctly, it said, 'Remember the diamond mine, the De Villiers family, and your brother's family.' It upset Father a lot and he wouldn't say anything. The police and the family thought it was a mean joke. He always regretted that he couldn't save his brother or his family during the mutiny. He couldn't bear to see their portrait and wanted it destroyed after his mother died, but Doris put it in the attic and had it put back on the wall when Father died."

"Do you still have that note?" asked Dermot with some excitement.

"It should still be in Father's room. Doris left everything in his room just as it was on the day he died."

Just then, Cora came in asking if they had seen Hector. Dermot greeted her and asked her to sit down and answer a few questions. Cora sat next to Flora and looked uncomfortable. Dermot asked Cora whether Allan had told her if he suspected anything untoward in the intelligence service when he visited the manor.

Cora thought for a second. "During the war, he rarely came home, except on some weekends. We were busy too because a part of the estate had been converted into a hospital to take care of wounded soldiers.

"He visited the weekend before he died and he looked upset. I forced him to tell me what was worrying him, and he told me that he suspected that a lady and her son who worked with him in the intelligence service were spies. He was going to set a trap for them to see if his suspicions were well-founded."

"Cora, you never mentioned that! So he may've been innocent after all?" asked Flora, surprised at the revelation.

"He swore me to secrecy. He had, after all, signed the Official Secrets Act and could've gone to prison or been executed for telling me that."

"I'm not surprised. Husbands are known to tell their wives things that they wouldn't tell other people... Did Lady Fitzhugh know about it?" Dermot asked.

"I told her when the newspapers were saying that he was a spy, but Doris forbade me to tell anyone. She said that people would think I was making it up to protect Allan's name," explained Cora.

"Now, did anyone in the family know the contents of the will or that her Ladyship planned to make changes?" asked Dermot.

The two women looked surprised and shrugged their shoulders.

"Doris never discussed her will with anyone. We only found out that Hector gets everything when the will was read. It wasn't a surprise to any of us though, since she was so fond of Hector because he is Allan's son," said Flora.

"Did she say anything about Arthur inheriting those antique guns that are in the library?" Dermot asked.

Flora looked surprised. "Not to us, but Arthur claimed that she had told him that she would make changes to her legacy. Bertram didn't seem to know anything about it though."

Dermot looked at Cora as Flora spoke; she had no expression on her face. He then asked Flora to take him to her father's bedroom. As he left the living room with Flora, he saw a portrait of a man in Tudor-style clothing.

"Is that your ancestor who first owned this estate?" he asked.

"Yes, Jeremiah Thomas Fitzhugh. This estate was gifted to him by King Henry VII for his services as a knight." Flora pointed to another portrait. "That's his son, Roy Fitzhugh. You see that crucifix on his chest? Family legend has it that he had it painted onto the portrait during the Catholic persecutions under Queen Elizabeth's reign. He also installed the statue of the queen in the chapel to show loyalty to her. The family pretended to be converts to the new religion, but secretly practiced the Catholic faith. It was during the Cromwellian period that the family switched to the Church of England. The library used to be a chapel until then and was converted into a library after that, but the statue of Queen Elizabeth remains even after the manor was renovated in the last century. Nobody knows why."

— — —

Dermot and Flora went up the stairs, walked along the corridor, and passed by Lady Fitzhugh's room. They stood in front of a door that looked like it hadn't been opened in a long time. Flora took a set of keys from her dress pocket and flipped through the key ring. She found the key she wanted and unlocked the door. The room was a bit dusty and dark. They entered and Flora went to the window and drew the curtains aside; the sun's rays lit up the room.

Flora pointed at the desk and gave Dermot permission to search it. Dermot went to the writing desk and looked at it. The desk still had papers that were yellowing with time and a pen next to an inkwell. There was a photograph of a woman dressed in the fashion of the mid-eighteenth century. Flora told Dermot that it was her mother and that Lord Fitzhugh had been devastated when she died, even though he had been unfaithful to her.

He opened the desk drawer and looked inside. There was an envelope that was postmarked two days before Lord Fitzhugh died. He opened it and took out the note. The note was yellowing and the ink was starting to fade. It said, 'Remember the diamond mine, the De Villiers family, and your brother's family.' It was not signed.

"The postmark says 'London'. Anyone could've sent this note. Have you received anything since?"

Flora shook her head.

"When did you and Mrs. Endecott come to live here?"

"A few months after Father left for South Africa. Doris was lonely and both our husbands had passed away. So she asked us to come live with her."

Dermot found a cheque book. He went through it and found certain payments made to a 'Portia Hartford'. He noted his discovery in his notebook.

"Who's Portia Hartford?"

Flora shrugged her shoulders. "I haven't the foggiest idea. Father never told us anything about his acquaintances. Maybe a woman who needed help? He once mentioned that coming close to death had made him realise that he needed to help people. He started giving to charity, which he never did before. He even donated money to build Meadowford Hospital. He was a changed man when he returned from South Africa."

"Some of the cheques were made to her account in the Bank of England. I wonder if Lord Fitzhugh was paying her because she knew something damaging about him?"

"Could be, because Father was very particular about keeping the family name free from scandal."

"Hello, what do we have here?" Dermot took a photograph from the drawer and held it up. It was of Lord Fitzhugh sitting on a chair and a man standing behind him on his right. On the back of the photograph was written 'Pretoria, 1898'.

"Oh, yes, that's a picture of Slattery with Father when they had just moved to South Africa. Slattery looked very different as a young man with a moustache – I can hardly recognise him there."

There was nothing else to pique Dermot's interest. After obtaining Flora's permission, Dermot put the note and its envelope in his breast pocket. He now had some leads that he had to follow.

Dermot went home and placed a call to the Metropolitan Police where he worked. He spoke to Detective Lloyd, his superior, and told him what he had learnt from his investigation. He also told Lloyd that he suspected that the deaths of Doris and Allan Fitzhugh could be related and wondered if he could view the file on Allan Fitzhugh's death, even if they were sealed. Detective Lloyd told him that an acquaintance of his at Scotland Yard, named Oswald Gardner, worked with Allan Fitzhugh in the War Office during the Great War, and he would speak to him about getting Dermot the files he needed.

Chapter 8: A Handful of Spies

In London, a man with his hat turned downwards to hide his face stopped in front of a red pillar post box. He furtively glanced around to see if anyone was looking at him. People walked past him, trying to escape the heat, without paying any attention. Satisfied, he reached into his pocket and took out an envelope. He quickly pushed it into the opening of the post box and hurriedly walked away. He was sweating, not only because of the heat but also due to nervousness. He had never done anything like this before. He slowed down and smiled. He knew his letter, which he had carefully typed, would make his victim nervous and pay attention. He was interested in what the outcome would be. Hopefully, it would be what he expected.

—   —   —

Dermot was in his car driving to London. The wind made the heat dissipate a little and he was grateful for that. He was excited about the case but at the same time he was unhappy – he had wanted his holiday to be a relaxing one.

On reaching Scotland Yard, Dermot went to the information desk and asked for Chief Inspector Oswald Gardner. A few minutes later, he saw a middle-aged man with greying hair and a big well-groomed moustache walk towards him. Dermot held out his hand and smiled.

"Detective Carlyle, I presume," the man said as he shook Dermot's hand. "Detective Lloyd has told me about you and the case. He mentioned that you suspect that the murder you're investigating may be linked to an incident that occurred during the war."

"Yes. It's the death of Allan Fitzhugh who worked for the War Office. He was found dead under mysterious circumstances and nobody has a clear answer as to what really happened."

"I remember that case; it was hushed up quickly. The files are all sealed, but I can get them for your investigation. Come this way and we can talk in my office."

Dermot followed Gardner to his office and sat down. It was a very tidy office; on his desk was a typewriter, a stack of files on one side, and some loose sheets of paper in a tray. Gardner sat down too as a secretary came in and gave him two files. He thanked her and she left, closing the door behind her.

Gardner opened the files and looked at them. He placed them in front of Dermot and then pointed to one. "This is his service record. Seems he had an exemplary service. He joined at the beginning of the war. His European travels before the war, particularly to Germany, made him a prime candidate to work in the intelligence service because of his language skills and knowledge of the area."

Gardner saw Dermot nod to indicate that he was aware of it. He pointed to the other file. "This file is on his death, which was very mysterious. He was found shot to death in his London office. He was clutching a piece of paper in his right fist, which came from top secret designs for a submarine that could go deeper than any other built at that time and could attack the enemy U-boats undetected. We never knew he was spying for Germany. We speculated that while he was handing over the plans to his accomplices, he probably changed his mind or demanded more money and they shot him. They made it look like suicide. He was shot through the heart and was found with the gun clutched in his left hand."

"But he was right-handed?"

"Yes, I believe so. Only his fingerprints were found on it, though, and it was ruled a suicide."

"Any idea who these accomplices were?"

"Yes, Mrs. Ethel Northam and her son, David. They had befriended Allan a year earlier while working in the War Office. Exemplary work, but they were very introverted and kept themselves to themselves. They were British subjects from South Africa..."

"South Africa?"

"Yes, they claimed they had worked for the British Army during the Boer War. The son, David, knew a lot about military manoeuvres and tactics. His mother, a widow, stated that her husband was killed in the Second Boer War and that helping England was like a tribute to her husband. They both spoke German and Dutch Afrikaans very well. Ethel worked as a typist, while David helped in decoding the messages we intercepted in German."

"Seems like South Africa comes into the picture all the time."

"What do you mean?" asked Gardner.

"The butler at Fitzhugh Manor, who was murdered, was writing his memoirs about his experiences in South Africa. He went with Lord Fitzhugh and was his batman during the war."

"May be a mere coincidence. Many people came to England after the Boer War, like the Northams did. During the Great War, we needed people with useful experience and so we recruited many who were capable of fighting on our side and also working in the intelligence service."

"What happened to them after Allan was killed?"

"They were reported to have died in a car crash. A guard heard the gunshot and saw those two get into a car and drive away from our office near the London docks. Road blocks were placed since the car was seen heading towards the coast. They managed to break through and were given chase. The coppers were gaining on them when they were separated by a flock of sheep. By the time the sheep got off the road, ten minutes had passed. All of a sudden, the coppers saw a column of smoke and went towards it. The car had gone off the cliff. Their bodies were never found and were presumed to have been washed into the sea. We did find scraps of clothing and some remnants of the secret plans for the submarine."

"So none of the plans could be salvaged?"

"No, they were burnt in the fire. The car exploded on the rocks below. We also found a remnant of a petrol can. The can must've opened when the car went down the hill and that probably helped accelerate the fire. We suspect that they were Boers who came to England with the influx of English settlers displaced during the war. Their opportunity to take revenge on England came during the Great War."

"If Allan Fitzhugh wasn't a spy, why go to all the trouble of befriending him, then killing and framing him as a spy? It just doesn't make sense. It seems like they had him in their sights all along."

"Everyone knew that Allan was from one of the prominent families in this region and that would make him trustworthy. His knowledge of Germany and other places gave him access to top secret documents and plans. So, these Boer spies for Germany knew that Allan was someone who could get those secrets for them. The only question is why he would betray his country?"

"He wasn't spying for Germany. His wife told me that he suspected them of spying and he wanted to trap them. He swore her to secrecy."

"If he had only shared his suspicions with us, then the two of them would have been put under surveillance. We can only speculate what happened from the evidence we have."

"What did they do before they joined the intelligence service?"

"They both worked at St. Cuthbert's Hospital in London. They had excellent references from the hospital. Their work was impeccable. Nobody had anything bad to say about them."

"Any pictures of them?"

"Unfortunately, no. It seems that after they shot Allan Fitzhugh, they burnt their files in the fire place. It mystified us as to why he would have their files in his office but, like you said, probably because he suspected them."

Dermot asked if he could take the files with him since he may find some clues in them. Gardner gave him permission to do so, with instructions that they must be returned because they belonged to His Majesty's Government.

As Dermot walked back to his car, he couldn't help but wonder why this case was so mysterious. Most murders were open and shut cases, but this case seemed to be linked to a mysterious death from a decade ago. He decided to visit St. Cuthbert's Hospital and find out more about the Northams.

— — —

Dermot showed his police badge at the front desk and asked to be shown to the director of the hospital. Dr. Butterworth was a stout and balding man with glasses. He looked like a strict school headmaster who wouldn't tolerate any insolence and he seemed annoyed for being disturbed.

"Police business. It's of the utmost importance," said Dermot, trying to sound very stern. He had faced such situations before and knew that saying he was from the police made people take him seriously.

Dr. Butterworth immediately put down his pen and set his papers aside. "What would you like to know, Detective Carlyle?"

"Do you remember two people who worked here and left just before the Great War began? Their names were Ethel and David Northam... a mother and son."

"I wasn't the director then, but I was a doctor performing surgeries. I hardly knew them. Nobody had any complaints about them that I remember and they both kept to themselves. David worked as an orderly and Ethel in the hospital dispensary."

"Were they close to any of the staff here?"

"Could be. You must remember that it has been several years since they worked here and many of the staff have now gone their separate ways. Some, like the Northams, volunteered during the Great War and never returned."

"There has to be someone here who remembers them well!"

"I don't know, Detective. That is all I can tell you. It's hard keeping up with files and paperwork, and it's definitely hard keeping up with people from many years ago. Why are you asking?"

"Can't reveal much, but they were involved in something untoward during the war years."

Dr. Butterworth shrugged his shoulders. "I read about that in the papers and it is hard to believe that they were spies. We never had any problems with them here."

Dermot could see that Dr. Butterworth was getting a bit uneasy. He thanked him and left his office. As he walked along the corridor, he passed by the hospital dispensary. It was a clean room, with a desk and a few chairs. There was an older woman standing behind the counter and placing bandages in the cupboard. Dermot went in.

"Excuse me. Have you been working here for a long time?" he asked.

The woman turned around and eyed him curiously.

"Who wants to know?"

Dermot took out his badge and showed it to her. "I work for the Metropolitan Police. I want to ask if you knew a Mrs. Ethel Northam and her son, David, who worked in this hospital before the war."

The woman looked at him. "My dear fellow, it's been many years since anyone came enquiring about them. My memory isn't what it used to be."

Dermot smiled. "May I know your name, please?"

"Sister Claudette Fleming. I've worked here for over twenty years."

"Perfect. It would be vital if you could remember anything about them."

She thought for some time and told Dermot that Ethel was quiet and kept to herself, but was close to her son. They came and went home together. When the Great War began, they decided to help with the war effort and claimed that their experiences during the Boer War would be of value to the British Government. They had even changed their accents to sound British.

"What did she do here?"

"She helped the chemist prepare medicines. Sometimes, she would accompany doctors and help dress wounds with the ointments we prepared here. All our dispensary workers did that. My assistant, Eunice, is doing that right now."

Dermot looked at the walls and saw a few pictures of the staff. A thought flashed through his mind and he asked Sister Fleming if she had any photographs of the Northams before they left to work for the government. She told him that there was a picture of the staff taken when the Great War began and that she had taken it for safe keeping when a part of the hospital was damaged in one of the German Zeppelin raids. She had kept the photograph in her attic and hadn't seen it since the war.

Dermot took out his card, wrote on it, and then handed it to her. "This is my telephone number in Meadowford where I will be staying for a few more days. Please call me when you find that picture. It's of utmost importance."

Sister Fleming nodded. He then asked her where the Northams had lived while they worked at the hospital and she told him that they lived at 245B Cheshire Street, which was just up the road.

—   —   —

Dermot walked out of the hospital and took a deep breath. He never thought that this case would be so complicated. Maybe the facts he was collecting were irrelevant to the murders and he should just focus on the household of Fitzhugh Manor. Perhaps it was just a robbery that went horribly wrong when Lady Fitzhugh woke up. The thieves killed her so she wouldn't identify them and Slattery had known who the killers were. However, he couldn't put out that aching feeling in his bones that he must follow this lead as well. The investigation was getting more complicated, as well as challenging.

He drove to Cheshire Street and located the building. It looked like a boarding house. There was a sign on one of the windows advertising rooms for rent. He knocked on the door and it was opened a few minutes later by an older woman holding a cleaning cloth.

"Yes, who is it?" she asked, eyeing him suspiciously.

"I'm Detective Carlyle from the Metropolitan Police. Are you the landlady?"

"Yes, what do you want?"

"I was wondering if I could talk to you about two former tenants of yours – Mrs. Ethel and David Northam?"

"Blimey, that was a while back. They left when the Great War started. Why do you want to know about them?"

"Their names came up during an investigation and I need any information you can provide about them."

"All right, come in and I'll put the kettle on. I knew those two would be trouble," she said.

Dermot followed her into the parlour and sat next to a small circular table. The landlady introduced herself as Sylvia Henderson and a few minutes later she brought over two cups of hot tea. She added sugar and milk and handed the cup to Dermot. Dermot took a sip of the tea and felt better.

"What sort of tea is this?"

"Indian, I suppose; tastes much better than Chinese." She sat down opposite him. "Now, about them Northams?"

He asked her to tell him anything she remembered about the Northams and she said that they were ideal tenants. They gave no trouble, paid their rent on time, and mostly kept to themselves. They arrived at her boarding house in 1903, because they had obtained employment at St. Cuthbert's Hospital. They told her that they were displaced by the Boer War and had recently come to England. They left in 1914 and lived close to the London docks. The next she heard about them was when she read in the newspapers that they had been killed in an accident.

"Did they have any visitors?"

"Mr. Northam had a few lady visitors and that upset his mother..." She lowered her voice and came closer. "You know, he was the randy type." She then spoke normally. "I heard them arguing once and he said that she shouldn't be bothered since she weren't his real mother."

Dermot grimaced. "That's strange. What else was out of the ordinary?"

"They had letters from Scotland, but they said they had never lived there when I asked."

Dermot sat up straight when he heard the word 'Scotland'. "From who? Do you know which part of Scotland?"

"Don't remember. Ain't my place to ask questions or pry into my boarders' lives."

"I'm sure... Any letters from South Africa?"

"No, but they did get a letter from France once, just after the Great War began."

"Was this the first time they received a letter from France?" asked Dermot with surprise.

"I can't say, but I remember Mr. Northam's face when he took the letter. He just said, 'It can't be him, after all these years...'"

"Why did you say that they would be trouble when you asked me to come in?"

"Because of the way they died. The coppers and reporters questioned me, but told me nothing. I reckon there was more to it than what them newspapers were saying."

Dermot finished his tea and thanked her. As he got up to leave, Sylvia held out a plate of biscuits.

"Here, Detective, have a biscuit. I baked them myself."

Dermot took one, thanked her, and left.

Chapter 9: The Mystery Woman

It was just after midday when Dermot left Cheshire Street and thought it was best to drive to the Bank of England and find out more about Portia Hartford. He went up to the teller and asked to speak to the bank manager. Mr. Perkins came out and greeted Dermot. He was a short, pot-bellied man with a balding head and glasses. Dermot introduced himself and told him that he needed information on the account that used to belong to Portia Hartford.

"Certainly, Detective. Do you know when the account was opened?"

Dermot took out his writing pad. "I think in 1903. That's when the first payment was made to Portia Hartford."

Mr. Perkins rolled his eyes. "Detective, that is more than twenty years ago. I'll try my best."

Dermot nodded and smiled. "I expect nothing less."

Mr. Perkins eyed him curiously and went to speak to his assistant. The assistant disappeared into a room. He directed Dermot into the office and they sat down. The assistant came in with a big book that looked like a ledger, which he deposited on the table.

After the assistant left, Mr. Perkins opened the ledger and looked at the records. He told Dermot that the account was opened on the third of September, 1903, and that ten pounds was deposited. When it was closed on the fourth of March, 1906, there was two hundred pounds in the account. The cheques were either mailed to the bank by Lord Fitzhugh or deposited by Miss Hartford, and she alone withdrew the money.

Dermot asked if he could see the ledger and Mr. Perkins handed it over to him. Dermot looked at his notes and also the recorded entries of the deposits.

"The amounts match. Now, was there an address listed on the account?"

Mr. Perkins turned to a page. "Yes, she lived at 34 Bishopsgate in East London. She must've been very poor to live there. I bet the money was a great help to her."

Dermot agreed, thanked Mr. Perkins, and left.

— — —

The East End had improved since the previous century, but it was still poorer than the other areas of London. As he drove through, he wondered how the woman had come to know any of the expensive secrets that Lord Fitzhugh had paid to keep silent. He asked for directions and in a few minutes he pulled up outside a building that despite its dilapidated state still looked better than the others on the street. Dermot's interest in the mystery was getting stronger.

He got out of the car and walked up the steps. He knocked and the door was opened by a plainly dressed woman.

"'Oo is it?" she asked in a cockney accent.

"Are you the landlady of this building?"

"Yes, what d'you want? I ain't got no rooms." She looked at Dermot's car. "Fancy car you got there, mister. Wouldn't catch me in a place like this if I 'ad a car like that."

Dermot smiled. "Madam, I'm a detective and here on police business. I'm not looking for a room to rent."

She stared at him. "S'pose you better come in then. Don't know what you'd want from me though. If it's about that robbery down the street, well Lord knows I ain't got nothin' to do with it."

"No, Madam. Now, may I ask your name please?"

"Blimey, aren't you full of them posh manners. Charmin' too. Hard to find that around 'ere. Mrs. Enid Potter's my name."

Dermot followed her into her flat. She offered him tea, but he kindly refused. Dermot asked her if she remembered Portia Hartford and she shrugged her shoulders and said that she didn't.

"She lived here probably from 1903 or earlier to 1906. Why don't you check your records?"

"I don't need t'look at any records. I've them all in 'ere," she said, pointing to her head.

"Mrs. Potter, this is a police investigation. I would urge you to check your records," he said sternly.

She mumbled under her breath, went to a shelf, and took out a book. She opened the book and looked at it for a few minutes.

"No, Detective, none by that name. Only one lady and her daughter lived here and left in 1906. Her name was Mrs. Frida Wilson. She came in December 1898..." She showed Dermot the book. He saw the dates and nodded.

"She was a strange un."

"Why do you say that?"

Enid told Dermot that when Frida Wilson came to live at her boarding house with a newborn baby, she was penniless. She had to work as a charwoman because her husband had died in an accident. Then, in 1903, she stopped working and started wearing nicer clothes. She even sent her daughter to a good school, saying that one day her daughter would be a lady. Frida even started talking 'like one of them aristocrats'. She bought a typewriter and started taking secretarial classes by correspondence. She told Enid that her uncle had died and left her some money. Then, in 1906, she left in a hurry and without a forwarding address, after selling some furniture and clothes, saying that she was going to marry someone.

"What did the mother and daughter look like?"

"Frida had brown hair and Adele, the littlun, had red hair. She said the red hair came from the girl's father. Frida was a looker though. Not surprised she got someone to marry her again."

"Before she left, was she happy or upset?"

"Come t'think of it, she was upset when she read in the paper that some lord had died. She kept sayin' that he was a good man. Methinks that she never met 'im but pretended like she 'ad. How could she, being lowly like us..."

"Did she have any gentleman callers?"

"If she did, she probably got 'em in without me or anyone knowing. She sometimes got right dressed up to go out, littlun too. Adele came back with chocolates and a stuffed bear once."

He took out the envelope that Lord Fitzhugh had received and asked Mrs. Potter if the handwriting on the note belonged to Frida Wilson, but she couldn't confirm it. Dermot thanked her and left.

— — —

Dermot reached home just as it was getting dark. His mother had kept his dinner out for him and he devoured it because he hadn't eaten since breakfast. He went to his room, looked at his notes, and read the files he received from Oswald Gardner. He wondered why the Northams claimed to be pro-British during the Boer War and the Great War and then spied for Germany? Was it a coincidence that they both worked at St. Cuthbert's Hospital where Lord Fitzhugh had his surgery just before he died? Did Allan find out something about his father's death and that is why they killed him then made him a scapegoat by framing him as a spy? Nothing made sense.

Chapter 10: Entering the Limelight

Dermot got up early the next day and drove back to London. He wanted to get to the London Library before it got crowded. He went into the reading room where two men were already there, reading the newspapers. Dermot walked to the front desk. Miss Cartwright, seated at the desk, raised her head and smiled at him.

"Good morning, Detective Carlyle. You're up and about early, I see."

Miss Cartwright was middle-aged and had worked at the library for nearly three decades. She was gifted with an exceptional memory and knew where every document and book was kept. Dermot knew he could always rely on her. Dermot greeted her and told her that he needed information on the Second Anglo-Boer War. Miss Cartwright told him to have a seat and went away. She returned a little while later wheeling a trolley stacked with papers and books and parked it next to Dermot. She informed him that there were letters, articles, and testimonies from both British as well as Boer soldiers. The books were written after the war and would provide him with the historical background of the war. Dermot thanked her. She smiled and went back to her desk.

Dermot looked through the newspapers and articles that were chock-full of the heroic exploits of British and colonial soldiers and also information about the various battles fought. Dermot also read some obituaries of the mostly young British men who had perished in the conflict.

As Dermot continued perusing, he stumbled upon an article about concentration camps that had been started by the British to intern the Boer farmers and their families. This aroused his curiosity and he read further articles about the shocking conditions of the camps. He noted that there was a concentration camp at Kimberley. The pictures of the emaciated internees sent a shiver down his spine. He couldn't believe that the civilised British Empire would treat Boer women and children in such a horrendous manner.

There was an article about the De Villiers' mine explosion and also the subsequent lawsuit for fraud brought by the Middleton & Price Insurance Company against Lord Fitzhugh. He perused the article and found that the company had paid a sum of one hundred thousand pounds to Lord Fitzhugh when he won the case. There was another article where he was interviewed when he returned home from South Africa after winning the case. He mentioned how much he had missed Meadowford Village and how he wanted to spend the rest of his days there.

Suddenly, an idea flashed through Dermot's mind. He got up and spoke to Miss Cartwright and then she disappeared into a room, closing the door behind her. Dermot perused through more articles about the war and noted certain points that interested him. When Miss Cartwright came back, she placed a newspaper from July, 1857, in front of Dermot.

"I forgot about this. You were right," she said excitedly. "Lord Fitzhugh was interviewed when he returned with his family after escaping the mutiny. The article is on the second page. Thomas Sutton, who worked for the *London Times*, interviewed him. There's also an artist's rendition of the family's escape in the caravan and of the grieving mother of William and Theo Fitzhugh."

After she left, Dermot read the article and found that it matched with what Flora Ainsworth had told him. He looked at the artist's drawing of the grieving mother and felt sorry for her. Dermot read a few more articles, letters, and portions of books. After he had finished, he thanked Miss Cartwright for her help. As he was about to walk away, he asked her what she meant when she said 'I forgot about this' when she handed him the newspaper.

Miss Cartwright tapped her forehead. "I know it's been a long time, but this lady came here several years ago. She was reading the newspapers and then asked me for the same newspaper from 1857 about Lord Fitzhugh's escape from the mutiny."

"Interesting... What happened then?"

"She started sobbing after reading the article. She looked like she'd seen a ghost. People stared at her and when I asked her what had upset her and she only said 'All lies, all lies...' She took her things and walked out. I never saw her again."

"What did she look like?"

"Very plain looking. Maybe middle-aged. Nothing unusual about her."

"Do you remember when this happened?"

"I think it was before Lord Fitzhugh died. I remember the newspapers had stories about him being close to death's door."

Dermot thanked her. He knew that Miss Cartwright's phenomenal memory was always right.

— — —

As Dermot walked towards his car, he saw someone familiar on the opposite side of the road. He realised that it was Pippa. When he had interviewed her, she had told him that she had a flat in London, that she worked for Selfridges on Oxford Street selling perfume, and that she also shopped at Oxford Street using some of the inheritance she received from her father after his death. However, now she was quite some distance away from Oxford Street where she usually shopped. Dermot decided to follow her.

People all around were hurrying to escape the blazing sun, but Pippa calmly headed towards her destination. She walked for some time and then stopped in front of a door. She knocked and it opened a few seconds later. He saw her greet someone and then enter. After the door closed, Dermot surreptitiously walked to the door and read the notice on it. It was the back door of a theatre.

"Pippa's an actress?" he said to himself and smiled. "Nobody mentioned it."

Dermot decided to investigate and walked around the building towards the front door. The door was locked. He knocked and the cover of the grille opened. He could barely see the face of the man on the other side.

"Who is it?" the man asked.

"This is Detective Dermot Carlyle from the Metropolitan Police. Is the theatre open?"

"No, we open on the thirtieth of next month for the production of *A Mistress at Hand*. You're welcome to come then. We're only rehearsing the play now."

"Can I come in? I've never been to a play rehearsal before. I'm sure you won't object, unless you're doing something illegal," he said, smiling.

The man hesitated, then said, "All right, you can come in and see. But you must be careful. If anyone asks, I will say that you would like to see how we perform before you decide to join us. Nobody needs to know that you're from the police. Once you're satisfied that there's nothing wrong, please leave us alone."

"You have my word, sir."

The grille closed and, a few seconds later, the door opened. Dermot walked in and he noticed that the man was slightly taller than him with a clean-shaven face and he wore a tweed hat. He held out his hand and Dermot shook it. He introduced himself as Francis Abernathy and he owned the theatre. He came from Leeds, along with his acting troupe, and was trying to market his play, which he co-wrote with the director. He bought the theatre building more than a year ago and then renovated it. He then asked Dermot to follow him.

Dermot followed Francis inside and they walked down a corridor.

"Normally I'm not at the theatre," Francis said. "I go around London and the suburbs to get some publicity for the play. If we have success on the opening night, then we can stay on in London."

He opened the double doors and they both walked in. Dermot found himself inside a large auditorium with several rows of seats. The actors were getting ready on the stage in front. Dermot and Francis sat in the last row, which was not well lit. The director of the play was sitting in the front, along with some of the cast. He gave the go ahead and the rehearsal commenced.

"We have a talented cast and some joined us in London," Francis whispered to Dermot.

Dermot watched the rehearsal and then he saw Pippa. She was playing the role of Celestine, the French mistress, in the play. She played her part to perfection.

"She's wonderful, isn't she? One wouldn't say she's British with that French accent," said Dermot.

"Yes, that is Philippa Fitzgerald. She's talented and charming."

Dermot looked at him and realised that Francis liked Pippa. "I thought her name is Pippa Fitzhugh, or is Philippa Fitzgerald just her stage name?"

Francis looked stunned. "Her family doesn't approve of her acting. She cannot reveal her real name."

"I understand. Mum's the word. Now, have other actors shown any interest in her?"

"Not really, but she's seeing this painter fellow. He's a lot older than her. Don't know what she sees in him. Some girls like older men, I reckon. He's been here twice and some of the other actresses have said that they find him very attractive."

Dermot could detect some jealously and silently chuckled, wondering whether Pippa knew that Francis liked her.

"He doesn't mind her acting?"

"Not at all, he is very Bohemian."

Dermot wondered what Pippa's aunts would say if they ever found out that she was acting. He looked at his watch and realised that he had to leave. He thanked Francis and wished him success with his play. Francis invited him to come on the opening night.

"I will try my best. Cheerio!"

Dermot left the theatre and walked back to the London Library where he had parked his car. He then drove home to Meadowford.

— — —

Dermot rang the doorbell of Major Havelock's modest home. Gerda let him in and showed him into the living room. The walls of the room had many trophies that Major Havelock had brought back from countries he had been stationed in or visited during his career in the British Army. Dermot looked around with awe. Lion and tiger heads mounted one wall and deer antlers mounted the other. Swords, daggers, and guns were either in a display case or mounted on the remaining walls.

"I see that you are admiring my souvenirs," said Major Havelock as he walked into the living room.

"Yes, Major Havelock. I've never seen so many on the walls of a living room. You must've had many adventures."

"I did. India, Africa, the Middle East, and South America – all have their own souvenirs to offer. I always felt I needed to bring a little piece of those places back with me, either to reminisce or to show off to the people who have never set foot out of Meadowford. If it were not for this damn leg, I wouldn't have retired early and probably would've become a general." He walked towards Dermot, wincing in pain. "Let me tell you one thing... the wounds you get when you're young do come back to haunt you in your later years."

Dermot pointed to two medals in a display case and asked him about them. Major Havelock told him that the King's and Queen's South Africa Medals were bestowed on him for his services during the Boer War.

Dermot and Major Havelock sat facing each other on armchairs. The armchair creaked under the weight of the old soldier. He looked at Dermot sternly and his blue eyes shone like diamonds. Then, in a gruff voice, he said, "I don't think you came here to ask me about these souvenirs. So out with it, Detective."

Dermot smiled at the brusqueness. "I understand that you served with Lord Fitzhugh in South Africa during the Boer War?"

"Yes, I knew him from here. Despite his advanced age, he volunteered to fight for his Queen and country, to subdue those Boers and help the British get their foothold in South Africa. A great man indeed."

"I'm sure," Dermot said, nonchalantly. "Was there anyone who held a grudge against Lord Fitzhugh when he commanded his regiment near Kimberley?"

Dermot could see that the question caught the major by surprise. Major Havelock thought for a moment. "No, we fought regular battles and he was a good general. The soldiers he commanded loved and respected him."

"I was told that you were close to her Ladyship. So, at the party, did she say anything unusual to you?"

"She said she had discovered that someone at the party wasn't being honest. She wanted to enjoy her party and planned on confronting that person the next day with the evidence she had."

"Was she talking about a man?"

"Yes, I believe so. I think she was talking about Arthur. He has always been a funny one. Lilian had a hard time disciplining him as a child. There was one instance when he was ten..."

"Yes, I know that he is a hard person to deal with, but that does not mean that he would murder his own aunt."

"Listen, Detective, when you've lived as long as I have and seen the things I've seen, nothing in this world will surprise you. He did say that Doris was his favourite aunt during the toast, but those were mere words. He's getting his inheritance since Doris is now dead."

Dermot thought for a second. "I think you're right. People have killed for a lot less. I thank you for your time, Major Havelock."

As he got up to leave, Major Havelock said, "I hope you find whoever did this to poor Doris. I shan't show him any mercy and would like to hang him from the lamp post in the village square."

— — —

The next morning, Dermot and Inspector Enderby went to Fitzhugh Manor. Inspector Enderby had placed two of his constables as guards the previous day and he wanted Dermot to meet them. The two constables went towards the two men when they saw them approaching. Inspector Enderby introduced them to Dermot. Andrew Barnaby was a young constable who had just joined the police force. He was of medium height and had red hair. Terence Jenkins was taller and had jet black hair.

"They will each work twelve-hour shifts and then be replaced by Constables Blackwood and Clarke. Jenkins will guard the front door, while Barnaby the backdoor, and he will make his rounds around the manor every two hours," explained Inspector Enderby as he handed Dermot a slip of paper containing the names of the four constables.

"Who's Aindrea Barnaby?" asked Dermot as he read the names.

"Me, sir. Me mum's Scottish and Aindrea is Scottish for Andrew," said Barnaby.

"Anything suspicious, Jenkins?" asked Inspector Enderby.

"No, Inspector. Very quiet and no one suspicious has come close to the manor. Just the regular staff and people who live here. Of course, the fellow that's courting Miss Fitzhugh comes and goes frequently."

"What about the backdoor, Barnaby?"

"Just the kitchen staff and people who deliver groceries. Nobody else. All have been checked and they've been coming here for many years. No one out of the ordinary."

"Very good! Remember your training and if anything out of the ordinary happens, or you get wind of any information, you know what to do."

The two constables nodded.

"How are the occupants of the manor?" asked Dermot.

"They're nice, Detective. The maids bring us our meals and tea. Miss Carter knows when I make my rounds and she likes chatting with us," said Constable Barnaby.

"The only person that's mean is that grumpy battleaxe, Mrs. Endecott. I think any man that meets her will reconsider marriage and be happy being a confirmed bachelor," said Constable Jenkins.

"You don't say... I've heard that Lady Fitzhugh was very kind. Wish somebody murdered Mrs. Endecott instead of her Ladyship," said Barnaby.

Dermot masked a grin, but Inspector Enderby looked furious.

"Barnaby, you're new here so I will let that go. Never joke about murder again. Is that clear? By God, I will make sure you'll be shovelling dirt by the roadside for the rest of that miserable life of yours."

Barnaby's face turned as red as his hair. "Sorry, sir, it'll never happen again. I promise."

"Good. Now get back to your stations, you two."

"Yes, sir," said the two constables. As they turned to leave, Dermot winked at Constable Barnaby to let him know that he understood why he had made an uncharitable comment about Lilian Endecott.

Chapter 11: Tea Time in the Library

Miss Carter entered the bedroom, carrying a glass of milk.

"Feeling better, Hector?" she asked.

"Yes, Miss Carter. I've been taking my tonic."

"Good boy, Hector. The doctor knows what's best for you." She placed the milk next to Hector and looked inside the bathroom. "Let me take that glass on the sink," she said as she walked inside the bathroom and took the glass.

"I'm glad you're taking your tonic. Your mother wants you to get better. She worries about you."

"Yes, I know, but that tonic is horrible. Never tasted anything like it."

"I understand." Miss Carter laughed. "Never liked tonics myself... Oh! Pippa's here with Mr. Seymour. She told me to ask you if you'd like to go out with them if you're feeling better."

"What do they plan to do?"

"They plan on riding the horses to the stream beyond the meadow. I know you'd like that." She looked at her pocket watch. "It'll be four o'clock in twenty minutes. Time for them to have tea. You better drink your milk and tell them if you want to go along so that Pippa can tell Charles to get your horse ready too. They plan to go riding at half past four." She smiled and left the room.

Hector was elated at the idea. He wanted to ride the horse that was gifted to him on his birthday two years earlier. He loved riding his horse, Lightning, in the fields and meadows around Fitzhugh Manor. His grandfather and father had been avid horsemen and so was his sister. The stables only had three horses remaining. Pippa and Richard would sometimes ride the horses when Richard visited Fitzhugh Manor.

He drank his milk, jumped out of bed, and ran to his mother's room. He told her that he wanted to go riding with Pippa and Richard.

"Hector, you've only just recovered from fever," Cora replied.

"I'm all right, Mother. You fuss too much. Please, Mother, I'm tired of being in the house all day," said Hector showing his irritation.

Cora sighed and relented, but not before lecturing him on being careful because he was the heir to the estate when he came of age. She then told him to tell Miss Carter to get his riding clothes ready and to tell Pippa that he had permission to go riding with them.

Hector went and told Miss Carter to get his riding clothes ready. He was happy that he finally had his mother's permission to get away and have some fun outside. Being the only heir was no fun for him. He was constantly being watched. He envied Pippa since she got to live in London in her own flat and did as she pleased. He was told that it was because she was older. Hector couldn't wait until he was older and got out of the clutches of his mother and aunts. They did not understand a young boy like him.

He wished his father were alive. Hector barely had any memory of his father, but from what he was told his father was very stern, but also very kind and understanding. Pippa had a lot of loving memories of him. He also missed Harrow. Even though some bullies taunted him about his father being a turncoat, he still had a few friends his age and loved being around them.

Hector went downstairs to the living room and told Pippa and Richard that his mother had given him permission to ride with them. Pippa told him to change into his riding clothes and be ready by four-thirty, while she and Richard had tea together.

A few minutes after Hector left, Miss Carter came into the living room with a tray containing tea, fish paste sandwiches, and apples.

"It's too hot in the living room, Miss Fitzhugh. The library is a lot cooler since I've opened the windows, so it would be nice to have tea in there."

"I think Miss Carter's suggestion is wonderful. Why don't we do just that?" said Richard sarcastically.

Miss Carter looked at Richard and sort of snorted at him.

"Sure, Miss Carter. Richard loves looking at the collection of books we have in there. The library seems to be his favourite place in the manor."

Miss Carter turned and walked away. "Just make sure that the books are not misplaced. I had to put *Moby Dick* back in its place."

After Miss Carter walked away, Pippa turned to Richard. "I can't understand why she doesn't like you. Give her some time. Just like my aunts, she will also come to like you."

"I suppose so. That old bird probably thinks I'm too old and not good enough for you."

They both got up and walked out of the living room. Richard headed to the library, while Pippa went out of the manor and walked down the hill to the stables. She told Charles to get all three horses ready. Then she walked back up the hill and into the manor. Constables Jenkins and Barnaby greeted her at the front door. Pippa went to the library and saw Richard sitting on one of the armchairs, reading a book.

"*Moby Dick*? Didn't you read it as a child, Richard?"

"No, but my father told me the story when I was young and I've always been fascinated by the story and about how the desire for vengeance can consume a person."

"You better put it back properly since Miss Carter doesn't like you misplacing the books. I didn't know that you had started another book. I thought you were still reading *The Count of Monte Cristo*, which you started on Aunt Doris' birthday."

Before he could answer, the clock on the wall struck four and Pippa got flustered.

"Oh! We must hurry up and have tea. We leave when Hector comes down. Knowing Hector, we may be out riding for a long time and you may get hungry," said Pippa, cutting an apple.

Richard got up and walked towards Pippa. She poured him a cup of tea and handed it to him. Richard held the saucer and it tilted, spilling tea on his shirt.

"Richard, what have you done? You will have to change your shirt or the stain will never come off," said Pippa, sounding annoyed. She looked at her blouse and saw that some tea had also spilled on hers.

"Oh, how clumsy of me! I'm very sorry. Must be this heat."

"Why don't you change your shirt quickly? I'll give it to one of the maids to wash or the stain won't go away. I too must do the same with my blouse."

"I don't have another shirt. I'm afraid I may not be able to go horse riding with you."

"I will ask Mother if she can give me one of Father's shirts. She wouldn't mind giving it to me if I asked."

"It is too far to walk to the bathroom on the other side of the manor," Richard said. "Let me remove the shirt here and give it to you. I'd better close the library door before your aunts see me without my shirt. I can sit by the window reading the book and finish my tea while you change your blouse and get me another shirt. You can be back here at four-thirty, in time to go horse riding as planned."

Pippa agreed, walked out of the library, and closed the door. A few seconds later, Richard partially opened the door and handed his shirt to Pippa.

"See you at four-thirty, my dear," she said, taking his shirt. She walked away while he closed the door.

—   —   —

Richard sat on the window sill drinking tea and eating the sandwiches and the apple that Pippa had cut for him. He continued reading *Moby Dick* when, all of a sudden, he heard someone speak.

"Hello there, Mr. Seymour. Everything all right?"

"Yes, Constable Barnaby. The library is very warm due to this nasty heatwave. Just need to be near the window to get some relief." He then told Barnaby how he accidently spilled his tea and that Pippa had gone to get him another shirt and to also change her blouse.

"Yes, those stains are hard to get out if not tended to immediately. You don't want those two old birds seeing you without your shirt though, especially Mrs. Endecott. That woman is…"

"Oh look, there's Charles. Looks like he's heading to the kitchen; hope he has our horses ready."

Richard saw Charles looking at them. He waved at Charles, who waved back.

"Well, I will let you get on with your book," said Barnaby. "I'm sure Miss Fitzhugh will not take long to get ready."

Richard grimaced. "You know how women are. They always take their time."

Just then the clock in the library started chiming.

"Is it four-thirty already? Pippa should be here… Oh, she's knocking on the door. Blimey! Time really flies when you're reading or talking."

Constable Barnaby nodded and walked away towards the side of the building.

— — —

Pippa knocked on the library door just as the clock began to chime, but there was no response.

"Richard, it's Pippa. I have a shirt for you. It is four-thirty and we have to get going." She knocked again.

"Coming, darling. Just talking to Constable Barnaby from the window. He just left."

Pippa heard the sound of something hitting the ground. "Richard, are you all right?" Then she heard the sound of something breaking.

"Yes, darling, it's just this confounded teacup. I accidently dropped it again and it broke."

"You better clean up the mess. You know, Miss Carter will have something to say about it."

Richard opened the door, stuck out his hand, and took the shirt. He closed the door and came out when he was dressed. Pippa went in and looked at the broken teacup on the tray, next to the other refreshments.

"No mess, darling, the cup was empty. I put the broken bits on the tea tray. Now... I have an idea that will cheer up Hector. Why don't we go to the caves while we're at the stream? I have the torch from the library desk in my pocket."

Pippa nodded and looked at the clock. "We better leave. It's getting late. Where's Hector?"

They both walked out of the library and saw Hector coming down the stairs.

"Hector, don't dawdle," Pippa said. "It's past four-thirty."

Hector shrugged his shoulders. "Miss Carter delayed in bringing my riding clothes. She had an errand to run."

"Richard, the shirt that I just gave you is drenched with sweat."

"It's hot in the library. I even sat on the window sill to cool off and it didn't help."

"So much for Miss Carter saying that the library is cooler due to the windows being open. The riding will cool you off... Come on, you two," said Pippa, impatiently. Richard looked at Hector and rolled his eyes.

They walked out of the front door, past Constable Jenkins, and down the hill towards the stables. When they reached the stables, they found the three horses were already saddled, but there was no sign of Charles.

"I saw him walking towards the kitchen a while back. I waved at him while talking to Constable Barnaby."

"He must've been summoned for an errand. We can take the horses out ourselves," said Pippa.

Chapter 12: An Afternoon Canter

Dermot was having his tea when the phone rang. He picked up the receiver and listened.

"Dermot, there's been another incident at Fitzhugh Manor," said Inspector Enderby.

"Another murder?"

"No, probably an attempted murder. This time it is the boy."

"Hector???"

"Yes, his saddle strap was cut. It came off when they were racing and Hector fell off the horse. Fortunately, he fell on some dried grass and he's not badly hurt."

"The poor chap. I'll get there right away," Dermot said.

Dermot changed and drove to Fitzhugh Manor as fast as he could. When he arrived, he saw a police car and an ambulance. He parked his car and got out. Inspector Enderby was waiting for him outside. He showed Dermot the saddle strap and he examined it. Inspector Enderby told him that he had already interviewed Richard Seymour, who had just left to catch the train back to London, and also Charles. Pippa was too distraught to talk and Hector was still being examined by Dr. Fielding. Dermot said that he would interview Pippa and Hector.

"Yes, they seem to like you. Maybe it is because you're young," said Inspector Enderby. Dermot smiled.

Inspector Enderby got into the car and drove off, taking the saddle to the police station. Dermot looked at his watch and decided to finish interviewing everyone before it got too late. He went into the manor and found Lilian Endecott sitting by herself in the main hall, looking sad.

"How's Hector?" he asked her.

"He's in his room. Dr. Fielding is with him. It was rank stupidity of Cora to allow Hector to ride the horse when he was not well."

Dermot heard footsteps and saw Dr. Fielding coming down the staircase.

"How is he?" asked Lilian.

"The fall has shaken him quite a bit. His arm is sprained and he has a slight concussion since he hit his head on the ground, but he'll be fine in a couple of days."

"That's good news. How are Pippa and Mrs. Fitzhugh?" asked Dermot.

"They're both upset and in the drawing room," said Dr. Fielding.

"Can I talk to Pippa?"

"Yes, but be careful what you say. She feels guilty about the accident since it was her idea to go horse riding," said Dr. Fielding.

Dermot went to the drawing room and saw Pippa and Cora staring at the floor, looking worried. He told them that Dr. Fielding had assured him Hector would be all right and he saw them breathe a sigh of relief. He then proceeded to ask Pippa to tell him what had happened.

Pippa composed herself and sat up straight. "Yes, of course." She cleared her throat and told Dermot about making plans with Richard to ride the horses to the stream and about Hector wanting to come along. She went to the stables to inform Charles about getting the horses ready. Dermot interrupted to ask her what time she returned from the stables.

"It was just before four. When I entered the library, I heard the clock chime and I told Richard to hurry up and have his tea. Richard was so engrossed in reading *Moby Dick*, that he didn't notice the time. I was surprised that he was reading it because the last time he was reading *The Count of Monte Cristo*, which he had begun on the day of the birthday party."

Dermot nodded as he made a note in his notebook. Pippa told him about Richard accidently spilling tea and that he decided to stay in the library while she took his shirt and got him a clean one. After she had changed her blouse, she got a shirt for Richard from Cora and went to the laundry room, but didn't find Abigail. So, she went to the kitchen and found Alice and gave her the blouse and shirt to wash.

"So Abigail was supposed to be doing the laundry at that time?"

"Yes. Don't know where she could've gone," said Pippa.

Just then, Abigail entered the room with tea and biscuits.

"Ahh, Abigail, you're just in time," Dermot said. "How come you were not in the laundry room between four and four-thirty?"

"Miss Carter told me to give Constable Jenkins a glass of lemonade... Am I in trouble, Detective?"

"No, just asking where you were."

Abigail nodded, placed the tray on the table in front of them, and turned to leave. Pippa continued and told Dermot about knocking on the library door and the clock chiming at four-thirty. Abigail suddenly stopped and looked at them.

"Anything the matter?" asked Cora.

"Um, no, Mrs. Fitzhugh."

"Then go about your duties, Abigail," said Cora firmly. Abigail walked away, while Cora muttered "Silly girl" under her breath. Pippa went on to tell Dermot about hearing Richard accidently dropping the teacup.

"So, you heard two noises?"

"Yes, Richard told me the teacup fell on the floor and when he was picking it up he dropped it again and it broke. He was just being clumsy again. He then opened the door quickly and took the shirt from me. When he finally came out, the shirt he was wearing was drenched with sweat."

"Must be the heat in the library," said Dermot.

"Yes. Hector came downstairs and we went to the stables. Charles wasn't there, but the horses were ready to be taken out. Richard told me he saw Charles leave the stables and go into the kitchen. So we took the horses and rode into the meadow towards the stream..."

Pippa reached for her teacup and drank from it. She put it down gently, composed herself, and continued.

"... After we crossed the meadow, Richard suggested that we race towards the stream to see who would reach the caves first. I wasn't keen because the terrain is very unstable and rocky. However, Hector said that nothing would happen and it was just a short distance. Hector loved the idea and so I reluctantly agreed, thinking it would buck him up.

"We began racing and Richard winked at me as if to suggest that I should let Hector reach the end first. He's very fond of Hector, but I suppose due to his recent illness and the murders, Hector seemed despondent. So I let him gain speed and ride ahead. Suddenly, the saddle came off and Hector's leg got caught in the reins. Hector's head hit the ground and the horse dragged him for a few feet. I couldn't believe what I was seeing.

"I raced towards him, got off the horse, and held Hector in my arms. He was motionless, but I could see that he was breathing. Richard rode over and told me to go fetch help. I felt Hector squeeze my hand, wanting me to stay with him. I told Richard to ride back and get help. He was hesitant, but being the understanding man that he is, he went back and brought help." Pippa started crying. "I should never have agreed to that race."

"It's not your fault," Dermot said. "The strap of the saddle was cut. When Hector rode the horse fast, the saddle came off and he fell off the horse. It is just providential that he didn't fall onto the rocks."

"You mean to say that it was deliberately cut?" asked Cora.

"Yes, that's what we suspect. I examined the strap and it looks like it was cut with a knife."

Cora and Pippa gasped at the new revelation.

"Do you have any idea who would want to harm him?" Dermot asked.

"No, Detective, he's just a child. He said he was feeling better since he was taking his tonic every day. So I let him go horse riding with Pippa and Richard," said Cora.

"I must speak to Hector," Dermot said. "Before that, I will speak to Charles. He may be able to tell me about the saddle... There's just one more question, why does Mr. Seymour read the books from the library whenever he visits the manor?"

Pippa seemed surprised at the question and replied that Richard liked reading books and, since he had no formal education, he didn't have the chance to read them as a child. The only problem was that he could never remember where to keep them as Miss Carter had her own system of arranging them. Since she was particular about the way she had shelved them, she would get upset when Richard or anyone misplaced any book. Pippa sometimes felt that he purposely misplaced books and liked telling her about it, because he knew that Miss Carter did not like him and it aggravated her.

"He just has a mischievous side to him, Detective," she said, smiling for the first time.

After bidding the two women goodbye, Dermot went out of the manor and walked down the hill to the stables. He saw Charles hauling hay as he approached the stables. He went to him and introduced himself. Charles dropped the bale of hay, wiped his hands on his handkerchief, and greeted Dermot.

"Now, tell me about the saddle on Master Fitzhugh's horse."

Charles looked upset. "I swear, Detective," he said slowly, "that saddle was all right when I left 'ere."

Dermot nodded. "Who called you to the kitchen?"

"That I don't know," Charles said, then he nodded towards the wall. "That panel there with them lights on and that bell, it connects to the servants' dining room. When they need me, they ring it. The bell rings whatever light comes on. Saves time, you see; instead of walking down 'ere and callin' me. That red light's kitchen staff and heavy chores they can't handle. That yellow light is the family needing me to drive 'em. I'm stable hand and driver here, you see. Today, the kitchen light came on."

"Interesting, and that happened just after Miss Fitzhugh came and told you to prepare the horses?"

"About fifteen minutes after, I went t'kitchen as the red light came on."

"Strange. When you returned the horses were gone?"

"Yes, I asked in the kitchen if they called me and everyone said they didn't. I thought it was a joke, so I came back 'ere."

"When did you hear about the accident?"

"Probably, half hour later. I saw Mr. Seymour riding his horse back t'wards the house. Miss Carter called me and I drove Mr. Seymour and Mr. Endecott t'where Miss Fitzhugh and her brother were."

"Did you hear or see anything out of the ordinary when you were getting the horses ready?"

"No. But the night Lady Fitzhugh was murdered, the horses were agitated. They started neighing, then stopped. Then, hour later or so, they started again. Thought it was this heat, but maybe something must've upset them... And there was something else..."

"What is it?"

"May not be important, but when the horses started the first time, I looked out of me bedroom window and there were a candle being waved from the library window. I thought it was Slattery and went back t'sleep."

"Did you mention it to Slattery?"

"Yes. After they found her Ladyship's body, he came to tell me about the murder. I told him what I'd seen and he looked at me strange like. He didn't say nothing; only smiled and went away."

The conversation with Slattery in the servants' dining room flashed across Dermot's mind. He remembered Slattery telling him that he did do his nocturnal rounds that night.

"All right, Charles, I will check your story. Don't disappear though. It won't look good for you," said Dermot.

— — —

As Dermot headed back to the manor, he thought about what Charles had told him. Charles seemed like an honest person. What possible motive would he have to cut the saddle strap and also lie that someone in the manor had called him to the kitchen? There had to be someone else involved. Was the murderer lurking near the stables on the night Lady Fitzhugh was murdered? It seemed like a lot of questions were coming up.

Dermot met Constable Barnaby as he was walking towards the front door.

"Ahh, Constable Barnaby, just the person I needed to talk to. I was told that Mr. Seymour was talking to you from the library window?"

"Yes, that's true. We spoke for quite a while. Strange how time flies when you're talking to someone."

"What are you implying?"

"I looked at my pocket watch before I started my rounds; it was exactly four p.m. When I was walking past the library window, I saw Mr. Seymour sitting by the window without his shirt on, reading and drinking tea. That may have been a few minutes after four. He told me why he was without his shirt and then we heard the clock strike four-thirty. Mr. Seymour told me that Miss Fitzhugh was knocking on the library door, so I left and walked around the building towards the kitchen. It seemed like we spoke for only a short time, but I suppose time does fly."

"Did you see Charles come out from the stables?"

"Yes, we both did, and Mr. Seymour waved at him and he waved back."

"So you went around the manor and came back?"

"Yes, but then Miss Carter came with lemonade and we talked for a few minutes. She's so nice to Jenkins and me; always giving us something to drink and talking to us."

"Did you notice anything out of the ordinary while you were talking to any of them?"

"No, I didn't notice anything. It seemed like I spoke to Miss Carter for a long time, but the time seemed to pass really slowly."

"Why do you say that?"

"After I finished talking to Miss Carter, I went around the manor and saw Mr. Seymour, Miss Fitzhugh, and her brother walking towards the stables. I looked at my pocket watch and it was only four-forty."

"Strange... I think it is all relative," said Dermot, shrugging his shoulders. "What did you and Miss Carter talk about?"

"I told her that I had been talking to Mr. Seymour and she obviously gave her opinion about him. We all know that she doesn't like him. She said what a mistake Miss Fitzhugh would make by marrying him and also how much Lady Fitzhugh despised him. She hoped he wasn't making a mess of the library books that she had carefully arranged. We also talked about the weather. Then she excused herself saying that she had to attend to some chores and that she would get me more lemonade another time."

"Did anything else happen?" asked Dermot.

"She seemed to stare for a moment while talking, like there was something happening behind me... But only the woods and the stables were behind me."

Dermot thanked him and walked to the kitchen to question Mrs. Withers. She admitted that Charles was in the kitchen asking who had summoned him, but everyone denied that any of them rang for him on the indicator board.

Dermot asked Alice about the indicator board in the servants' dining room. She took him there and showed him two boards.

"This board 'ere ain't the same as the one down in the stables. It connects to every room in the manor, as you can see on the board. The coloured disc moves under the room the person is ringin' from. So when Mrs. Endecott wants someone in 'er room, she pulls the cord next to 'er bed and the disc moves under 'er room and then that there bell rings. The board down in the stables is only connected to 'ere." She pointed to the second smaller board with two buttons marked 'Kitchen' and 'Driver'.

"If we need Charles, then we press the button 'ere and then he knows that he is wanted in the kitchen. It's instead of us walkin' down to the stables, you see," said Alice.

"Who thought of this system?"

"Slattery told me that when they was electrifying the manor a few years ago, Lady Fitzhugh asked the electricians to use this system to summon the person from the stables. She got the idea from the summoning bells they used to have in the old days apparently."

"By Jove, Lady Fitzhugh was an intelligent and remarkable woman," said Dermot with admiration.

"She was, sir. Mind you, you daren't get on her wrong side. Irene Shaw was foolish stealin' that necklace; dismissed without a reference she was."

"Did Slattery mention to you about seeing anything unusual when making his rounds on the night her Ladyship was murdered?"

"He... he didn't make his rounds that night."

"Why?"

"After I found the body, he and Miss Carter brought me down to the servants' dining room. When Miss Carter went to get me some tea, Mr. Slattery slammed the table with his fist. He said that if he hadn't drunk the wine, then he would've gotten up like he usually did and probably could've prevented her Ladyship's murder. But he only had one glass, like we all did. Miss Carter poured it out for us as she didn't want us gettin' drunk."

Dermot was now certain that Slattery had lied to him because he had known who the real murderer was. He thanked Alice and left.

As he was leaving the kitchen, he almost bumped into Miss Carter. He apologised and asked her if she had seen anyone at the stables earlier when she was talking to Constable Barnaby.

"No, Detective, I don't think so... I cannot remember anything; I'm still in a state of shock at what happened to that poor boy."

"What's your opinion of Charles?"

Miss Carter looked upset. "That man is just trouble..." She looked up at Dermot. "If you ask me, that Charles is up to no good. He's careless and I don't know why he's not been fired already... His carelessness almost cost Master Fitzhugh his life. If only Lady Fitzhugh were alive." Then she choked up and got teary eyed.

Dermot comforted Miss Carter and said that he would find who tried to kill Hector.

—   —   —

Dermot went upstairs and knocked on Hector's bedroom door. Hector asked him to come in. Dermot opened the door and entered. Hector was in bed, with his right hand bandaged and his face bruised.

"How are you, Hector? Some nasty fall, eh?"

Hector moved a bit and tried to smile. "It hurts, but the doctor said that I'll be all right."

"That's nice... Is it okay to ask you a few questions?"

"Sure. I'm not going anywhere."

Dermot smiled, took a chair, and sat next to the bed. "Now... How did you know about Pippa and Mr. Seymour going horse riding?"

"Pippa told Miss Carter to ask me whether I would like to go riding with them. She knows that I like riding my horse, Lightning."

Dermot asked Hector to tell him about his accident. Hector looked blank for a second and told Dermot that he never suspected anything. It was only while the horse was gaining speed that he suddenly felt the saddle slipping and then it was too late. Before he could react, he was on the ground and Pippa was by his side. The next thing he remembered was waking up in his bed.

"Pippa told me that you held her hand and didn't want her to leave your side when Mr. Seymour suggested that she go get help."

"Yes, now I remember. You know, Detective, I may be young, but I know a lot of things. This is the first time that any man has shown great interest in Pippa. She always does what Richard tells her to do. I think she's afraid of losing him, if you know what I mean. I know he loves her because on the night that he was here for the first time, I was sent to bed early and I couldn't sleep. So I snuck down to the library to get a book and then I heard footsteps. I hid behind the curtain by the window and I slowly looked to see who it was. I saw Richard coming into the library. He went to the book shelf and put a note in one of the books."

"Does Pippa read any books from the library?" asked Dermot, bewildered.

"She used to read sometimes, but hardly anyone else ever reads those books, especially with Miss Carter complaining if they haven't been placed back in the proper order."

"Did you tell anyone about Richard leaving that note in the book?"

"No, I know that my aunts don't like Richard and Mother doesn't either, but she is happy that someone is finally interested in Pippa. She wants Pippa to get married and for me to inherit this place."

Dermot smiled at Hector. He could see that Hector was an astute child.

"And... did you see what was in that note?"

Hector smiled boyishly. "No, Detective. Pippa would have been upset with me if I did that. Please don't tell her what I saw."

"I won't... but why leave a message in a book when he could tell her in person?"

Hector shrugged his shoulders. "Lovers have their own way of communicating."

Dermot chuckled and then noticed the washbasin in the bathroom and realised that he was thirsty. He asked Hector if he could drink from the tap and Hector told him to use the glass from the medicine cabinet. Dermot opened the cabinet and took the glass. As he was about to open the tap, he smelled something. He bent towards the sink and found that the smell came from there. It brought back memories of a tonic given to him as a child. After drinking the water, he opened the medicine cabinet and took the bottle marked 'Fowler's Solution'.

"Hector," he said, walking back towards the boy. "You've been a naughty boy, haven't you? You've not been taking your tonic."

"How did you know?" asked Hector, startled.

"The washbasin smells of it. You put a spoonful of it in your mouth when your mother is looking and then slowly spit it into the sink – am I right?"

Hector looked at Dermot in stunned disbelief.

"You're right," Hector said with a sheepish grin. "I hate the taste, but I've noticed that ever since I stopped taking the tonic, I've been feeling better. I know it's strange, but I've been trying to tell Mum that and she never listens."

"Mothers are like that."

Dermot looked at the tonic bottle and smiled. He asked Hector if he could take the bottle with him. Hector said he could since Dr. Fielding had given him medicines for his current injuries. Dermot hid the bottle inside his coat pocket and told Hector not to tell anyone that he had taken it. He bid Hector goodbye and left the room.

— — —

Half an hour later, Dermot was at Inspector Enderby's office. He produced the tonic bottle and Inspector Enderby gave him a quizzical look.

"It's Hector's tonic bottle. I need to get it tested."

"For what?"

"I don't know, but I have a hunch. Something that Hector said to me tells me that we need to test the contents of this bottle. I'm not sure what will be found, but we'll know the answer as to why Hector was getting worse when he took the tonic."

"All right! I will have the chemist at the hospital test it. Your hunch better be right."

"I hope so. If not, then I must stop detecting," Dermot said with a grin.

Chapter 13: What's in the Tonic?

The next morning, while having breakfast, Dermot received a phone call. After listening to what Inspector Enderby had to say, Dermot went to the breakfast table, drank his coffee, took a piece of toast, and ran out, leaving his parents speechless.

Ten minutes later, he was pulling up in front of Meadowford Hospital. Inspector Enderby was waiting for him in the car park.

"I came as soon as I could. What did the chemist find?"

"He hasn't told me everything but, like I mentioned on the phone, he will have to explain his findings to us."

They walked into the building and towards the laboratory. On the way, Inspector Enderby told Dermot that Dr. Heathcliff was the chemist who worked at the hospital and that he also helped the Meadowford police with any chemical analyses they needed, instead of sending the samples to London. They knocked on the laboratory door and went in. Dr. Heathcliff turned around and greeted them. He was in his forties, of medium height, and his brown hair was starting to go grey at the temples.

Inspector Enderby greeted Dr. Heathcliff and introduced Dermot to him.

"Detective Carlyle, you were right indeed. There was an excess of a necessary ingredient in the tonic."

Dermot smiled, but at the same time he was becoming impatient with Dr. Heathcliff since he was not very forthcoming with the details. "What do you mean by a necessary ingredient?"

"I used the Marsh Test to see if the tonic contained what I suspected. I was not disappointed with the results. The test came out positive for arsenic."

"Arsenic?" asked Inspector Enderby.

"Yes, but it was carefully administered. Fowler's Solution has arsenic in it. It is an important ingredient for making the tonic. The normal concentration would be approximately 7.6 grammes per litre. However, tests on this solution revealed that the concentration was higher than the prescribed limit."

"Isn't arsenic poisonous?"

"Not in small quantities," Dr. Heathcliff explained. "Homeopaths also use arsenic in their medicines. It's actually good for you in small quantities."

Inspector Enderby and Dermot looked at each other. They knew that arsenic was used as poison to get rid of pests and to murder people, but now they were being told that it was good for them.

"The child was prescribed this tonic by Dr. Fielding?" asked Dr. Heathcliff.

"Yes, he suffers from acute asthma. He had a mild attack a few weeks ago after he got back from a trip they made to the stream. I was told it was a chilly day," replied Dermot.

"The bottle says that it should be shaken before taking a tablespoon of the tonic. Shaking the bottle made the arsenic spread inside the bottle and enter the child's body every time he took the tonic. That's why he started feeling sick, with flu-like symptoms, every time he consumed it."

"So you mean that it was slowly killing him?" asked Dermot.

"Yes, and if he had continued taking his tonic regularly, as Dr. Fielding prescribed, arsenic would have accumulated in his body. It would've been enough to kill the poor child by the time he finished the bottle."

"He was not taking it regularly and complained that he didn't like the taste. His mother was after him to have the tonic regularly, but he only pretended to take it and then spat it out into the washbasin in his bathroom," said Dermot.

"That was what probably saved him. The poor child would've died an agonising death at the end. Ironically, his disobedience is a good thing. Usually arsenic has no taste, but it's just that he did not like the taste of the tonic. Whoever put excess arsenic in it, knew that if the tonic was tested, the high amounts of arsenic would've been attributed to the chemist making a mistake while preparing the tonic. Nobody would've been any the wiser in this case."

"Good, God... We have a poisoner on the loose," said Inspector Enderby.

"Did anyone know that he wasn't taking his tonic?" asked Dr. Heathcliff.

"Everyone knew. His mother and aunts were after him to take his tonic," said Dermot.

"Someone may not have wanted to wait until he finished the bottle and that is why they tried to kill him by cutting the saddle strap," said Inspector Enderby.

"Or may've realised that he wasn't taking his tonic. I must go back to the manor and warn them," said Dermot.

Inspector Enderby grabbed hold of Dermot's arm and suggested that they first go to Dr. Fielding and find out where the bottle came from. Dermot agreed and, after thanking Dr. Heathcliff, the two men headed to Dr. Fielding's office. They knocked on the door and went in. Dr. Fielding was surprised to see them.

"Is something wrong?" he asked.

Dermot asked whether he gave the tonic bottle to Hector and Dr. Fielding said that he merely prescribed it but the tonic was probably purchased from Mr. Harris, the chemist, in the village. Inspector Enderby told Dr. Fielding what the tests had found and Dr. Fielding's jaw dropped in disbelief.

"No wonder he wasn't getting any better. We thought he wasn't taking his tonic," said Dr. Fielding.

"Yes, he was getting sick when he took it and got better when he didn't," said Dermot.

"The arsenic must've been inserted into the bottle by someone in the manor. Couldn't have happened at the chemist's shop," said Inspector Enderby.

Dr. Fielding looked at Hector's medical report. "Yes, he did get better when he took it at first and then started getting worse. So that explains it."

The two men thanked Dr. Fielding and drove to the chemist located in the village square.

— — —

Mr. Harris was an older man with grey hair and glasses. He looked just like a character from a Dickens novel. He knew the two men and was surprised to see them in his shop. After the customer he was serving had left, the two men came forward and greeted him.

"Nice to see you two again, but I think this isn't a social call. Am I right?"

"Nothing to alarm you, Mr. Harris. We just want to know if anyone from the manor bought any arsenic recently," said Inspector Enderby.

"Ahh, yes, their gardener, Mr. Lacey. He came here a few weeks ago and bought a big tin of arsenic. Said that he needed it for getting rid of pests. He even signed the poison registry."

He showed them the poison registry and they looked at the date it was bought.

"A day after the wills were stolen," said Dermot. "So, whoever stole the wills is also responsible for tainting the tonic with arsenic."

They thanked Mr. Harris and, as they left, he called out to them.

"Just one thing, that cook of theirs – Mrs. Withers. She came by a day after her Ladyship's murder and bought some sleeping powders. She claimed that two of her sleeping powders went missing on the night her Ladyship was killed. Each box I sell contains fifteen powders and when she went to bed that night she was surprised to find only three remaining instead of five."

Dermot looked perplexed and thanked Mr. Harris for the information.

— — —

The two men drove to the manor and went in search of the gardener. Mr. Lacey was an older, heavily tanned man. He sat outside the gardening shed, smoking a cigarette.

"Mr. Lacey, I presume?" asked Inspector Enderby, showing him his badge.

"Yes, 'ow can I help ya, Inspector?"

"We spoke to the chemist, Mr. Harris, and his records show that you purchased some arsenic a few weeks ago. For what purpose, may I ask?"

"Well, Inspector, I have t'battle with the rats 'ere. They attack the vegetable garden and I need it ta poison them, you see. The strange thing is though that tin I bought was nearly half empty the day after. I thought someone had taken it for the rats, but since you're here now it mayn't be so."

Dermot and Inspector Enderby looked at each other.

"So we were right, Dermot," said Inspector Enderby.

"Who knew about you buying the tin of arsenic?" asked Dermot.

"All t'staff knew. When we was having lunch, you see, someone said they was seeing rats round the manor as it's getting warmer. I told Miss Carter that I'd need some money to get some poison for 'em and that I'd keep it in me shed."

"This was before Irene was fired?" asked Inspector Enderby.

"Yes, I think so, Inspector."

Dermot and Inspector Enderby thanked Mr. Lacey and walked back to the manor.

"Wonder who could've pinched the arsenic?" asked Dermot.

"It could be anybody, but none of them will admit taking it. At this point, all of them are under suspicion, perhaps with the exception of Pippa because she had a chance to murder Hector when she was alone with him after his accident."

"You're right, but surely you wouldn't suspect the elderly sisters and Mrs. Fitzhugh."

Inspector Enderby looked at Dermot. "Dermot, I know you're young, but there are mothers who will do anything for money. If you've heard of Mary Ann Cotton, then you can safely assume there are women who will murder their children for money. That damned woman used arsenic too.

"Mrs. Fitzhugh had access to the tonic bottle and she also worked as a nurse, dispensing medications to soldiers convalescing here during the war. So, she knows a thing or two about poisons. She also had a motive to kill Lady Fitzhugh so that Hector could inherit the estate and she could be in control and not be under three dotty old ladies... She also could've let her accomplice into the manor house," Inspector Enderby explained.

They went to the drawing room and found Alice dusting. They asked Alice to let Cora know that they wanted to talk to her. Alice went away and Cora came into the drawing room a few minutes later. They asked her to be seated and Cora sat down without saying a word.

"Mrs. Fitzhugh, from where did you get the tonic for Hector?"

"From the chemist, Mr. Harris, in the village. Why do you ask?"

"Was it opened?"

"No, it was sealed. Why? Is this relevant?"

Inspector Enderby told Cora what the chemical analysis of Hector's tonic bottle had revealed. He also told her that they suspected the extra arsenic could have been stolen from the gardening shed and added to the tonic to slowly poison Hector.

Cora looked horrified. "Why would anyone want to do that? He's just a child and has never harmed anyone."

"We don't know why. It seems odd that someone would target the oldest and the youngest members of the family. There must be a reason for it. Do you know if anyone wanted to harm Lady Fitzhugh and Hector?"

"I don't know. Hector inherits everything with others being provided for, but I don't think anyone in the family would want to harm him. Everyone's fond of Hector."

"There is something I wanted to clarify. I had the Toronto police investigate you and your family. They weren't wealthy, am I right?"

The question stunned her. "No, Inspector, we weren't."

"You were also fired from your job as a teacher because money from the school safe went missing?"

Cora looked perturbed. She excused herself and went and closed the door. She then came back to them. "It was a misunderstanding and the real thief was eventually caught. However, mud sticks and I couldn't find a job. I was working as a waitress when I met Allan and he was so kind..." She then raised her voice. "Am I a suspect? Why did you have me investigated? You think that I would kill my own son for money? How dare you!"

"Just routine questions, Mrs. Fitzhugh. All part of the investigation," answered Dermot, trying to calm the situation.

Cora looked at them. "Then find the killers," she said firmly. "It's your job, damn it!" She then took a moment and calmed down. "I must leave this manor house. I only stayed here after Allan died because of the children... His sisters, especially Lilian, resent me because I'm not from the same standing as them and because I'm not English either. It got worse after the American and Canadian soldiers who were convalescing here during the war were a bit unruly."

"If you leave, you'll not be safe. My constables cannot be sent to wherever you go. Everyone needs to be here and then my constables will make sure that nobody gets in or out. Is that understood?" said Inspector Enderby sternly.

Cora looked disappointed. "Yes," she said sharply, "but if anything were to happen again then I am taking my children out of this horror house and will probably move back to Canada. Let the police try and stop me then." She then turned and walked away.

Dermot looked over at Inspector Enderby. "Now, does that sound like a mother who would kill her child?"

"Believe me, that Cotton woman was just the same."

"It's not her. I guarantee that."

"Sorry, you've lost me."

"According to the will, Cora handles the estate only if Hector is alive and only until he turns twenty-one – so Cora has everything to lose if Hector dies because Pippa is next in line."

"Which means that Pippa is back to being a suspect, but then who are her accomplices?"

Dermot shrugged his shoulders and suggested that they go to the kitchen and talk to Mrs. Withers. They met her in the servants' dining room and asked her about the two missing sleeping powder packets. She told them that she was sure there were five in the box the night before and was surprised to find only three when she went to bed after the party. She questioned the staff and they denied taking them.

"Why would anyone want to steal sleeping powders?" asked Inspector Enderby as they left the manor.

"I think I know why. The killers needed two people to be asleep and one of them was Slattery."

Chapter 14: Comeuppance is Served

Dermot's father, Edmund, reminded him about the billiards game at the Meadowford Country Club that night. Edmund's friends – who had fought alongside him in the Boer War – wanted to meet Dermot after his father had told them that he was a detective with the Metropolitan Police. However, Dermot didn't want to go because he was overwhelmed with the case.

"There has to be a first time for everything, Dermot," Edmund said. He understood his son's plight. "Experience is the best teacher, and you will learn what your strengths and weaknesses are when you're by yourself. Come and enjoy yourself tonight. It'll do you some good and you may learn something."

Dermot knew his father was right. He needed some respite and going to the club would be a good opportunity to feel reinvigorated.

Meadowford Country Club had a swimming pool, tennis courts, a gymnasium, and also a billiards room. Edmund was a regular member along with some of the villagers. They were greeted by the receptionist, who took their hats. They walked through the corridor and entered the billiards room. There were four men already there.

"Edmund, nice to see you again," said a man wearing a brown suit. "This must be Dermot, the great detective."

"Yes, Malcolm, this is my son, Dermot. Poor chap, he is supposed to be on his holiday, instead he's investigating those two murders at Fitzhugh Manor," said Edmund proudly.

The four men came and shook hands with Edmund and Dermot. The other three men introduced themselves as Ernest, Owen, and Donald. Malcolm said that after the Boer War, he was stationed at various locations in India and retired as a colonel after nearly thirty-two years of service. Ernest left the army after the Boer War and became a chartered accountant. Owen joined the diplomatic service and travelled all over the empire before retiring. Donald came back to Meadowford and continued his profession as a stone mason.

"There's another friend who hasn't retired. He lives in South Africa and his name is Elmer Griffin. He's a detective with the Pretoria Police Force," said Donald.

"Maybe he could help you with your case," said Owen, laughing.

"Oh, come on, Dermot's here to forget about the case and relax. Let's start with a game, shall we fellas?" asked Edmund, applying chalk to the tip of his cue stick.

They began playing and the older men began talking about their war experiences. Dermot listened and felt out of place.

"Is that all you ex-servicemen talk about?" asked Dermot. The men stopped talking and laughed at Dermot's candour.

"Yes, Dermot, what you say is true," said Owen. "Believe me, hardly anyone likes war. Most of us hated going into combat, but when it's all over we like to reminisce about it, especially when we get together here at the club for sundowners on some evenings, just like we used to do in Africa."

"Edmund, do you remember when the Boers ambushed us in the veld?" asked Donald.

"Yes, I do. They caught us by surprise, but we overpowered them."

"A few of them were taken as prisoners to the camps."

"What camps are you talking about?" asked Dermot with great interest.

"The ones where the families of the Boers were interned for the duration of the war," replied Donald.

"I read about them and I heard that the camps were horrendous, with people dying like flies."

"Yes, and some of us, like your father and me, were assigned to those camps as guards."

Edmund looked at Donald and gestured to him to stop, which did not go unnoticed by Dermot.

"You never told me that you were a guard at a concentration camp," said Dermot, taken aback.

Edmund showed his annoyance at the revelation. "Son, I'm not proud of that, but it was what we were commanded to do. We asked no questions but obeyed our superiors."

"I learnt about those camps because of this case and also how cruel the British military were to the Boers. Many innocent women and children perished due to starvation and disease in those camps."

"Yes, it was a terrible mistake. I've heard that even her majesty Queen Victoria was upset about the war and that it could've hastened her death. I wouldn't be surprised if the Boers still harbour resentment or join forces with others who have a grievance against the British Empire to harm us," said Owen.

"Well, I would not put it past them to join forces with the Irish Republican

Army or the Scottish Independence Movement to weaken the British Empire. I heard that some of the IRA joined forces with Germany during the Great War to fight against the empire," said Malcolm.

A waiter entered with a tray of glasses and drinks and placed them on the table beside the billiards table.

"Here come the sundowners. Let's finish our game and then we can have our drinks," said Donald as he positioned himself to take a shot. The others agreed with him.

— — —

Bertram Kerr sat next to the window in his room at the Carlton Inn, facing the street and drinking his scotch and soda. He smiled, satisfied with himself. The errand that Lady Fitzhugh had sent him on had given him power over someone. He had the greatest regard for Lady Fitzhugh, but he had decided to use that information for his own advantage now that she was dead. He had to be careful though because he had contacted that person about his secret past and he knew that the person would do anything to keep that information hidden.

Sending that letter had worked. When Bertram telephoned from a pay phone, the person had agreed to meet with him. Bertram had insisted that they meet at the Carlton Inn in Meadowford, somewhere where he had never stayed before and so nobody would recognise him. If anyone in London had gotten wind that he was involved in blackmail, he would no longer be allowed to practice law. Not that it mattered. The items that his victim would give him in exchange for the proof he had would ensure that Bertram lived a life of luxury for the rest of his years. But he had his reputation to uphold and he needed to hold his head high in society.

Bertram heard the knock on the door and felt nervous. Maybe he shouldn't be doing this, but it was too late now. He went and opened the door. His victim had lowered his hat so that he could not be recognised. Bertram relished the surprised look on his victim's face when his victim recognised him. He smiled and let his victim in.

— — —

Dermot parked his car and walked to the entrance of the Carlton Inn. Inspector Enderby had called him a few minutes earlier about the discovery of a dead body by the chambermaid that morning. Dermot, by now, was familiar to the constables and they let him pass. The guests were clustered in the dining room and were being served tea and refreshments. The women looked distressed. The owner of the inn, Mr. Jessup, a middle-aged and balding man who stood at the bottom of the staircase, greeted Dermot and told him to go upstairs. He looked perturbed. Dermot guessed that Mr. Jessup was worried that his business would suffer because of the murder.

He reached the top of the staircase and walked to the end of the corridor to the room that had the number four marked on the door. He knocked on the door and then walked in. Inspector Enderby was inside with a police constable who he introduced as Constable Drake. The body of Bertram Kerr was on the floor and his eyes were bulging out. He had been garrotted and the cord was still around his neck. Dermot couldn't believe that only a few days earlier he had eaten with Bertram Kerr and that now he was looking at his corpse.

"Probably a former client of his that didn't like him, or perhaps he knew who was involved in Lady Fitzhugh's murder," said Inspector Enderby.

"I think he chose the Carlton Inn as a rendezvous point on purpose, because he did not want to be recognised by the staff of the Meadowford Inn. He told me that he always stayed there whenever he came to Meadowford," said Dermot.

"You're right. He used the alias Thomas Morrow when checking in," said Inspector Enderby.

"Did anybody see or hear anything?"

"Nothing from the guests; they were all in the dining room as it was lunch time. The chambermaid was passing by and she heard a sound. She knocked on the door and, when there was no response, she was about to unlock the door with her key when a voice told her that he was all right and that he had knocked down something. He asked not to be disturbed and thanked her. She went about her business after that. When she came to clean the room in the morning, she discovered the body."

"I must talk to her. Has the room been searched?"

"No, we just came in and examined the body. Nothing seems to be disrupted or unusual, except for the body on the floor," said Inspector Enderby.

"Exactly, the room looks immaculate," said Dermot. "Whoever was here must've been careful not to touch anything so as to not leave any fingerprints or evidence. However, I have learnt from previous cases that, when a murder is committed, the murderer leaves in a hurry and inadvertently leaves behind some evidence. I suggest that we search the room ourselves."

After Constable Drake took some pictures of the room and the body, the three men began searching the room. A few minutes later, Constable Drake said that he had found something. The two men came to him and looked at what he had in his hand.

"Looks like a stone," said Inspector Enderby.

"Blimey, that looks like an uncut diamond! Let me take a look," said Dermot.

Constable Drake handed the piece to Dermot and he held it to the light.

"Looks very expensive. I'm positive this diamond, or maybe there are more of them, has something to do with the murder of Mr. Kerr. Thank you, Constable," said Dermot. Constable Drake smiled and nodded.

After the body was taken to the morgue, Dermot and Inspector Enderby went to meet the chambermaid. She was a petite brunette in her thirties, with her hair tied in a bun. She looked upset but managed to maintain her composure.

Inspector Enderby introduced her as Violet Moran. She told Dermot about the voice in the room and discovering the body in the morning.

"What sort of a sound did you hear?"

"A choking sound. It was very low, but then I heard the chair fall and the sound of stones or marbles falling on the floor."

"How did the voice sound when it answered you?" asked Dermot.

"It sounded a bit like he was scared... I asked if he wanted help, but he said that he was fine and asked not to be disturbed." She suddenly sat upright, looking anxious. "Should I have gone in, Detective? I could've seen who the killer was."

Dermot smiled. "You did the right thing by not going in. You're alive because of that. If anything had happened to you, nobody would've heard anything because it was lunch time."

Violet Moran stared for a second, then nodded and leaned back on the chair.

— — —

After leaving the Carlton Inn, Dermot drove to Fitzhugh Manor. Cora came out to greet him and was smiling, which was unusual since she always had a dour look on her face.

"Detective, I have some good news. Pippa called from London to tell us that she's engaged to be married. Richard proposed to her yesterday and wants to get married at the earliest. He spent all day finding her an engagement ring. She can't wait to show it to us."

Dermot was stunned. "How have your sisters-in-law taken the news?"

"They're not too happy. Lilian thinks it's disrespectful to Doris. Flora thinks it's too soon, but Richard feels that it's the right thing to do. He told Pippa that the tragedies of the past few days had made him realise that death can come at any time, and so he wanted to marry her before anything happened to either of them." She smiled and then added, "I couldn't care less what they think. They resent me because of my background and lack of finesse, but Allan chose me. In the same way, Pippa has chosen Richard and after all it's her happiness that counts."

Dermot smiled. "Please tell the happy couple that I've congratulated them... I must go in and see Mrs. Ainsworth. Please excuse me."

"Of course. She is with Lilian in the library, reading the newspaper."

Dermot went to the library and saw the two sisters sitting together and reading portions of the newspaper. He went in and greeted them. He could see the exasperated look on Lilian's face, but Flora greeted him with a smile.

"What is it you want, Detective Carlyle?" asked Lilian without hiding her annoyance.

"I need some answers about the mine your father owned. It may help me understand what the motives could be behind these murders."

"Go right ahead, Detective," said Flora. "Don't let Lilian's behaviour bother you. She's just upset because of Pippa's engagement."

At the mere mention of the engagement, Lilian grunted, showing her disapproval.

"Oh, yes, Mrs. Fitzhugh told me about it. Congratulations, nevertheless," said Dermot.

"It is not just the news of Pippa's engagement, but the torch in the library is missing," said Lilian with exasperation.

"Now, Lilian. Let's not waste Detective Carlyle's time... Go ahead and ask your questions, Detective."

Dermot cleared his throat. "Mrs. Ainsworth, did your father bring back any diamonds from South Africa?"

"As a matter of fact, he did. There were ten uncut diamonds in a pouch. He said that Mr. De Villiers gave them to him when they became partners."

"Where are those diamonds?"

"After Father's death, Doris kept them in a safety deposit box in the Bank of England. They've been there ever since."

Dermot reached into his pocket and took out a small box. He opened it and the two elderly sisters gasped.

"What are you doing with that? I haven't seen them in donkey's years. This one looks just like the diamonds that Father showed us," said Lilian.

"Are you sure?" Dermot asked.

"Yes, I'm certain, Detective."

"I will obtain permission to check if the diamonds are still in the safety deposit box at the bank."

"They should be. Why wouldn't they be there?" asked Lilian.

"Lilian, be quiet. Let the detective do his job," admonished Flora.

"It's okay, Mrs. Ainsworth. We found this diamond in the room where Bertram Kerr was murdered..."

"Whaaattt... there's been another murder? Doris' solicitor? Why on earth?" said Flora, stunned.

"Oh! So that horrid little man is dead," said Lilian nonchalantly.

"Why was he horrid?" asked Dermot.

"Because he never acknowledged us in any way; it's as if we never existed. He was nice to Doris because she paid him and held him in high regard. She even called him 'Bertie' affectionately. He always wanted to be the centre of attention, maybe because he was suffering from a Napoleonic complex due to his short stature," said Lilian.

Dermot nodded in agreement and the scene at the Meadowford Inn with the waiter came to his mind.

"I have a hunch that these murders could be connected to the diamond mine back in South Africa. Do you know if the De Villiers have any surviving family members?"

"His only child, a son, who was studying in Germany when the war broke out, returned to fight for the Boers and died towards the end of the war," said Flora. "If I remember correctly, Father mentioned in passing that Mr. De Villiers had a sister in Scotland. Her name was Lady Argyle."

Dermot smiled. "I'm curious to know what Lady Fitzhugh thought of Richard Seymour."

"Hmm... she thought he was a vulgarian. Doris felt that he pretended to be something he wasn't, even though he's gotten a bit rich because of his paintings. He seems very unconventional with that facial hair and also his hair being longer than usual. It's beyond me why Doris allowed Pippa to invite him for the birthday party," said Lilian. "Doris even mentioned that Mr. Kerr once saw Pippa and Richard together in London and even he did not approve of Richard."

"Do you know why her Ladyship wanted to talk to Mr. Seymour and Pippa the day after the party?"

Flora shrugged her shoulders. "Doris knew that Pippa always wanted a husband. I suppose that's why she finally gave in and decided to accept Richard courting our Pippa. Make no mistake, Detective, Doris may have been a very kind and generous woman but, if you crossed her, she could be nasty," said Flora.

"Even though Pippa seems complaisant now, she was always a rebel, especially after Allan died. Maybe that's why she's attracted to Richard, because he looks like a rebel," said Lilian. "She was suspended from finishing school for two weeks for having those books."

"Which books?" asked Dermot.

"You know, those banned books: *Fanny Hill* and *The Lustful Turk*," said Flora.

Dermot managed to stifle a laugh.

"A classmate gave them to her and, when she refused to reveal who it was, the headmistress suspended her," explained Flora. "We didn't know anything about sex at that age. Even when we got married, a few years after Allan was born. Mother told us about it on our wedding day and I was aghast."

"I know I was," said Lilian with some disgust.

"Even my own two daughters didn't know anything about sex. I told them what my mother had told me."

"What was that?" asked Dermot.

"She told me what all Victorian mothers told their daughters at that time. 'Just lie there and think of England.'"

Dermot laughed loudly and then noticed that the elderly sisters were looking at him sternly. He quickly composed himself and left after wishing the sisters a good day.

He went out of the manor and drove to London, laughing to himself all the while.

— — —

After obtaining a warrant from the judge, which Detective Lloyd got expedited, Dermot went to the Bank of England and produced it to the bank manager, Mr. Herbert Perkins, whom he had met before. Mr. Perkins read the warrant and escorted him to the bank's vaults.

The safety deposit box in Lady Fitzhugh's name contained a pouch and a manila envelope. They opened the pouch and counted the diamonds. There were ten uncut diamonds. Dermot wondered where the diamond they had found in Kerr's room came from. He opened the manila envelope and found a photograph of two men. Dermot recognised Lord Fitzhugh, but he did not recognise the other man. He looked at the back of the photograph and it said 'Pretoria 1898, De Villiers and Fitzhugh'. He requested permission to take the picture with him, citing that he required it for investigation. Mr. Perkins at first was reluctant, but when Dermot insisted he relented and gave the picture to Dermot.

Chapter 15: Abigail's Revelation

The next day, Dermot was at the Meadowford Police Station bringing Inspector Enderby up-to-date on the investigation. He informed him that the diamonds that Lord Fitzhugh had brought back from South Africa were still in the vault in the Bank of England. With the discovery of the diamond in Bertram Kerr's room, a new mystery emerged as to who else had possession of the diamonds that were supposed to be in South Africa and how was Bertram Kerr's murder connected to the murders and the attempted murders at Fitzhugh Manor?

They decided that Charles was a possible suspect because he was the last person to handle Hector's saddle. However, there was nothing connecting him to the other murders. Was he just an accomplice following orders? If so, why would he and Pippa join forces to commit these heinous crimes? They had three suspects so far and although they all had clear motives, there was no proof that any of them had committed all of the murders.

Inspector Enderby had found out that none of the three suspects were near the Carlton Inn on the day that Bertram Kerr was murdered. Arthur and Charles were at Fitzhugh Manor and Pippa had gone to London the previous day, catching the early morning train, and had then come back to Meadowford the evening after Kerr's body was discovered.

After talking to Inspector Enderby, Dermot drove to Fitzhugh Manor. He needed to ask Pippa about the missing torch from the library. She hadn't mentioned the torch to him when Dermot had questioned her about the events leading up to Hector's accident. He greeted Jenkins as he walked past him towards the front door. Miss Carter opened the door and he asked to see Pippa. She asked Dermot to wait in the living room and she went to call Pippa.

Dermot entered the living room and sat on the armchair facing away from the door. A few minutes later, he felt like he was being watched. He turned around and saw Abigail standing at the door, looking at him.

"Oh, Abigail, you gave me a fright," said Dermot, relieved as he got up.

"Can I talk to you, Detective?"

"Sure."

Abigail entered the room and stood in front of Dermot. "The day Master Hector 'ad his accident... strange things happened that don't make sense."

Dermot looked perplexed. "Such as?"

"For instance, a person sayin' that they were at a place when they weren't."

Dermot was puzzled by the reply. "Please, tell me more."

"On the day of the accident, before they went horse ridin', I was about to air the laundry outside when Miss Carter told me to take a glass of lemonade to Constable Jenkins guarding the front door. She took one to Constable Barnaby as he came towards the kitchen while making his rounds. As I passed by the library, I heard the clock inside strike four-thirty and the door was closed. However, she weren't there."

"Who wasn't there?"

"When I came to the library while you were interviewing Miss Fitzhugh about the accident, Miss Fitzhugh said that she 'eard the clock strike four-thirty when she knocked on the library door. But that ain't right."

Dermot chuckled. "Sorry, Abigail, you must be mistaken. Constable Barnaby, and even Mr. Seymour, told me that Miss Fitzhugh knocked on the door when the clock struck four-thirty."

"It's impossible. I know I wear spectacles and I ain't bright, but I'm sure she weren't there. And another strange thing... when I was in the laundry yard after, I heard the clock..."

All of a sudden, Dermot looked beyond Abigail and she turned and saw Pippa and Miss Carter standing at the door.

"Come along now, Abigail, you mustn't keep the detective with your idle talk. There's work to be done," said Miss Carter firmly.

"Yes, Miss Carter."

Abigail turned to Dermot and apologised for wasting his time and then walked out. Miss Carter sighed. "Sorry, Detective, I'll see that she does not waste your time any more."

Dermot nodded; Miss Carter turned and followed Abigail.

Pippa came towards Dermot, smiling, and asked why he wanted to talk to her. Dermot noticed that she had a very flirtatious demeanour about her. Even her gait was sensual and seductive. When he had first interviewed her, she had insisted that he call her Pippa rather than Miss Fitzhugh. It seemed like Pippa was attracted to him. Whilst she wasn't particularly pretty, she had a nice figure and was far from unattractive.

He asked her about the missing torch from the library and added that her aunts had happened to bring it to his attention. Pippa looked perplexed and then her eyes brightened. She told Dermot that Richard took the torch and put it in the saddle bag on Hector's saddle. He wanted them to explore the caves near the stream. The torch could still be in the vicinity where the saddle fell off the horse. Dermot realised that could be true because Inspector Enderby had made no mention of a torch.

"Oh, forgive me," Dermot said. "I hear congratulations are in order on your engagement to Mr. Seymour. Seems like it is rather sudden, isn't it?"

"Yes, I was surprised when Richard proposed. He spent the whole day searching for the perfect ring. He came to Selfridges where I work, just as I was about to leave, took me to my flat, and proposed." She held up her hand and showed Dermot the diamond ring.

Dermot told her that the ring looked beautiful and then asked her when Richard had started painting. Pippa replied that Richard started painting after he had recovered from his injuries in the Great War; after all, he needed money to make ends meet and his government pension was limited.

"I'm lucky he loves me. Women think he's dishy, but he chose plain-looking me. He sought me out in the art gallery and told me that he noticed me at Selfridges and thought I was someone special... I just don't understand why my aunts and Miss Carter don't like him."

Pippa was about to say something more, when they heard a scream.

"Help... Miss Carter... help me..."

"What was that?" asked Pippa, horrified.

"It sounded like Abigail," said Dermot as he ran out of the living room. He tried to discern where the screams had come from. Pippa came running behind him and told him they were from the laundry room.

"Quick, show me where it is."

The two of them ran along the corridor and through a doorway. From the top of the stairs they saw Miss Carter sitting on the landing, leaning against the wall. They ran down the stairs to the landing. They slowly moved Miss Carter, who was moaning in pain, and saw that the back of her head was a bit bloodied. She was semi-conscious and was now slowly moving her lips trying to say something.

Pippa let out a scream and pointed to the bottom of the stairs. Dermot looked and saw Abigail at the bottom of the stairs with the laundry basket next to her and clothes strewn around her. Dermot ran down the stairs and took Abigail's hand, looking for a pulse. There was none. He looked at her face; her eyes were staring upwards. Her spectacles were on the floor next to her. From the corner of his eye, he saw something move and he looked towards the door. It was the cat that Abigail used to feed.

"I suppose you saw the whole thing," he said to the cat. The cat looked at him and then ran outside through the open door.

Dermot went up the stairs to where Pippa was trying to help Miss Carter get up. He asked Miss Carter what had happened and she faintly said that a man had come down the stairs and attacked them. They tried to defend themselves and the last thing she heard was Abigail scream as she fell down the stairs.

"Is... is... she alive?"

"No, she broke her neck in the fall. He must've gone down the stairs and towards the woods through the open door. Constable Barnaby must be making his rounds. We may be able to catch him."

Cora and Arthur came down the stairs and looked petrified.

"Oh my God, Miss Carter," said Cora. She looked at Abigail's body and let out a faint scream.

"Take care of Miss Carter," yelled Dermot as he turned to go back down the stairs.

Dermot ran around Abigail's body and the clothes. He ran past the washing tub and the wringers and out of the door. The bright sunlight hit his eyes and he had to blink a little to get used to it. He looked to his left and saw Barnaby walking down the hill. He called out to him and told him what had happened. Barnaby said that he hadn't seen anyone run past him, but anyone could've run into the woods and down into the meadow.

Barnaby blew his whistle and Jenkins came immediately. Dermot found that Jenkins was the more athletic of the two and he told Barnaby to wait while he and Jenkins went in search of the killer. They ran towards the woods and split apart to cover the area. They entered the woods and ran through them into the meadow and down the hill towards the stream. They saw no one. They converged at the stream, panting heavily. Constable Jenkins told Dermot that due to the lack of rain there were no footprints showing which way the attacker went and so it was futile attempting to find him. Dermot agreed and suggested that they head back.

The two men headed back and went into the laundry room. Dermot looked at the body of Abigail and shook his head in disbelief. A few minutes ago, she was alive and talking to him. She had been just about to tell him something. What was it she was trying to tell him before they were interrupted? Something about the clock when she was in the laundry yard. It just didn't make sense.

Dermot went upstairs and enquired about Miss Carter. Pippa said that Miss Carter was in her room resting and that Dr. Fielding was on his way. She had also called the police. Cora then became distraught and announced that she wasn't going to stay in the manor any longer. She was going to take Hector and move into the Meadowford Inn where she would make arrangements to go back to Canada. No amount of convincing would make her stay. When Inspector Enderby arrived, she told him her plans and was adamant that she be allowed to leave the manor. Inspector Enderby finally relented and granted her request.

Chapter 16: The Butler's Memoir

As Dermot drove home, he began thinking about the events that had unfolded – three murders and two attempted murders, all within the span of a few days. They were connected somehow, but he couldn't see how. Was he missing any clues? He knew he had to find the killers before more people died. He reached his parents' house and went in. He barely acknowledged his mother's greeting and invitation to have dinner. He told them that he was unwell and wanted to go to bed early. He went upstairs to his room and looked at his table. He saw the two files that Oswald Gardner had given him, and then he noticed something else. It was the memoirs of James Slattery. He hadn't opened it since he had placed it on the table. Maybe, there was a clue in it to be discovered. He took the book, sat on his bed, and began to read.

Slattery described his journey with Lord Fitzhugh on the *SS Durban* to Cape Town, South Africa. He was excited about the prospect of seeing a new country. The first few pages were about the country, the wildlife, and the scenery. Slattery chronicled in detail Lord Fitzhugh's meetings with several people who owned diamond mines. Lord Fitzhugh decided to go into partnership with a Boer farmer named Christiaan De Villiers, whom he met at a country club in Cape Town. He and his son, Peter, who was currently studying in Berlin, had discovered the diamond mine accidentally, while clearing a small hill on the land they farmed near Kimberley.

Christiaan was intent on obtaining financial help to excavate the diamonds, as he was a farmer of modest means. When the Boer War began, soon after they agreed to become partners, Lord Fitzhugh had assured Christiaan that although their two countries were fighting each other, he wouldn't pull out of his financial backing for the mine and that he would protect them.

In the next chapters, Slattery mentioned Lord Fitzhugh accepting an offer from the British Army to lead a small regiment of British soldiers. His military experiences in India and England were sought by the British Army. Slattery also mentioned that a young private from Meadowford, named Percival Havelock, was in the regiment. Private Havelock soon became Lord Fitzhugh's confidant.

The next few chapters described Slattery's experiences during the war and some of the battles he had witnessed. He mentioned the bullet wound that Private Havelock received to his leg during a battle and his return to the unit after convalescing in a hospital in Pretoria.

Dermot noticed that the colouring of the ink now looked brighter and realised that this was where Slattery had continued writing his memoirs, a few months earlier.

"So he was writing from memory after almost a twenty-five year hiatus," Dermot said to himself.

Slattery briefly mentioned how his obsession for getting up in the middle of the night to check the doors and windows began. Lord Fitzhugh and Slattery had stayed with the British family a week before they were murdered. It was determined that the perpetrators had entered through a window. Nobody knew whether the perpetrators who had killed the family were natives or Boers. During the war, Slattery would check whether the tent flaps were secured. When he was in a building, he would check the doors and windows.

He wrote about the ending of the war and how relieved Lord Fitzhugh and he were because they had escaped unscathed. He described witnessing the mine exploding on the day it was to be inaugurated and the subsequent trial brought forth by the insurance company. He had started writing another chapter about Lord Fitzhugh being exonerated and then the memoirs stopped rather abruptly. Dermot realised with sadness that this was because Slattery had been murdered.

By the time Dermot finished, it was close to dawn. As he closed his eyes, he realised that Slattery had not mentioned anything about the De Villiers family. Even after Lord Fitzhugh became sole owner of the mine, Slattery had not written that they had perished. His last mention of them was when the Boer War began.

—   —   —

After sleeping for a few hours, Dermot drove back to Fitzhugh Manor. He needed to know how much the elderly sisters knew about the mine. Maybe they could tell him why Slattery had not mentioned the De Villiers family again in his memoirs. Constable Jenkins greeted him as he arrived. Dermot went in and found the two sisters in the drawing room, with tea in front of them. Lilian was embroidering, while Flora drank tea. He greeted them and told them why he was there. Lilian looked at him angrily and reprimanded him for being impertinent by barging in while they were having their tea. She demanded to know how the mine could possibly be related to Abigail's death.

Dermot knew that Lilian was a very difficult woman, but he had been blessed with the patience of a saint. He showed her Slattery's memoirs.

"Mrs. Endecott, I know they don't seem to be related, but Slattery wrote about his time in South Africa and I'm afraid there are many questions I need answered to help me with this case."

The explanation seemed to calm her down and Lilian began sipping her tea.

"Sorry, Detective. Lilian is just upset at what happened yesterday, and also about Cora and Hector leaving. They have moved to the Meadowford Inn and Cora's planning on taking them back to Canada," said Flora.

Dermot asked Flora who had informed Lord Fitzhugh of the huge deposit of diamonds in the mine if he was in the veld fighting the Boers.

Flora thought for a moment. "Father told us that he had received a letter from Christiaan telling him about the discovery and that the geologist who examined the mine also confirmed it. That letter from Christiaan and the geologist's report helped exonerate Father at his trial."

"That makes sense... Now, Slattery's memoir doesn't mention what happened to the De Villiers family. Did your father ever mention how Christiaan and his wife died in the war? He would've had to have known that to get ownership of the mine."

Flora shrugged her shoulders. "Father didn't want to talk about how they died and forbade anyone from asking about the mine, the war, or the trial. We just respected our father's wishes and did as he asked. Slattery would've known, but he is..."

Dermot nodded disappointingly. He did not get his most important question answered. Was there any particular reason why Lord Fitzhugh didn't want to talk about his time in South Africa? Maybe he was just interested in putting the past behind him and moving on.

He requested Flora to search through Lord Fitzhugh's papers and find the letter or any documents related to the trial and the mine. Flora said that she would.

"Did Slattery ever meet the son?"

"No. I distinctly remember Father saying that none of them had met him because by the time they met Christiaan his son had already sailed for Germany. As you know, he came back and perished in the war."

Dermot nodded. "How's Miss Carter?"

"She is fine. Thank God. Dreadful being attacked and seeing someone being murdered in front of your eyes," answered Lilian, which surprised Dermot.

"Yes, she's the best housekeeper we've ever had," chimed in Flora. "She came in at the last minute too."

"What do you mean?" asked Dermot.

"We interviewed many women for the position and we had already decided on one when Miss Carter arrived. Strangely, as we interviewed her, we all felt that we knew her. She gave us the feeling that we had met her before. We unanimously agreed that we would hire her," said Flora.

"Strange... Where had she worked before?"

"She worked for a Mrs. Mable Evans for nearly twenty years. Her employer succumbed to cancer a few months before we hired her. She even showed us Mrs. Evans' obituary from the *London Times* and the reference letter from her was most impressive."

"Where is she? I would like to speak to her."

"She's in the living room, polishing the silverware. Even though she had that awful ordeal yesterday, she's up and about doing her duties as if nothing happened to her," said Flora.

Dermot thanked them and went to the living room. He found Miss Carter polishing the silverware. She looked up and peered at him through her pince-nez. Dermot greeted her and asked how she was feeling. Miss Carter got emotional and said she was fine but was upset that she couldn't prevent Abigail from being killed, even though she had cried for Miss Carter to help her. She then composed herself and looked at him quizzically.

"Are you here to question me, Detective Carlyle?" she asked.

"Yes, just routine questions because of what happened yesterday. I suspect that the man who attacked you and Abigail was intending to kill you. He may've noticed that you saw him near the stables while you were talking to Constable Barnaby. Now, please think carefully and tell me what you remember seeing when you were talking to Constable Barnaby."

Miss Carter looked flustered. "You know, Detective, I've tried, but I cannot see that far very well, even with these on... I vaguely remember seeing his back. He was wearing a grey coat and a bowler hat. The man who attacked us was wearing the same thing. He was dressed like a vagrant."

"Maybe that was just a disguise. It is strange that he got into the manor in the first place. The front door is guarded by Constable Jenkins, and Constable Barnaby walks around the manor every hour. Was the laundry door unbolted?"

"Abigail was very scatterbrained; she must have left the door unbolted. All

I remember is that he suddenly came running down the stairs from the main floor and pushed me. I fell against the wall and then he pushed Abigail and she..."

"I understand... and he went out through the laundry door, the way he came in. He must have been wandering in the manor and saw you both going down the stairs, then decided that it was the perfect opportunity to get rid of you... Now, there's something else I wanted to ask you; did you see a knife when you entered Lady Fitzhugh's bedroom?"

"No. The shock of seeing her Ladyship dead was too much to take and then I saw the empty box. I remember thinking that she was probably killed for the necklace."

"It must've looked stunning on her neck."

Miss Carter glared at him, as if looking through him. "Yes, it was very beautiful and it looked very elegant on her neck. Now, nobody else will wear it... nobody should... it was meant only for her neck." She started crying, which startled Dermot, making him uncomfortable. She wiped her eyes and composed herself. "Well, Detective, if you have no more questions for me, I will get back to work."

"Just one more... Where did you live before coming here?"

Miss Carter seemed taken aback at the question, but she quickly composed herself. "I lived in Cumbria for nearly twenty years working under Mrs. Evans, a widow with no children. She taught me to be a good housekeeper and I was also her companion. When she died, I was not wanted by her niece as she was travelling to the Far East to be with her husband. Fortunately, I saw the advertisement in the *London Times* and applied for this job."

"Thank you, Miss Carter. I will let you carry on with your work."

—　　—　　—

Dermot headed to the kitchen and found Alice chopping vegetables. She looked distraught and her eyes were red like she had been crying. Dermot said that he wanted to talk to her. After obtaining Mrs. Withers' permission, they headed to the servants' dining room.

They sat down and Alice stared at the table. Dermot said soothingly, "Alice, I know you're distraught over the loss of Abigail, but it would help if you can answer a few questions."

"Yes, Detective Carlyle," she said softly.

"Was Abigail seeing anyone?"

She looked at him in surprise. "No, Detective, she never said nothin' about it to me."

"Now think carefully, did she tell you about anything strange happening on the day that Hector had his accident?"

"We talked just before goin' to bed that night and she said it was strange that she didn't see Miss Fitzhugh in front of the library door at the time she said she was there."

"Is that all she said?"

"She also said that if she'd been in the laundry yard instead of takin' lemonade to Constable Jenkins, then she would've seen the person goin' into the stables after Charles left."

"So she did not think that Charles had anything to do with it?"

"No, she saw Charles walk past the laundry door to the kitchen. She didn't believe that he would harm the boy. Why would he want to hurt his little master who hadn't done him any harm?"

"Anything else?"

She shook her head.

"What about the clock striking when she was in the laundry yard?"

"Oh... yes... she kept goin' on about that. She said she heard the clock strike four-thirty twice. I told her that it does, once in the morning and once in the evening. But she said it was only a few minutes after she heard it strike the first time when Miss Fitzhugh said she was at the library door. She then saw the three of 'em go into the stables and ride off towards the meadow."

"Yes, she was beginning to tell me about that when we were interrupted. It didn't make sense to me either."

"Abigail was a little dim-witted. Even at school and when we trained to become maids, she made silly mistakes. She was my friend and I tried to 'elp her. I suppose she wanted to show off that she knew somethin', but it may've been nothin'. I think she may have made it up, because a clock don't strike the same after a few minutes."

Dermot nodded. "You two grew up together?"

"Yes, Detective. Been friends since we were small. Her family was glad we got hired together because they knew I'd look after 'er. She may've been a silly girl, but she was kind and didn't deserve to die like that," Alice said, teary eyed.

"Did you see anything unusual on that day?"

Alice wiped her tears. "Now that you mention it, when I fetched the tray from the library, I saw some dried mud and a leaf on the carpet. I saw the same on the day her Ladyship's body was found. Probably don't mean anythin' though. Loads of people went into the library at the party, could've come from their shoes."

"You're right; anything else?"

She smiled. "Mrs. Withers was upset that the knife was a bit blunt."

"Which one?"

"The knife Miss Carter put on the tea tray for Miss Fitzhugh and Mr. Seymour. Miss Fitzhugh said that she used it to cut the apple, but I don't think that would've made the knife blunt."

"Interesting," Dermot said and then he thanked Alice and left.

Chapter 17: Painter's Muse

Dermot took the lift to the floor where Richard lived in Mayfair, London. He knocked on the door of the flat and Richard opened it, wearing a shirt with paint stains on it and holding a colour palette.

"Ahh, Detective Carlyle," Richard said, looking taken aback. "What a pleasant surprise. What brings you here?"

"I was in the vicinity and I wanted to talk to you about Hector's accident."

Richard rolled his eyes. "I've already told Inspector Enderby everything that happened. It was just an accident... Please come in."

As Dermot entered, he got the smell of paint. He looked in the corner of the room and saw a blonde woman, wrapped in a sheet, posing in front of a half-finished painting on an easel. She winked at Dermot and greeted him. Richard introduced her as Felicity, his model.

"Ooooooo, so you're really a detective like Sherlock Holmes? Never met a detective before."

"Sort of, but without Dr. Watson."

Felicity chuckled.

"You're painting her for your next gallery exhibition?" asked Dermot with a smile.

"Yes. I know what you're thinking, Detective, but an artist has to be open-minded and paint everything, including beautiful women," Richard replied.

"By the way, congratulations on your engagement. Mrs. Fitzhugh mentioned it to me."

Dermot noticed the frown on Richard's face and immediately looked over at Felicity.

"Richard, you cheeky devil, you never told me that you're engaged to that girl you're seeing," said Felicity, sounding hurt.

"It just slipped my mind... Now, Felicity, why don't you put on some clothes and run along. The detective wants to talk to me. We can finish your painting another time."

She giggled. "Yes, darling." She got up with the sheet wrapped around her, went into the bathroom, and closed the door.

Dermot asked Richard to tell him what happened on the day that Hector had his accident. Richard began by telling Dermot about making plans with Pippa to ride the horses and about Hector wanting to join them. He then told Dermot what happened after the three of them took the horses from the stables and about Hector's accident.

"Hmm, I can see nothing wrong with your story, but... well, Abigail said something strange to me a few minutes before she was attacked and killed..."

The bathroom door opened and Felicity came out. She kissed Richard on the cheek, wished them both goodbye, and left.

After she left, Dermot continued, "Abigail told me that she did not see Pippa outside the library door when the clock in the library started chiming at four-thirty p.m. She was passing by the library, taking a glass of lemonade for Constable Jenkins at the front door. Only you can corroborate whether Pippa was really at the library door when the clock chimed. It will help strengthen Pippa's alibi."

"Detective, you have my word that Pippa was knocking at the library door at four-thirty. Constable Barnaby also heard the clock chime and I told him that Pippa was at the door knocking.

"Maybe Abigail was mistaken."

"Yes, she was. We all know Abigail was not a bright girl. She probably invented that just to make herself sound smart. The door was closed because I didn't want one of those old birds seeing me without a shirt and throwing a fit. They get upset very easily... especially Aunt Lilian."

"Yes, I know. But why didn't you want to change in the bathroom?"

"You see, Detective, I was reading a book. It was so engrossing that I didn't want to idle away my time in the bathroom doing nothing. Pippa was okay with me being in the library because the bathroom was at the other end of the corridor. The shirt needed to come off immediately so that the stain wouldn't have time to set."

"Which book were you reading?"

"*Moby Dick*. My father told me the story as a child. I was fascinated with the story of Captain Ahab and how doggedly he pursued the whale, but ultimately his passion for revenge got the better of him and killed him. I was reading it as I waited in the library while Pippa went to the stables and told Charles to get the horses ready. Miss Carter had already put the tray with the tea, sandwiches, and apples in the library. The book was interesting and I didn't want to put it down."

"Pippa told me about hearing a breaking sound twice..."

"Yes, I was very clumsy that day. The teacup I was drinking from fell on the floor as I was placing it on the tray and then when I picked it up it slipped from my hand and broke."

Dermot nodded slowly and continued.

"Pippa also told me that you took the torch from the desk in the library."

"I found the torch in the desk and used it to look for pieces of the teacup on the floor. I then took it along with us since we had decided to take Hector on a tour of the caves near the stream. I put it in the saddle bag on Hector's horse. It must still be lying where Hector and the saddle fell."

"Now, speaking of clothes, does Pippa know that you paint women with hardly any clothes on?"

Richard laughed. "Detective, what are you? The morality police? Yes, she does. All painters have to paint people in the nude or with hardly any clothes on."

"I hope that you're aware that Pippa thinks that you love her and are faithful to her. She wouldn't fancy you fooling around with a saucy dish like Felicity."

A wave of anger swept through Richard's face.

"Well, Detective, it really is none of your business," he said. "You can be sure that once Pippa and I are married, this will all stop. Felicity is one of those flapper tarts, good for a little nookie." Richard then lowered his voice. "Pippa would make a good wife, but Francis – who as you know owns the theatre where she acts – seems keen on her. I could tell when I met him and I've seen him following us to Meadowford and around London. I haven't told Pippa. I don't want her thinking I'm against her being an actress, like her mother and aunts."

"How did you know that I met Francis?" asked Dermot, surprised.

"Pippa told me. Francis mentioned to her that a detective knew who she was and she gathered that it was you. She's very grateful that you've kept her secret. Her aunts still adhere to the Victorian mentality that only loose women become actresses and they would do anything to prevent her from becoming one."

Dermot tried not to smile and then said in a serious tone, "Pippa mentioned that you fought in the Great War."

Richard was caught by surprise and responded, "Yes, I was injured in France. Recovery was long and hard. I had no family... only my talent to help me. I worked as an odd job man while I painted. Once I got an art gallery in London to take my paintings, things started working for me."

Dermot spotted a picture of a young girl on the table. "Who's that?"

Richard looked at the picture and his expression changed. He picked it up and gazed at it with sadness. "That's my daughter. She died during the Spanish flu epidemic. Her mother died in childbirth."

Dermot sympathised with him and then tactfully asked if he knew the reason why Lady Fitzhugh had invited him to her birthday party.

"No. I was surprised when she invited me a few hours before the party and also when she asked me to meet her the next morning. Pippa felt that maybe she had finally come to accept me. We'll never know," he said, shrugging his shoulders.

Dermot thanked him. Then as he was about to leave, Richard said, "Detective, if I were you I would take a closer look at Charles. He isn't trustworthy."

"Why do you say that?"

Richard began narrating an incident that he witnessed when he first visited Fitzhugh Manor. Pippa had told him that they had horses at the stables and he went alone after dinner to have a look. As he approached the stables, he heard two people talking. He crept on slowly and saw Charles talking to Irene Shaw. Irene was telling him that Lady Fitzhugh was going to call her solicitor and add her to the will since she knew who she really was. Then Charles said how marvellous it would be if Irene would get that money immediately, instead of waiting for her Ladyship to die. They could elope and then go to Paris for their honeymoon.

Dermot interrupted him to ask if he had heard what Irene meant about who she really was, but Richard just shrugged his shoulders. Dermot then asked him to continue.

Richard explained that the pair had heard footsteps approaching. Irene looked outside and saw that it was Pippa coming down the hill. Irene left the stables from another door and Charles went to his room. Richard went up to Pippa and she was startled to see him. They both went into the stables and, as they petted the horses, Charles came down from his room and pretended that he was up there reading a book. He had no idea that Richard had heard a part of his conversation with Irene.

"Why didn't you mention this before?"

"Irene had been fired many days prior to the murder and Charles sleeps in the stables, so I didn't think it was important until now. I haven't even told Pippa about it. When you mentioned that Abigail told you that nobody can be in two places at the same time, I thought of Charles and Irene. An accomplice could've let them in."

Dermot smiled. "Mr. Seymour, I thank you for that important piece of information."

— — —

As Dermot was heading to the lift, he almost bumped into Felicity.

"Oooooo, Detective. I forgot my purse in Richard's flat. I need it to pay the taxi or I cannot go home... Cheerio!"

She touched his shoulder, giggled, and walked away. Dermot couldn't shake off the feeling that there was something strange in her behaviour.

Chapter 18: A Woman Unveiled

The next morning, Dermot drove to Fitzhugh Manor and went to the stables. From a distance, he could see Charles holding a bucket and feeding a horse. Charles saw Dermot approaching.

"Morning, Detective. What brings you 'ere?"

"You've not been completely honest with me."

"What's that supposed to mean, eh?" said Charles, putting the bucket with the horse feed down. "I told you and that Inspector Enderby what happened that day Hector had his accident."

"Yes, I've no doubt about that, but you didn't tell us that you were seeing Irene Shaw or that you were planning on eloping together when she got some money from Lady Fitzhugh's estate."

Charles' eyes widened and he stepped back, steadying himself against the wooden door of the horse's stall.

"How... how'd you know that?"

"Never mind. Now tell me, how were you two planning on getting Irene's inheritance early? Was it by murdering Lady Fitzhugh?"

Charles looked like a cornered animal and slowly began speaking. "No... You see, Detective, Irene is the illegitimate daughter of Frida Wilson, who worked as a maid at the manor many years ago. Lord Fitzhugh..."

Dermot was startled when he heard the name. He asked Charles to continue.

"Her Ladyship dismissed Frida when she discovered she was pregnant... On the urging of her mother, Irene obtained work here as a lady's maid and, when she grew close to Lady Fitzhugh, she told her who she was and also showed her proof. Lady Fitzhugh had mellowed down a bit in her old age and she felt that she had wronged Frida. So she said that she would give Irene a legacy under certain conditions."

"What were those conditions?"

"I'm saying nothing. You'll have to ask Irene... We thought we'd not have to wait long as Lady Fitzhugh was very old and would die soon."

"You know, this new revelation doesn't look good for Irene and you.

Besides, you were the last person to handle Hector's saddle."

"Detective, I swear that we never had anything to do with what happened. Irene was never mentioned in the will."

"How'd you know that?"

"…because she was fired for stealing that necklace, which she didn't."

Dermot nodded, he knew very well that Charles had a point. Dermot cautioned Charles about leaving Meadowford and told him that if he did the law would be after him. Charles nodded with relief and wiped the sweat from his face.

—   —   —

Dermot drove out of Meadowford and headed to St. Crispin's Village and the Boar's Head pub where Irene Shaw worked. When he entered the pub, he saw Irene behind the counter serving drinks to two men. A look of surprise swept through her face when she saw Dermot.

"What can I do for you?" she asked, trying not to make it obvious that Dermot was connected with the police. He moved closer to her and whispered, "We need to talk. I need to ask you about the inheritance Lady Fitzhugh was about to leave you."

Irene's eyes widened and her expression betrayed that she was hiding something.

"Let me ask the landlord if I can take my break now."

Dermot nodded and Irene walked through the curtain behind her. She emerged a few minutes later and an older bearded man followed her and stood behind the counter. Dermot surmised that he must be the owner.

Irene followed Dermot outside and they sat down on a bench. Dermot told her that he knew who she really was and about her conversation with Charles.

"It's true that we said that," she said, looking ashamed. "But we had nothing to do with the death of Lady Fitzhugh. You must believe me."

"This new revelation makes both you and Charles suspects. It would be best if you tell me what happened."

Irene became a little calmer and told Dermot about her mother being seduced by Lord Fitzhugh when she was a maid at Fitzhugh Manor. Frida told him of her pregnancy before he left for South Africa, and he told her to get rid of the baby. When Frida told Doris Fitzhugh this, she accused Frida of lying and dismissed her to avoid a scandal. She was given three months' salary in advance, a good reference, and was warned never to reveal the paternity of the baby.

"How did you get employed at the manor?"

"I saw an advertisement for a lady's maid and I applied through the agency. I have many years of experience working as a lady's maid for one of the ladies here in the village and also in London, and they gave me good references. So I got the job."

"How did you manage to tell her Ladyship who you really were?"

"She once remarked that I reminded her of someone, but she couldn't remember who. When I managed to gain her trust, I told her who I really was. I also told her about my mother being an invalid. She got upset and apologised to me. She said that she would leave me a legacy in her will on one condition: nobody was to know who I really was. She didn't want the family involved in another scandal like when her brother died. I agreed. When the solicitor arrived a few days later, the wills went missing and so she was not able to add me to her will."

"So it wasn't you who stole those wills and then put them back?"

"No. I swear I didn't know that Mr. Kerr was there until we were ordered to search for those missing wills."

"Yes, it would seem pointless for you to steal the wills, but there is a possibility that you needed to know who was going to inherit the estate and the line of succession. So that doesn't completely put you above suspicion... What proof did you show Lady Fitzhugh to show that you were the illegitimate daughter of Lord Fitzhugh?"

"After Lord Fitzhugh returned from South Africa, my mother wrote to him telling him about me. He agreed to meet us and we met in secret. He acknowledged me and promised to help us. I showed Lady Fitzhugh the letters that her father wrote to my mother. He used to send my mother some money, but of course that stopped when he died.

"Life got even harder for us after my mother developed arthritis and she had to stop working as a secretary. She knew that most people mellow down in their old age and I had a right to get an inheritance. So we planned for me to get employment at the manor and gain Lady Fitzhugh's trust, which I did, and it would've worked. However, that incident with the necklace ruined everything for me."

"Yes, the mysterious necklace," said Dermot, making a wry face. "Now, tell me, how did you get involved with Charles?"

Irene bit at her nails, but she stopped and composed herself. "Charles had come to work at the manor a few months before I did. He never got along with Miss Carter. Once I got close to Lady Fitzhugh, Miss Carter was not nice to me either. Seems she didn't like anyone being close to her Ladyship. One day,

Miss Carter got me upset and I ran into the woods behind the stables. Charles followed me and comforted me. He spoke to me with that soothing voice of his. I knew I could confide in him and I told him who I really was and why I was at Fitzhugh Manor. He encouraged me to tell Lady Fitzhugh and I did."

"What happened after you were fired?"

"Mother and I decided to cut our losses and get on with our lives. Charles wanted to leave, but then Lady Fitzhugh got murdered and now he's a suspect in the attempted murder of Master Fitzhugh. I don't know what will happen." She began to cry.

Dermot comforted her and asked if he could meet her mother. Irene obliged and, after obtaining permission from the pub's landlord, they drove for nearly five minutes until they came to a row of houses. They stopped in front of a house with the number fifteen marked on it and walked to the front door.

Irene knocked on the door. "Mother, it's me." The door opened and in front of them stood a frail middle-aged woman with a walking stick. Irene introduced them and told her mother why they were there.

"Come in, I'm going to have some tea," Frida said nonchalantly. She then turned around and walked towards a settee, using her stick for support. They followed her; Dermot sat on the opposite settee and Irene sat next to her mother.

"What would you like to know, Detective?"

"Miss Shaw, you worked for Lord Fitzhugh..."

"Detective," Frida interrupted. "It's Mrs. Shaw. My husband is deceased and his son owns the Boar's Head pub where Irene works... After we moved back to St. Crispin's Village, Mr. Shaw, who was keen on me when I was young, proposed marriage since he was then a widower."

She chuckled when she saw a look of surprise sweep through Dermot's face.

"I will tell you the whole story since I know why you're here." She then proceeded to tell Dermot about Lord Fitzhugh seducing her and Doris Fitzhugh dismissing her on account of the pregnancy. Her parents disowned her after she secretly had her baby in St. Crispin's Village. So she moved to London and worked as a char to support herself.

"What made him acknowledge Irene as his daughter?"

"He was an old man by the time he came back from South Africa. He was upset that Allan and he didn't get along. After he narrowly missed being killed in the mine blast, he thought he was given a second chance to right certain wrongs he had done in India and South Africa. He secretly met with us in

London. I would write to him when we needed money, using the moniker 'Miss Portia Hartford'. After burning my letters to prevent anyone from finding out, he would send us a cheque to the bank account he opened in London under my moniker. He didn't want anyone to know that he had a child out of wedlock – he had his family name to consider."

Dermot nodded. "So you're the mysterious Portia Hartford. We thought you were trying to blackmail Lord Fitzhugh because you knew a secret he wanted suppressed. Did he ever tell you what he had done in South Africa and India?"

"No, he never mentioned them and I never asked since it wasn't my business... However, one day he met us after his visit to St. Cuthbert's Hospital. He was sweating profusely and looked scared. I asked him what happened and he said he thought he'd recognised a man from South Africa following him from the hospital onto the street. But it was doubtful as the man was dead. That's all he said."

Dermot took out an envelope and placed it in front of Frida. She opened it and read the message.

"I think you want to know if I sent this to Lord Fitzhugh?"

"Yes, he received it just before he died of septicaemia. We thought it was the mysterious Portia Hartford that sent this to him."

Frida shook her head. "No, I did not," she said firmly. "Because of his generosity, Irene attended a good school and I learnt to be a secretary and improved myself. When he died and the money stopped coming, my work as a secretary helped us survive; until this illness made me incapable of typing or doing anything useful."

She then asked him to go to the table close to him and look at the note she wrote before she developed arthritis. Dermot walked to the table and saw a picture on it. The picture was of a very attractive woman who was dressed in the style of the late 1890s.

"Mrs. Shaw, is this you?"

"Yes, Detective, a far cry from what I look like now. This illness has taken its toll on my body."

Dermot took the note and came over to the settee. He compared the two handwritings and they were completely different.

"Well, a new mystery now emerges as to who wrote this note."

"I'm glad we solved one mystery for you... Now, would you like some tea before it gets cold, Detective?" said Frida smugly as she gingerly held the teapot over a teacup.

Chapter 19: Long-forgotten Memory

Flora handed Dermot a stack of documents.

"Detective, here are Father's papers. I found the reference letter that Miss Carter gave us. Surprising that Doris had it with her," she said.

Dermot was in the drawing room with the two elderly sisters. Flora mentioned that she had found Lord Fitzhugh's papers in Doris' bedroom, along with the reference letter in the same drawer. It mystified her because she had expected to find them in her father's bedroom.

Dermot read the reference letter written by Mrs. Mable Evans on her death bed. It painted a glowing picture of Miss Carter as a highly competent and loyal housekeeper, and Dermot realised why she was hired even though she was interviewed at the last minute. He then perused through the documents regarding the settlement made by the insurance company and the report by geologist, Gregory H. Huddleston from the Parr & Monroe Geology company, about the mine having a huge diamond deposit. He also went through the deed that made Lord Fitzhugh the sole owner of the mine. However, there was still nothing to indicate how the De Villiers family perished during the Boer War.

Dermot noticed a brownish envelope with handwriting that had faded with time. He looked closer and saw that it was addressed to Lord Fitzhugh in South Africa. With Flora's permission, he opened the letter and read it. It was from Christiaan De Villiers and dated the twenty-fifth of August, 1901. Christiaan gave Lord Fitzhugh the good news of having excavated the mine a little further and finding more diamonds. The geologist had also confirmed that the mine had a vast deposit of diamonds. Christiaan said that he was now sealing the mine for the duration of the war. The last paragraph caught Dermot's attention. It stated that Christiaan was planning on sending his share of the uncut diamonds to a safe place.

While Dermot was wondering as to where Christiaan could have sent his share of the diamonds, Miss Carter came into the drawing room and announced that Sister Fleming from St. Cuthbert's Hospital was on the telephone wanting to talk to Dermot. He excused himself and followed her.

The phone was located next to the staircase that led to the kitchen.

After Miss Carter went down the staircase, Dermot picked up the receiver and greeted Sister Fleming. She said that his mother had told her to call Dermot at Fitzhugh Manor. She told him that she had finally found the photograph of the hospital staff taken before the war in one of her old trunks in the attic. Dermot told her that he would head to London immediately and that he would meet her at the café in front of the hospital in an hour and a half. After bidding the two elderly sisters goodbye, Dermot got into his car and headed towards London.

— — —

Sister Fleming came back from the Records Room after looking at the file of a long-deceased patient. What Dr. Butterworth had said to her earlier, when she showed him the photograph, had brought back a long-forgotten memory she hadn't thought was important until now. She must tell Detective Carlyle about it. She picked up her bag in which she had the envelope that contained the picture. Looking at the photograph brought back a lot of recollections from before the Great War, from when things were different. She recognised some of the staff who used to work at the hospital. They went off to war and never returned.

Sister Fleming adjusted her hat, spoke for a few minutes, and said goodbye to Eunice, her assistant. She looked at the clock as she walked out of the hospital. It was almost time to be at the café. Detective Carlyle would be pleased with her. She walked out of the gate to the edge of the pavement and she was about to cross the street when she saw a man approaching her. Even though the man's hat was lowered in an attempt to hide his face, the evening sun highlighted his visible features and Sister Fleming gasped in shock as she recognised him.

"Oh, it's you. I thought you were dead. Where...?"

Without warning, the man grabbed for her bag. Clinging to it with both hands, she yelled out for help as she fought wildly with him, but he was too strong and ripped it from her grasp. He then pushed her hard towards the road. The sound of brakes squealing and the thud of the car hitting her body brought people to the spot and the man quickly walked away with the bag tucked under his arm.

— — —

The evening traffic into London had been heavy and Dermot's progress had been slow. His body was tense from his concern of being late for his meeting and from suffering the frustrated drivers yelling expletives and blaring their horns. His nose stung from the exhaust fumes that filled the air while he had queued. But as he finally drove away from the congested areas towards the hospital, Dermot glanced at his watch and smiled. He was relieved that he would be on time; and he felt the tension ebb away and his shoulders slowly began to relax.

As Dermot drove up to the hospital, he saw that a large crowd had gathered by the road at the entrance. There were people of all ages and even some in hospital uniforms, but all were jostling and peering towards the road in front of a car. As he looked at them, Dermot saw two constables run towards the onlookers and push their way through.

Dermot pulled over at the side of the road and got out of the car. He pushed through the mass of people and when he finally saw what they were all crowding around the shock hit him like a punch to the stomach. He forced himself to take another look as bile burnt at the back of his throat. On the hot tarred road and lifeless like a doll was the body of Sister Fleming. Her blank, glazed eyes stared upwards towards the sky and her limbs were contorted around her body. Blood was oozing from her mouth and angry welts and bruises covered the exposed skin of her face and hands. The driver of the car was trying to explain to the constables what had happened.

"Detective Carlyle from the Metropolitan Police," Dermot said as he moved hastily towards the constables. "What happened?"

"The lady was hit by this car. I saw a man grab her bag and push her in front of it," said a woman wearing a brown hat. The colour had drained from her face and her hazel eyes showed the horror she had just witnessed.

"Did she know the man? What did he look like?"

"I was standing a few metres away. I saw the look of surprise on her face and she said something to him, when he suddenly grabbed her bag. She fought back and after he took the bag he pushed her in front of that car. He was slightly more than medium height. I couldn't see his face because he had lowered his hat to hide it. That's all I saw," said the woman.

Dermot felt his head spin. Who could've known that he was meeting Sister Fleming? He had spoken to her barely two hours ago and now she was dead. The orderlies from the hospital arrived with a stretcher and asked everyone to move away. They lifted the body onto the stretcher and covered it with a sheet.

Dermot took one last look at the body as it was being taken through the hospital gates. He pushed through the crowd and went back to his car. He climbed in and put his head on the steering wheel. When he felt the dizziness pass, he started his car and drove back to Meadowford Village. One thing he now knew for certain was that David Northam was still alive.

—   —   —

The next day, Dermot drove back to St. Cuthbert's Hospital. When he entered the hospital, he saw that it was business as usual, but he could tell that many of the staff were very distraught. He went to Dr. Butterworth's office and knocked on the door. When Dr. Butterworth gave him permission to enter, he went in and expressed his sympathies. He asked if Dr. Butterworth had met Sister Fleming the previous day.

"Yes, she told me that she found the staff photograph taken when the war began. She showed it to me; I glanced at it and went on my way. That was the last time I saw her…" He choked a bit and tried to hold back tears.

"I understand, Dr. Butterworth," Dermot said soothingly. "When you glanced at the picture, did you recognise any of the staff?"

"It's been a long time, Detective. Most of the staff joined the war and some never returned. Some that did went to work in other places. Ethel and David Northam were in the picture and so was I. Dr. Steward, who was the head of surgery, was in the middle… Oh… I said to her that I remember the day it was taken because it was the day that Dr. Steward decided to join the Royal Army Medical Corp. The death of Lord Fitzhugh a few years earlier had upset him a lot. He had never ever lost a patient until then. I recognised his face in the photograph and it brought back memories of that day. He still looked upset."

"Lord Fitzhugh developing septicaemia was a mystery, right?"

"Dr. Steward could never comprehend how it happened. He blamed himself for being negligent, even though the family didn't complain. When the war began, he volunteered and died in France. I think he felt he had to make restitution for being negligent."

"Did Sister Fleming tell anyone that she was meeting me?"

"I don't know. You can check with Nurse Eunice with whom she worked. She's very distraught, so you'd better be careful when talking to her."

Dermot thanked Dr. Butterworth and promised him that he would find the person who killed Sister Fleming.

Dermot then went in search of Nurse Eunice and found her in the office that she had shared with the late Sister Fleming. Nurse Eunice was in her thirties, with brown hair; her blue eyes showed the pain of losing her supervisor. Dermot went in and introduced himself. He asked her if she had seen the photograph and if she knew that Sister Fleming had been on her way to meet him.

"Yes, Sister Fleming mentioned that she was going to meet you to give you the staff photograph taken in 1914. She showed me the two people you wanted to see, but the faces could barely be made out. Ethel Northam was wearing a veil on her head and David Northam had a moustache."

"Did she say anything else?"

"She said that what Dr. Butterworth had said to her about Dr. Steward had brought back a memory. It reminded her of the day that a patient by the name of Lord William Fitzhugh was about to be discharged after having gall bladder surgery. She went through the records and found that there was a patient by the name of Franklyn Hayworth who had an infected leg. He was in the room next to Lord Fitzhugh. The leg had to be cleaned often due to the infection.

"Sister Fleming remembered seeing Nurse Northam coming out of Mr. Hayworth's room with a tray containing soiled bandages belonging to Mr. Hayworth. She then entered Lord Fitzhugh's room. Sister Fleming didn't think anything of it, but she said that it struck her as odd."

"Why did she think that was odd?"

"I don't know. That was the last thing she said to me." Eunice starting tearing up; she took out her handkerchief, wiped her eyes, and composed herself.

"What happened to Mr. Hayworth?"

"Let me take you to the Records Room. I know exactly where the file is kept."

Dermot followed her to a big room where the files were stored. Eunice went to the cabinet with the year 1906 marked on it and opened it. She looked through the files and pulled one out. They opened the file and read the notes.

Franklyn Hayworth had a boil that had to be lanced. However, the infection was so bad that he had died of septicaemia a few days after.

"That's exactly what Lord Fitzhugh died of. Nobody could understand how he got septicaemia when he was recovering so very well from the surgery," said Dermot.

"Probably what Sister Fleming wanted to tell you, in addition to giving you the photograph, was that she suspected that there was a connection between the deaths of the two men."

"She suspected that Lord Fitzhugh's death was not due to negligence but deliberate," said Dermot. "Nurse Northam must've infected the bandage with the pus from Hayworth's bandage and then given it to Dr. Steward to dress Lord Fitzhugh's wound. That's how he got septicaemia and died. No wonder Dr. Steward blamed himself; he thought that he'd been negligent."

—   —   —

The next morning, Dermot was having breakfast with his parents. Edmund was reading the newspaper, which annoyed Edna and she finally decided to say something about it.

"Edmund, put down that paper at once. Your son rarely eats at home because he's on a case and now that he's here you're reading the paper... May I ask what's so interesting?"

Edmund put the paper aside. "If you must know, my dear, I'm reading an interesting article about one of the German spies from the Great War."

"Who?" asked Dermot.

"Gerhard Von Schultz. He spied for Germany during the Great War and has written a book about his experiences as a spy. He says that he placed spies in the War Office who acted as double agents."

"Is that so?"

"Yes, and he was in South Africa during the Boer War. His mother was Boer and his father was German. Because he spoke fluent French, he was in France during the Great War, spying for the Germans. He passed on to the Germans the information he obtained from his spies in England and from the French."

Dermot suddenly sat upright. "Did you say he was in South Africa?"

"Yes, he fought against the English there. So when the Great War began, he continued to fight the English for the Germans. He said he was going to get important information from his spies in England that would've helped the Germans in 1916, but it didn't happen."

"Please let me read the article, Father."

Edmund handed the newspaper to Dermot. Dermot read the article and became thoughtful.

"What is it, Dermot?"

Dermot snapped his fingers. "Thank you, Father." He put a few spoonfuls of scrambled eggs into his mouth and drank his coffee. He got up from the table and went upstairs to his room with a piece of toast sticking out of his mouth. He looked at his notes and smiled. He had a lead that had unexpectedly fallen into his lap. He went back downstairs.

"Father, I think I'll need to send a telegram to your friend, Elmer Griffin, in South Africa."

Chapter 20: A Suspect in Custody

Inspector Enderby was at his desk, writing his report. He was overwhelmed with the direction of the case and there was no end in sight. They had a chief suspect, but no concrete evidence to arrest or charge him with the crime. The phone rang and he picked up the receiver. It was Constable Lyons, whom he had asked to shadow the chief suspect. Inspector Enderby smiled. It was an answer to his prayers – they now had the evidence to charge the suspect with murder.

Inspector Enderby took Constables Beckett and Clarke with him and headed to Meadowford Train Station. They went to the ticket counter and Inspector Enderby asked the man behind the counter what time the next train from London would be arriving.

"At quarter past five, sir."

Inspector Enderby thanked the man and beckoned to the two constables to follow him to the platform. In a few minutes, people began arriving on the platform and the crowd grew bigger with each passing minute. They heard the whistle of a train and saw smoke in the distance.

"Be on the lookout. We cannot afford to let him escape." The two constables nodded.

The train approached the station and the crowd started moving forward. As the train stopped directly in front of the platform, the doors opened and the passengers began alighting. The three policemen searched the faces of the passengers for their suspect, but none of the faces looked familiar. All of a sudden, one of the constables pointed to a man standing next to the door of the train carriage.

"There he is."

The man jumped onto the platform and tried to run towards the exit, but the crowd prevented him from passing through. He turned and ran towards the back of the train, jumping onto the tracks. He looked back and saw the three men pursuing him. He stumbled on one of the sleepers and fell. Before he could get up, the two constables grabbed him and Inspector Enderby came closer.

"Arthur Endecott, I am arresting you on the charges of robbery and the murder of your aunt, Lady Doris Fitzhugh."

—   —   —

Inspector Enderby and Dermot walked into the interrogation room. Arthur was sitting down, sulking. The two men sat opposite him and Inspector Enderby produced the diamond earrings.

"Mr. Endecott, you're in serious trouble for selling a pair of stolen diamond earrings and for resisting arrest. Not to mention that you are a suspect for murdering your aunt."

Arthur looked up. "I knew that I was a suspect, but I'm innocent."

"How did you know that we suspected you?"

"Everyone knew that I was there to ask Aunt Doris for some money. She wasn't sympathetic when I told her why I needed the money..."

"What do you need the money for?" asked Dermot.

"It's private. Nothing to do with this case."

"Mr. Endecott, you need to tell us everything," said Dermot.

Arthur explained that he was part of Delhi's high society and that he loved gambling. Before marrying Cecily, she made him promise that he would give up gambling. The new set of friends he made in Delhi, however, had got him into gambling again and he had squandered his money. Cecily had threatened to leave him and take their three children with her. A friend of his had told him about a coffee plantation in Kenya. Cecily and he thought it was a good idea to move to Kenya for a fresh start and she promised to stay with him if they moved. The only problem was that he didn't have any money to move or to buy the plantation.

Arthur had explained the situation to Lady Fitzhugh, but she wasn't sympathetic. However, while she was getting ready for her birthday party, she called him to her bedroom and told him that she was waiting for some news because she had received a telephone call earlier. Depending on the report she got, she would consider giving him the money he needed, but he had to give up gambling.

"What news was she waiting for and from whom?" asked Dermot.

"She didn't tell me. It was on a need to know basis with Aunt Doris."

"Why did you steal the diamond earrings?"

"When I saw her lying there dead, I knew that I wouldn't receive the money. Nobody would believe that she had made all those promises to me the previous night. I'd seen her put those diamond earrings in the drawer. I knew that Miss Carter was familiar with all the jewellery in Aunt Doris' jewellery box, but I thought nobody would miss the diamond earrings because they were in the drawer.

"When Slattery and Miss Carter were outside attending to Alice and also preventing the others from entering the bedroom, I saw my chance. I opened the drawer and took the earrings. Then I left the bedroom and acted shocked like everyone else. I knew that these earrings would fetch me some money and I would be able to pay a part of my gambling debts and move to Kenya."

"Is that all you took?" asked Inspector Enderby.

"Yes, I swear. Honestly, Inspector, I didn't take anything else."

Inspector Enderby looked at his notepad. "We know that you didn't take the emerald necklace because Miss Carter entered before you and saw the empty jewellery box. However, when we interviewed you just after your aunt's body was discovered, you said that you only entered the room and stared at the body for a few minutes in shock. Now you've admitted that you pinched these earrings. So you lied to us, which is a serious crime. I ask once again; did you take anything else?"

"Just the earrings, I swear," said Arthur, sounding upset.

Dermot and Inspector Enderby looked at each other and knew what the other was thinking – that Arthur was hiding something.

"One last question; do you have an accomplice?" asked Inspector Enderby.

Arthur looked surprised and shook his head.

"All right, Mr. Endecott. Constable Clarke will escort you back to your cell."

—   —   —

A few hours later, after obtaining a search warrant, they drove to Fitzhugh Manor in Dermot's car. They went to the living room where the two elderly sisters were having tea.

"What's the meaning of this?" asked Lilian when she saw them.

Inspector Enderby told her about Arthur being arrested and also about Constable Lyons seeing him pawning the earrings in London. He showed them the earrings.

"Good heavens! Those are our mother's earrings. Haven't seen them in donkey's years. Where did he get them from?" asked Flora.

"Mr. Endecott stole them when he entered the bedroom after Lady Fitzhugh's body was discovered. He lied about not taking anything from the murder scene, but he did. He was always our prime suspect from the beginning. He doesn't have a solid alibi for the murders of Lady Fitzhugh or Slattery, not like he has for Kerr and Abigail's murders, but we suspect that he has a partner or two. We cannot figure out who they are... Any idea why he came back to England?" asked Dermot.

Lilian Endecott looked annoyed. "Well, he said that he came to celebrate Doris' birthday. I knew it wasn't true because I could tell that he wanted something from her. Doris refused to tell me what it was. She told me at the party that she had an important matter to deal with and that she would let me know once things were settled."

"What did she mean?" asked Inspector Enderby.

"Doris was always secretive. She never told us anything until she felt that it was the right time to tell us."

"It's true," said Flora. "It drove us crazy that she treated us like children. She would go to any lengths to keep the family name and the fortune secure, just like Father."

"Did her Ladyship and Mr. Endecott get along?" asked Inspector Enderby.

"He was upset and resented that Father gave everything to Doris because he expected to be his heir, being the only grandson at the time of Father's death."

"Any idea why that happened?" asked Dermot.

"He was probably aware that Arthur was just like him. Unfortunately, Arthur inherited Father's penchant for gambling and excitement. Cecily changed him somewhat after they met and married in Shimla. Father felt that Arthur would squander his inheritance and Doris knew much more about running the estate than Arthur did," explained Flora.

"Did you know that Arthur's marriage is on the rocks and that we also received a telegram saying that he's wanted by the Delhi police for assaulting a high-ranking British civil servant?" asked Dermot.

"No, we never knew about that," said Lilian. "It wouldn't surprise me one bit though. Cecily isn't one to take any nonsense and I'm surprised that she's stayed with Arthur all this while. Arthur must've acted like a martyr and she must've fallen for it. Probably, she's had enough and wants to move on."

"All right. Well, we have a warrant to search Arthur's room. We have a feeling that he's hiding something," said Inspector Enderby.

Dermot and Inspector Enderby went up the staircase and entered Arthur's room. They began searching, but after an hour they were still empty-handed.

"Maybe we're wrong. He may've just taken the earrings."

"Probably," said Dermot. "But wait, the painting of the landscape looks a bit tilted." Dermot pointed towards a painting on the wall. "There could be something hidden within the frame. If not, then perhaps I should find another job," said Dermot.

Dermot took the painting down slowly. He heard something move inside as he turned the frame. He took off the clips and removed the back, then he looked at Inspector Enderby's eager face and smiled.

"You know we're missing the murder weapon... Well, here it is, along with the handkerchief he wrapped it in. I'm positive that the blood on the handkerchief is Lady Fitzhugh's."

Inspector Enderby looked shocked.

"Blimey," he said as he caressed his moustache. "He looks like a simpleton. I never thought he'd be capable of committing cold blooded murder."

"Yes, it's an Indian dagger. The design on the hilt will have left that bloody impression on the carpet under the bed."

"I believe we have our killer," said Inspector Enderby with satisfaction.

—   —   —

Inspector Enderby and Dermot stood in front of Dr. Talbot who had Lady Fitzhugh's autopsy file in front of him. He had taken a close-up photograph of her throat where it had been sliced.

"May I?" Dr. Talbot asked as he reached for the dagger.

"Sure, our fingerprint expert at the police department has already taken a partial fingerprint from the dagger. It had been wiped clean, except for the fingerprint on the side of the handle. He's comparing it with Arthur's fingerprints that we took when we arrested him and I'm positive it'll match," said Inspector Enderby.

Dr. Talbot held the dagger and examined the blade. "The blade is blunt like I suspected, and the width of the blade seems to match the cut on the victim's throat. I believe that this is the weapon that killed her. It sliced the carotid artery and she would have died within a few minutes."

"Thank you, Doctor. I believe that Mr. Endecott will start talking when we confront him with the evidence we have," said Dermot.

—   —   —

Inspector Enderby and Dermot once again sat in front of Arthur, who now looked scared and worried. He gazed at the table as he was afraid to look at the two men.

"Looks like you're in a lot of trouble, Mr. Endecott," said Inspector

Enderby sternly.

Arthur looked up, surprised and upset. "Why?"

"We've just received a cable from the Delhi Police. It says that you're wanted in Delhi for assaulting a Mr. Lipton at the Delhi Country Club."

"It... it's not what you think. He started going after Cecily when I asked him for a loan to pay off my gambling debts and he wouldn't leave her. He was drunk and wouldn't listen when I asked him to let go of her hand. So I hit him."

"That's not what we were told. The police didn't know that you're in England. They thought that you're in Calcutta and have been searching for you there."

"I had my friends spread false rumours that I was in Calcutta, while I went to Bombay and boarded a ship that brought me back to England. I did not mean to assault Mr. Lipton, but he just wouldn't leave Cecily alone. He's well connected with the Delhi Police Commissioner and I knew nobody would believe me. So Cecily and I decided that I would come to England, get money from Aunt Doris, and then we could all move to Kenya."

"It's not just that; we found this in your room," said Inspector Enderby.

Arthur's eyes widened when the dagger, wrapped in the bloodied handkerchief, was placed in front of him.

"Where... where... did you find that?"

"In the painting where you hid it. Did you think that nobody would find it? You didn't clean it very well. We even found a partial fingerprint on the handle and we have compared that fingerprint to the one we have on file, and it's yours."

"Please... I can explain. I did not kill Aunt Doris. I..."

"All right, let's hear what you have to say," said Inspector Enderby.

"After I put the earrings in my robe pocket, I turned around and I suddenly spied the dagger under the bed. I was shocked to see it. It was the dagger I had brought from India and it should've been in my suitcase. I knew I would be accused of murder. I took my handkerchief and grabbed the dagger, and then I put it in my pocket and walked out like nothing had happened. That's the truth, I swear. I was just scared that I would be arrested for a crime I did not commit."

Inspector Enderby banged his fist on the table. "Liar... Do you think we're fools? Do you think that acting like a martyr will get you some sympathy? I've dealt with criminals like you before, and I can tell when someone is lying. You're in big trouble for murder, assault, avoiding arrest, and theft. The long arm of the law has finally got you."

"Please… I was scared; I did not murder Aunt Doris."

"What about the blood stain on the window sill?" asked Dermot.

"I took the bloodied handkerchief to the window sill and wiped some blood on it to make it look like someone had left by the window – so that people wouldn't suspect that I had something to do with the murder."

"Mr. Endecott, we know that you have two very good motives for murdering your aunt because you felt that you should've inherited the estate from your grandfather and because you also needed money. Besides that, you also tampered with evidence and stole from the crime scene," said Dermot.

Arthur looked at Dermot almost tearfully. "I did, but I just wanted to tell the truth because I realised that it wouldn't be in my best interest to withhold anything. Eventually, it would come out in the open and it wouldn't look good for me."

"I'm certain your aunt didn't approve of the way that you gambled away your money. She knew that once a gambler, always a gambler. Am I right?" said Inspector Enderby.

"Yes, she did. I just wanted her to give me what I was going to inherit. She finally relented just before the party. I swear that's what she told me."

"All right. You can go back to your cell." Inspector Enderby motioned to Constable Clarke, standing near the door, to take him away.

Arthur got up and went with the constable.

Chapter 21: Lucky Finds

Dermot walked into the woods behind the stables. Ever since Charles had told him about the horses being anxious the night that Lady Fitzhugh was murdered, he knew he needed to investigate the cause. He had only walked a few metres when he heard a rustling sound. He stopped and slowly turned to his side.

"Who's there? Come out with your hands up," he said, slowly putting his hand on the gun that was hidden inside his coat.

The rustling got louder and then a grey cat walked slowly out from one of the bushes. Dermot recognised the cat.

"Hello, puss. You're Abigail's cat, aren't you? What the dickens are you doing out here?"

The cat meowed and walked ahead of him, then turned back and looked at him with its green eyes, as if beckoning Dermot to follow her. He wasn't sure what to do, but then felt that the cat wanted to show him something. He followed the cat deeper into the woods and then found himself standing in front of a stone slab half hidden in the undergrowth. If one were not paying attention, they would surely have missed it.

"Hello there, what've we here?"

The cat looked at him and went towards the slab. It crawled under a small bush and then disappeared. Dermot was stunned. Nobody had mentioned that this stone slab existed in the woods. He bent down, parted the bushes, and found a hole just big enough to allow a cat to pass through. The slab was warm to the touch due to the hot sun, but Dermot slowly lifted it and found that it wasn't too heavy. The slab looked old, but he could tell that it had been moved recently because some of the bushes around it had a few branches broken. On removing the slab, Dermot saw some steps behind it that led below and into the darkness.

Dermot never liked smoking cigarettes, but would smoke to keep others company. He kept a matchbox and a few cigarettes with him, just in case. Dermot took out the matchbox and stood on the steps. The sun shone partially through the canopy and lit part of the opening. Dermot could see that when the stairs ended there was a tunnel that led into the darkness. He slowly went down the stairs and then lit a match. The tunnel was leading towards the manor and he began walking along it slowly. Whenever a match burnt out, he lit a new one. He could see the cat in the distance and tried to keep up with it.

In some areas of the tunnel, the rocky ground was moist and the cat occasionally stopped to lap up some of the water that seeped out of the rock. 'Must be an underground spring,' Dermot thought. He treaded carefully and eventually he felt the tunnel start to lead upwards. He walked slowly until he came to a dead end. Dermot lit another match and found himself in front of a wall with a small entryway approximately three foot square. One part of the wall surrounding the entry looked older than the other. The newer portion looked like part of the mansion that was renovated in the early 1800s.

Dermot looked down and saw a mechanism that had recently been oiled. He tried it and nothing happened. He then realised that the means to open it was on the other side of the wall, probably in one of the rooms in the manor in order to prevent anyone from entering the manor through the tunnel. As he put one foot back, his shoe touched something and he heard a faint clink. He bent down and saw that the object had jagged edges. He picked it up carefully and put it in his coat pocket. Dermot realised that he only had two matches left. He lit another and quickly retraced his steps back to the opening. He put the slab back in its place, keeping a small opening for the cat. Satisfied, he turned and walked towards the meadows.

—   —   —

Dermot and Inspector Enderby stood outside Bertram Kerr's home in Chelsea. It was a plush flat with his office attached to it. They were let in by Kerr's secretary, Miss Livingstone, a hefty woman in her forties. The slightly sallow complexion of her face betrayed her grief at the tragic loss of her employer and complemented the spectacles that perched on her nose. They thanked her and asked her to wait outside while they searched the place. They entered the office, which was well furnished and had antiques in some corners and paintings on the wall.

"Fancy place, eh," said Inspector Enderby.

"Certainly is. I can't see why he would need to blackmail someone for a few diamonds," said Dermot.

"I called some of my contacts and one of them told me that Kerr collected antiques, paintings, and precious stones. His precious stones are all in a safety deposit box in the Bank of England and they're worth quite a fortune."

"Good work, Inspector. It seems that his greed got the better of him and he sank very low. We can start by searching his bedroom and then come back to the office."

"Good idea."

They searched the bedroom until Dermot called Inspector Enderby over to the briefcase that he found in the cupboard. Dermot recognised it as the briefcase that Kerr had with him when they dined together at the Meadowford Inn. They opened it and looked through the contents.

"These are the wills of Lady Fitzhugh and her father," Inspector Enderby said as he pulled out two envelopes from the briefcase.

"Yes, Kerr told me something about Lady Fitzhugh's will. If I remember correctly, Hector will inherit the estate when he turns twenty-one, Pippa will inherit the estate if anything were to happen to Hector, and if Pippa were deceased then it goes to Arthur and then to the oldest daughter of Flora. I can clearly see that Arthur had a motive to kill Lady Fitzhugh and Hector, and he certainly had the opportunity to kill his aunt. He could've put arsenic in the tonic Hector was taking, but he certainly couldn't have cut the saddle on Hector's horse because he was with the two elderly sisters in the drawing room. Pippa should have been next on his list, but nothing has happened to her so far."

"Maybe whoever cut the saddle strap meant it for Pippa," said Inspector Enderby.

"No, everyone knows that Hector rides that particular horse because it was gifted to him on his birthday; we can assume that the killer knew that too."

"Is it possible that Arthur may have slipped out of the manor and gone to the stables and cut the strap without being seen?" asked Inspector Enderby.

"No, both Mrs. Endecott and her sister swore that he was with them all the time until Richard came riding to tell them about the accident. It couldn't be Arthur. Also, who's the man who attacked Miss Carter and Abigail? Surely Miss Carter would know if the attacker was Arthur?"

"It's all too confusing. None of this makes sense, except Lady Fitzhugh's murder and the attempted poisoning of Hector."

Dermot nodded. "Let me see what Lord Fitzhugh's will says." Dermot read the will for a few minutes. "It just tells us what we already know. Doris Fitzhugh would inherit everything, with some legacies bequeathed to his other two daughters and a small legacy to Slattery, his wife, and to the other staff. However, there's a clause here that doesn't make sense. It says that if the estate is in danger of being inherited by a non-family member, for any reason, then the next male family member could contest the will and get that inheritance if he wins the contestation. This clause has to be followed for all time to come."

The two men looked at each other, perplexed.

"Lord Fitzhugh disinherited his only son and made Doris Fitzhugh his heir. When this will was made in 1905, the only male member of the family would've been Arthur Endecott because Hector was not yet born," said Inspector Enderby.

"Right. Allan Fitzhugh only returned after his father died. Remember, he blamed his father for his mother's early death. Once Allan and his family were back in the picture, Doris Fitzhugh made her will to favour Allan and Hector because she brought up Allan and felt that they had more right to the inheritance."

"This makes it complicated, but doesn't look good for Arthur Endecott. When was Lady Fitzhugh's will made?"

Dermot looked at the date. "On the thirteenth of July, 1917; a year after Allan was killed. It was witnessed by Slattery and the housekeeper, Matilda Slattery."

"Arthur must've felt betrayed that Hector was going to inherit everything, so he murdered Lady Fitzhugh and then tried to murder Hector," said Inspector Enderby.

"He was at the picnic when Kerr came to visit Lady Fitzhugh," said Dermot. "So his accomplice must've stolen the wills and put them back in Kerr's briefcase after reading them. When his accomplice told him about the contents of the wills, Arthur planned how he would eliminate Lady Fitzhugh and his two cousins who were in the way of his inheritance. He planned to frame Pippa for the murders so that she would be tried and sentenced to death. That way he didn't have to bump Pippa off, but let the law do it for him. By Arthur's own admission, we know that her Ladyship was going to make changes to her will the day after the party, and I'm sure he was going to be disinherited. It makes perfect sense."

"What about the dagger? Why would he use his own dagger and then hide it?"

"That's what's puzzling me. Why was that particular dagger used? Even though he's a simpleton, surely he would have enough sense not to use his own dagger. He probably thought he'd make himself a martyr and then realised his folly. So he used the opportunity to enter the bedroom, while everyone else was outside, to take the dagger. He could've stolen the earrings and the necklace after killing her. If so, then where is the necklace?"

"That could be a possibility... Now, maybe Slattery was killed because he was blackmailing Arthur. Perhaps he saw Arthur take the dagger or somehow suspected him."

"Could be. We'll have to prove all this, and connect Kerr's murder to the other murders. However, the other murders don't seem to connect with Sister Fleming's murder. Remember, Allan was killed by two people who he thought were spies. We cannot connect Arthur to them," said Dermot.

"You really think they're all connected, don't you?"

Dermot nodded. He glanced into the dustbin and saw some papers. He bent down and went through them.

"Just torn papers. Nothing of importance but, hello, what do we have here?" Dermot picked up a piece of paper and looked at it. "It looks like we have a stub from a train ticket."

Dermot called Miss Livingstone in and asked her if she knew why Kerr had visited Scotland on the fourteenth of June. She pursed her lips and told him that Kerr had never given her any specific reason other than a client had requested him to help find out something of grave importance.

"Do you know who that client was?"

"No, he never told me. He said that he would go directly to Meadowford Village for Lady Fitzhugh's birthday party and would be back two days later."

Dermot thanked Miss Livingstone and they left. As they were walking the street, he said to Inspector Enderby, "We have to go to Scotland."

"Why?"

Dermot held up the ticket stub. "On the day of the party, Bertram Kerr travelled from Scotland back to London. He went to Argyle Village. I think that whatever information he found there, he was using to blackmail the person who killed him. That's the only explanation I have at the moment. I have a hunch that our answer lies with what he discovered at Argyle Village. Mrs. Ainsworth told me that a relative of the De Villiers family lives there."

"Where exactly in Argyle Village?"

"Argyle Castle," Dermot said. "Time to pack, Inspector."

Chapter 22: Highland Bound

Dermot and Inspector Enderby bought their tickets at London's King's Cross Station. They boarded the train and a day later they were in a quaint little Scottish village with a twelfth-century castle. When the two men stepped off the train, the cooler Scottish air greeted them – a relief from the heatwave in Meadowford. As they made their way to the front of the station, Dermot's eyes were drawn to the imposing castle and the splendid turrets and spires that disappeared into the mist.

They took a taxi to the inn close to the village square and the clerk at the front desk greeted them with a strong Scottish accent. They took the key from the clerk and deposited their luggage in their room. After a quick lunch, they asked the clerk for directions to Argyle Castle. She gave them the directions and then added that they had heard rumours that Lady Argyle was probably on her last breath. They thanked her and headed to Argyle Castle on foot.

"I don't understand why Kerr would want to come to Argyle Castle."

"Perhaps Lady Fitzhugh wanted him to investigate something," said Dermot. "Mrs. Ainsworth told me that she found Lord Fitzhugh's papers concerning his time in South Africa in Lady Fitzhugh's room. So she must've read the letter that Christiaan sent to her father and she could've also told Kerr about the diamonds that Christiaan kept for himself. If I'm right, Christiaan sent the diamonds to Lady Argyle for safe keeping. What I cannot understand is, what did Kerr find out here that he then used to blackmail the person who killed him?"

"I suppose we'll find out if Lady Argyle is well enough," said Inspector Enderby as they approached the castle.

Dermot knocked on the door; it was opened by a pretty brunette with brown eyes. Something about the woman caused Dermot to pause, but he quickly came back to his senses. "Excuse me, we've just arrived from London and would like to speak to Lady Argyle."

The young lady's smile vanished and she looked crestfallen.

"Who is it, Nancy?" came a voice from behind her.

"Two men from London. They want tae speak tae her Ladyship."

An older woman came to the door, wiping her hands on a dirty apron that was tied around her waist.

"I'm Mrs. Blair. Why do ye want tae speak tae Lady Argyle?"

"That's between her Ladyship and us," Inspector Enderby said sternly. "Would you please be kind enough to let us in and let Lady Argyle know that we're here to see her?"

"All right, but first ye'll hae tae meet with her grandson, the future Lord Argyle. I'll fetch him for ye."

Mrs. Blair opened the door and let them in. She scurried away while Nancy took them to the living room. Portraits of the former lords and ladies of the castle hung on the walls.

"People like lookin' at them," Nancy said when she noticed the two men admiring the paintings. "On the wall over there is Lord Clyde Argyle who built this castle. He fought alongside William Wallace against the English. The Argyles have always been strong proponents for breaking away from England."

The last painting was of a beautiful woman with blonde hair, dressed in Victorian clothing, and wearing a tartan sash across her torso. The name plate at the bottom told them that the woman was Lady Aileen Argyle and was painted in 1880.

"She was a beautiful woman," Nancy said, smiling.

A few minutes later, a man of medium height in his late twenties came into the room. Without a smile, he introduced himself as Gerard Argyle and bluntly enquired why they wanted to talk to his grandmother. Inspector Enderby introduced himself and Dermot, and told him that they were investigating the murder of Bertram Kerr and that they wanted to talk to Lady Argyle about Kerr's visit to the castle.

"I'm afraid you cannae speak tae her."

"Why not?" asked Inspector Enderby.

"My dear grandmother is on her death bed. She's asleep and can barely talk. I dinnae want tae disturb her."

Inspector Enderby and Dermot looked at each other.

"This is a murder investigation and we must know what transpired between them," said Inspector Enderby sternly.

Gerard Argyle looked at them and shook his head adamantly.

"Four people have been murdered: Lady Fitzhugh, her butler, her maid, and Bertram Kerr, who was her solicitor. A thirteen-year-old boy was almost murdered twice. We believe that Mr. Kerr was murdered because he found out something about the murderer from Lady Argyle and then attempted to blackmail him."

"All right," Gerard said reluctantly. "But only for a few minutes. Remember she's weak."

"We promise to try not to upset her. We'll be quick," said Dermot.

Gerard told the two men to follow him. They entered the bedroom of Lady Argyle. The curtains were drawn and the room was dark and cold. They could see a person lying in bed and almost fully covered; only her hair on the pillow was visible. Gerard switched on the table lamp and they could see a face clearly; a face that was once beautiful, but was now covered with wrinkles and looked worn out.

Lady Argyle opened her eyes and looked at the three men. In a weak voice, she asked Gerard who they were. Gerard introduced them and told her why they were there.

"He... he... told me that a will written by Christiaan surfaced in South Africa and that he wanted to talk to me about it," said Lady Argyle very quietly. "It was just a ruse."

"Did he ask about the diamonds that belonged to the De Villiers family?" asked Dermot.

Lady Argyle took a deep breath. "He said... he... knew about... the diamonds from the firm in South Africa and I told him that Christiaan sent them to me during the war... I showed him the family photographs. He suddenly got nasty when he saw one of the photographs and forcibly took it... He was not... not a nice man. Threatened me about... exposing... I... I am so tired." She took two deep breaths and fell asleep.

"Gentlemen, please, I must insist that ye leave now. She cannae tell ye any more," said Gerard angrily.

Dermot and Inspector Enderby nodded and left the room. They waited outside the bedroom door. Gerard came out and closed the door carefully behind him.

"She's resting and I don't know when she will wake up. She's too weak."

"All right, Mr. Argyle... I understand that you will inherit this place from Lady Argyle?" asked Inspector Enderby.

"Yes, I'm her only heir. My parents died when I was a wee boy and my grandmother raised me after their deaths."

"Where were you on Tuesday of last week?"

"I was here. Why do you ask?"

"Mr. Kerr was killed by an unknown person," said Dermot. "We believe that it was a man he was blackmailing. That man had the diamonds with him and could be from this castle."

"You think I'm that man?"

"Not accusing you, Mr. Argyle. Merely trying to tie up all loose ends," said Inspector Enderby with a smile.

"You can ask the staff and they will all vouch for me. With my grandmother being so sick, I dinnae want tae be away from her in case something happened tae her. I certainly wouldn't go tae London, which is a full day's journey from here by train. Most of us Argyles would never step foot into England unless it was absolutely necessary."

"We'll question the staff about your whereabouts on that day. Now, did you know about the diamonds?" asked Inspector Enderby.

"I've nae idea about the diamonds you're talking about. I ken that my grandmother's brother owned a diamond mine in South Africa and that the mine was destroyed after the Boer War."

"Didn't she tell you that he had kept some uncut diamonds from the mine for himself and that he gave the rest to Lord Fitzhugh?" Dermot asked, astonished.

Gerard looked stunned. "No. Grandmama was distraught over the loss of her brother and his family. Then with my parents dying of pneumonia when I was a bairn, we rarely discussed her family because it upset her so. She once flew into a rage when I asked what happened to Lord Fitzhugh and she told me ne'er tae mention his name again."

Dermot and Inspector Enderby looked at each other.

"Was Lady Argyle born in South Africa?" asked Dermot.

"Yes, her mother emigrated from Scotland tae South Africa in the last century. She married a Boer and settled there. Grandmama met my grandfather when he went tae South Africa on a hunting trip, and she came tae Scotland more'n fifty years ago."

Dermot asked Gerard if he had met Mr. Kerr when he visited the castle. Gerard replied that he did meet Mr. Kerr in passing. Gerard and his secretary, Nancy, had been about to leave to go to the registrar's office to register his new car. Kerr had showed Gerard his card and told him that he wanted to talk to Lady Argyle. Gerard and Nancy left after telling Kerr to wait for Lady Argyle in the living room. When they returned a few hours later, Mr. Kerr had already left and Lady Argyle was distraught but she refused to say what had transpired between them. Lady Argyle had been sick for a long time and meeting with Kerr made her worse.

"In her delirium, did she say anything about the missing photograph?" asked Inspector Enderby.

"Not really! I'm nae even sure which photograph she is talking about. She only has one of me as a bairn with my parents and also the one of grandfather next to her bed that you just saw. As I said, she hardly spoke about her family or showed me any pictures of them because it was very painful for her."

"What did she mean about Mr. Kerr wanting to expose her? Was she involved in anything untoward?" asked Inspector Enderby.

"Inspector, my grandmother is a respectable lady. She would nae be involved in anything untoward, is that clear?" answered Gerard sternly.

Inspector Enderby rolled his eyes. "All right, you have my apologies. These are just routine questions that we have to ask."

Gerard grunted with distaste.

"Now, tell me," said Dermot, "how come you don't have a butler or a lot of staff working in a big place like this?"

"Ruiseart, our butler, joined one of the Scottish Regiments tae fight in the Great War alongside the British Army; as did some of the other male servants. Ruiseart was the only one in his regiment who survived the gassing and bombing in the Somme trenches. He was discharged and brought here to recover, but sadly he died a few years later. Fortunately, we had Alister and Jane come tae work for us during that time...

"Strange thing is that Grandmama started getting the *London Times* right after they arrived and stopped around the time Ruiseart died..."

"Why's that strange?"

"She ne'er liked anything English here... Our family has ne'er been a great supporter of the Sassenachs since the days of William Wallace."

"What happened to Alister and Jane?" asked Dermot.

"They left after Ruiseart died. Grandmama was sad tae see 'em go; Jane was a good companion tae Grandmama and doted on Nancy, so did Alister. Grandmama started getting sick after Ruiseart died."

"What did he die of?"

"Most probably of his war injuries. He was ne'er the same after the gassing and suffered from lung problems. He got sick suddenly and died in agony one night. Grandmama once told me that she feels guilty for his death. Don't ken why... and she mentioned his name once when she was delirious."

Dermot and Inspector Enderby thanked Gerard for his help. They then questioned the staff and every one of them confirmed that Gerard Argyle was at the castle on the Tuesday that Mr. Kerr was murdered in Meadowford Village. None of them had heard what Lady Argyle and Bertram Kerr had discussed. Mrs. Blair heard the front door slam and found Lady Argyle shaking with fright when she went to investigate.

Dermot questioned Nancy Blair and she confirmed that she went to the registrar's office with Gerard on the day that Bertram Kerr came to Argyle Castle. She also confirmed that Gerard was at the castle the day that Kerr was murdered. Finally, Dermot asked her if they had met before.

"Detective, am I under suspicion? I haven't been out of Scotland for a number of years. I was brought up in this very castle by my grand-aunt, Mrs. Blair, after my parents died in London. In fact, Lady Argyle was very kind tae me and had me educated. She even made me her secretary. I'm very grateful tae her... Why do you ask?"

"It's just that you look familiar. When you opened the door, I thought I had seen you before. You probably look like someone I know but I cannot remember who."

Nancy laughed. "Detective, I'm sure it will come tae ye. Now, will that be all?"

As Dermot and Inspector Enderby were preparing to leave, Dermot asked Gerard to find out about the missing photograph when Lady Argyle was lucid and to send him a telegram immediately.

—   —   —

On the walk back to the inn, Dermot and Inspector Enderby reflected on their visit to the castle.

"Either they're telling the truth or the staff have been paid off or threatened with the loss of their jobs if they admit that Gerard wasn't here on the day that Mr. Kerr was murdered. Did you notice how he tried to divert the conversation to his dead butler? Perhaps he has something to hide," said Inspector Enderby.

"Could be a possibility and, yes, I did. Why did Mr. Kerr take a photograph from Lady Argyle? Did he recognise someone? Is that why he was killed?"

"I can't say, but this is the most complicated case that I've ever worked on, Dermot; feels like we're getting nowhere. At least you were right about Lady Argyle having those diamonds. I wonder who has them now."

"Well, we'll have to find that out ourselves. I think we have all the answers, but we need to fit them in the right order and then things will be clear," said Dermot disappointedly.

The next day, on the way to Argyle Train Station, Dermot requested that the taxi go to the registrar's office. Inspector Enderby looked perplexed.

"Won't take long," said Dermot. "Just need to check if Gerard Argyle and Nancy were really at the registrar's office that day."

Chapter 23: The Major Explains

Dermot needed to unwind after the tiring journey to and from Argyle. This case was taking a lot out of him. The whole village was talking about the latest murder and the arrest of Arthur Endecott. Everyone knew that Dermot was working on the case and some villagers even pointed at him when he drove around the village. Even his parents were being asked about the case by friends and acquaintances.

Dermot decided to go to the country club for a relaxing swim. As he walked towards the diving board, some of the women, who were sunning themselves, looked at him and smiled. Dermot had an athletic body. He used to play cricket and rugby in school and maintained his physique by swimming and playing tennis. Whilst he knew that women found him attractive, he was a bit shy so he simply smiled back and continued walking. The cool and refreshing water enveloped him when he dove into the pool from the diving board. Refreshed, he began swimming and the tension in his body ebbed away.

After his swim, Dermot lay on a pool chair and closed his eyes. When he opened them again, he saw a portly man looking down at him.

"Oh, hello, Major Havelock, how nice to see you. It's a nice day for a swim."

"Yes, it's been so hot lately." Major Havelock winced as he moved to get a pool chair.

"Are you all right?" asked Dermot, quickly sitting up.

"Yes, just this damn leg! The bullet wound still gives me trouble in my old age."

Major Havelock placed a pool chair alongside Dermot and sat down; the chair creaked at the weight that was suddenly thrust upon it.

"This heat reminds me of South Africa and India. It can last for a long time there."

"Say, do you know anything about the De Villiers family in South Africa?"

"You are talking about Lord Fitzhugh's business partner, am I right?"

"Yes. Do you know what happened?"

"Not really, but I heard that they were killed during the Boer War."

"Do you know how?"

Before Major Havelock could answer, Gerda Havelock came by. "Darling, there you are... We've got to get going." She recognised Dermot and greeted him. "Yes... you came over a few days ago to talk to Percival. Would you like to come over for dinner tonight?"

Dermot was startled and hesitated for a moment. "Yes, I would love to..."

"All right, we'll see you at seven-thirty. Dinner will be at eight... Come along, dear."

"See you later," said Major Havelock as he slowly got up. "We can continue our conversation over dinner."

Dermot leaned back on the chair and realised that this would be a good opportunity to ask Major Havelock about what happened during the Boer War. Reading Slattery's memoirs had brought up a lot of questions for which he needed answers. He decided to go home; he had to read some of the chapters again to see if any new questions would come up.

— — —

That evening, Gerda Havelock ushered Dermot into the living room where Major Havelock was sitting drinking scotch and soda. He greeted Dermot and pointed to the drinks on the table. Dermot got himself a glass of brandy and took a seat opposite the major. As they slowly sipped their drinks, Dermot began the conversation by telling Major Havelock that his father, Edmund, had been in the Yorkshire Regiment during the Boer War. Dermot knew it would put the major at ease and he hoped he would then be willing to answer his questions.

Major Havelock took a sip from his glass and told Dermot that he was in the newly formed Imperial British Regiment, commanded by Lord Fitzhugh, which was disbanded after the war. His father had been one of Lord Fitzhugh's tenant farmers. Lord Fitzhugh was glad to have someone from Meadowford Village in the regiment and he trusted the major just as much as he trusted Slattery.

Dermot told the major that in his memoirs Slattery had briefly mentioned the meeting between Lord Fitzhugh and Christiaan De Villiers when they become partners. However, after the war began, there wasn't any mention of Christiaan and his family at all. Dermot had learnt from Flora that they had perished during the war, but she couldn't give him any further details. Major Havelock recounted how Lord Fitzhugh had learnt that the entire De Villiers family had perished in the concentration camp and that the son had died in battle towards the end of the war.

When he heard the words 'concentration camp', Dermot's interest was piqued and he sat forward.

"Which concentration camp were they in?"

"I believe it was the one in Kimberley."

"Do you know what happened?"

Major Havelock took another sip of scotch and looked up at the ceiling as if trying to remember.

"In late August, 1901, I was convalescing in a hospital in Pretoria from a gunshot wound to the leg," he said. "When I rejoined my unit in Kimberley on the tenth of September, Lord Fitzhugh told me that he had heard that the De Villiers family had been sent to the concentration camp in Kimberley a few days earlier. Their land had been destroyed and the house had been burnt to the ground. He tried his best to get them out, but there was nothing he could do. After the war ended, we heard that they had all perished in the camp due to disease and starvation."

"But… why imprison innocent women and children?"

"The British Army tried to demoralise the Boer population by imprisoning the families of the Boer soldiers. Lord Kitchener began the scorched earth policy, where they killed the livestock and also ruined the fertility of the soil. The De Villiers may've been imprisoned because their son was in the Boer Army."

Dermot shook his head, trying hard to comprehend what he had just heard. The pictures of emaciated people in the concentration camp, which he had seen in the London Library, came to his mind. He took a sip of brandy and felt a little better; however, there was still something bothering him.

"Did you ever meet Christiaan De Villiers?"

"No," Major Havelock said, looking at Dermot and making him feel uneasy. "I did not have that pleasure."

"I wonder why Slattery didn't mention the incarceration of the De Villiers or about Lord Fitzhugh trying to get them out."

"Maybe it wasn't his story to tell. Most people only put their experiences in their memoirs, not someone else's."

"I know, but he did write about things that didn't concern him. As Lord Fitzhugh's batman, he was with him all the time and he meticulously documented everything that took place, like meetings with other British soldiers and high-ranking officers from the army. But, strangely, he didn't mention anything about Lord Fitzhugh trying to help the De Villiers."

"Possibly because Lord Fitzhugh did not succeed. You have to remember that Slattery was a very devoted butler and that loyalty will have continued, even after the master's death. Keeping your master's secrets and not ruining his reputation are all part of being loyal. Too bad he was murdered and his body was stuffed in the cupboard. What an ignominious end for a faithful butler."

"Yes indeed! Did you ever meet Lord Fitzhugh after he left South Africa?"

"No, I returned to England many years after he died. He was a good man. He knew how to reward loyalty and his recommendation helped me move up in the army. My late father spoke very highly of his Lordship."

Dermot took another sip of brandy just as Gerda Havelock came into the living room and announced that dinner was served.

"Hope you like my roast lamb with mint sauce. It's Percy's favourite."

Dermot nodded and smiled. He got up and followed the older couple to the dining room.

—   —   —

That night, before he went to bed, Dermot re-read some portions of Slattery's memoir. Something that the major had said made him uneasy. As he read further, he finally realised what it was. The next morning, Dermot went to the telegraph office and sent two telegrams, marked urgent, to Elmer Griffin in Pretoria.

Chapter 24: Things Fall into Place

It was the day of Henrietta Howard's annual garden party, which was always held on the vicar's birthday and always followed a service of thanksgiving. Dermot was looking forward to hearing Reverend Howard's sermon. When he entered the church, he was surprised to see that it was filled to capacity – it looked like the whole village was there. He looked ahead and saw the two elderly sisters from the manor seated in the front row that was always reserved for them, along with Cora and Hector Fitzhugh. Henrietta began playing the church organ and the service began.

The vicar's sermon was about God's divine providence existing even in hard times, such as that which the village was currently facing. After the service, the Fitzhugh family departed because they were in mourning, and the remaining congregation went to the vicarage garden for the party.

"Do I have to go, Mother?" Dermot asked.

"Yes, Dermot. They're all waiting to meet you. It's not every day that people in Meadowford get to meet my son, the detective," she said proudly.

As they entered the vicarage garden, Dermot was greeted by the sweet and heady scents of roses, hyacinths and rhododendrons. The dazzling colours of the flowers framed the evenly mown and lush-green lawn upon which large white marquees had been erected ready for the day's festivities. Laughter and chattering filled the air as the guests took their places at the garden tables or gathered refreshments from the elaborate buffet and bar in one of the marquees.

Edna Carlyle introduced Dermot to the people around him. They questioned him about the case and asked when it would be solved. A group of women, who looked like the village gossips, wondered aloud whether they were going to be the next victims, because the murderer could be lurking amongst them.

Dermot sat down to eat while his parents spoke to the people around them. Henrietta Howard came by and greeted them. She was very loquacious and gathered the attention of some of the people seated at Dermot's table and also the next. She told them that she missed Lady Fitzhugh because she always attended her annual garden party and the two of them would reminisce about the days when Lady Fitzhugh taught her at the village school.

"We would talk about Lily Anderson, a classmate of mine, who was the class clown. She had a knack for making things up just to avoid getting into trouble with the teachers. I remember…"

Dermot was lost in thought. Something that Henrietta had just said had got him thinking. He had always suspected that someone was not being entirely honest with him. He sat for a few minutes, deep in thought, and then suddenly got up. Dermot realised that everyone's eyes were on him.

"What is it, Dermot?" asked Edmund, baffled.

"Sorry, Father… but thank you, Mrs. Howard, for telling me what I need to take a closer look at. I have to get going…"

Dermot left with everyone staring at him.

"Duty calls, I'm sure," said Edna, embarrassed, as she sipped her tea to avoid the many pairs of eyes on her.

Dermot ran to his car and drove home. He picked up the phone and asked for the operator to connect him to the London Library. After a few minutes, he heard a familiar voice on the phone.

"Miss Cartwright," Dermot interrupted. "Sorry to disturb you, but I need a favour from you…"

Dermot packed a few clothes and left a note for his parents. Then he drove to the London Library. Miss Cartwright smiled when she saw him.

"You were right," she said. "I've found what you wanted…"

Dermot then drove to King's Cross Station, bought a ticket, and had just enough time to catch the train as it pulled away. He returned home the next day, satisfied that his hunch was correct.

— — —

Edna called out to Dermot, telling him that four telegrams had been delivered. Dermot went down the stairs and Edna pointed to the telegrams on the table and continued dusting. Three telegrams were from Mr. Griffin in South Africa and one was from Gerard Argyle. Dermot opened and read them. Then he re-read them and thought for a second.

A few hours later, Inspector Enderby and Dermot were standing in front of Major Havelock's door. Gerda Havelock opened the door and was surprised to see them.

"Whatever is the matter, Gentlemen?"

"Good afternoon, Mrs. Havelock. Is the major at home?" asked Inspector

Enderby.

"Yes, he's reading the newspaper."

"Good, we'd like a word with him."

The ageing major looked surprised as the two men went into the living room.

"Major Havelock, we need to talk to you about what really happened when you rejoined your unit after convalescing in Pretoria," said Dermot.

"Whatever for? I was wounded in my right leg and have the scar to show you." He bent down, fighting against the rotund stomach that prevented him from bending any further.

"No need to, Major Havelock, we know about your injury. However, you were not completely honest with me when I came here for dinner..."

Major Havelock was silent. Dermot handed over two of the telegrams from South Africa and Major Havelock read them. Beads of perspiration appeared on the major's brow.

"When I came here for dinner, you told me that Slattery was very loyal to Lord Fitzhugh."

Major Havelock nodded slowly.

"I assume that you too have that same loyalty to Lord Fitzhugh. It's because of his recommendation that you had a distinguished military career and a promotion from a Private to Lance Corporal after the war. You also got those medals because of his recommendation. That's why you're still loyal, am I right?"

The major's silence was deafening.

"Percival," said Gerda from the door. "You don't have to be loyal to his Lordship any more. He's dead... Inspector Enderby can arrest you for thwarting a murder investigation. You've got to tell him what happened, my dear. Tell them the truth and I will see you through this."

Gerda sat down next to the major and took his hand. He looked into her eyes and then slowly began to speak. "After I arrived from Pretoria..."

— — —

That night, Dermot sat at the table in his bedroom, looking at his notes. He had two suspects, but he couldn't determine their motives or whether they had any accomplices. There were so many unanswered questions; if he could only glean the answers from the evidence he had before him! Frustrated, he decided to go to bed. As he cleared out his pockets, he found a folded piece of paper in his coat. It was the list of the constables that Inspector Enderby had placed to guard Fitzhugh Manor. There was one name that stood out again. Two hunches came to Dermot's mind; he had to see if they were correct.

The next morning, Dermot placed two calls: one to Miss Cartwright at the London Library and one to Oswald Gardner in Scotland Yard. He needed them to check out his two hunches. While he waited, he re-read the two wills, his notes, and the telegrams. He looked at the photograph of Lord Fitzhugh and Christiaan and remembered what Flora Ainsworth had told him. Another idea flashed across his mind. After Dermot got confirmation from Miss Cartwright and Oswald Gardner, he made arrangements with Oswald Gardner to take the next step. He then drove to Meadowford Police Station with the photo of Lord Fitzhugh and Christiaan, and spoke to Inspector Enderby about putting his theory to the test.

— — —

Argyle Village – That same day
As evening approached, Inspector Sean McDonald and his team of men entered the graveyard of St. Drostan's Church in Argyle Village equipped with shovels. Inspector McDonald had received a phone call from Chief Inspector Oswald Gardner asking him to exhume the body of one of the denizens of the graveyard. It had taken a few hours to obtain the exhumation order from the judge, but now they were ready to begin. Inspector McDonald cleared the overgrowth from the relatively new five-year old headstone and read the engraving.

"All right, men, this is it. Start digging!"

— — —

Meadowford Village – The next day
After dropping Inspector Enderby at the Meadowford Train Station, Dermot went to the Meadowford Inn with two constables. He asked the receptionist for Cora Fitzhugh's room and then they climbed the staircase. Dermot knocked on Room 26 and Cora opened the door.

"Is Miss Pippa Fitzhugh here?" asked Dermot.

"Yes... she has come to say goodbye. Hector and I are about to travel to Liverpool to catch the boat to Canada. Why are you here?"

"To arrest Pippa," said Dermot curtly.

"Why? What has she done?"

"She and her lover, Francis Abernathy, who owns the theatrical company where she acts, planned the murder of Lady Fitzhugh and also the attempted murder of Hector so that she could inherit the estate."

"No, Pippa would never hurt Hector," said Cora tearfully.

"Please step aside, Mrs. Fitzhugh. We have a warrant for Pippa's arrest," said Constable Blackwood abruptly.

Cora stepped aside reluctantly and the three men went in. They found Pippa sitting at the desk. She was taken aback when she saw them.

"Wha... what... is it?"

"Miss Pippa Fitzhugh, you are under arrest on suspicion of the murders of Lady Fitzhugh and Mr. James Slattery, and also for the attempted murder of your brother, Master Hector Fitzhugh. We have also arrested your accomplice, Mr. Francis Abernathy. Please come with us."

Stunned, Pippa slowly got up. "Mother, this isn't true," she said with a quivering voice.

"I know, Pippa. I will find a lawyer who will get you out of this mess."

"Where's Hector?" asked Dermot.

"He's having tea with another boy he met here... Please don't let him see Pippa getting arrested," pleaded Cora tearfully.

Dermot nodded and told Cora to take Hector to the manor, where they would be safe from the reporters.

Constable Blackwood handcuffed Pippa and led her away.

—　　—　　—

Inspector Enderby was on a train heading to Argyle Village. He was reading a newspaper that had been left behind by a previous passenger. The front page had pictures of Lady Argyle lying in state at Argyle Castle and of her funeral cortege with the hearse flanked by her grandson. He felt the train slowing down and when he looked out at the people on the approaching platform he saw two men wearing trench coats. When the train finally stopped, he alighted and walked towards them.

"Inspector Enderby, I presume," said one of the men, holding his hand out.

"Yes, you must be Inspector McDonald," said Inspector Enderby, shaking the man's hand.

"Right y'are, chum. Sorry about the wee bit of rain. This is Sergeant Mackenzie."

Inspector Enderby shook the other man's hand. "It's a relief from the heat back in Meadowford to be honest."

"Dae ye have the documents?" asked Inspector McDonald.

"Yes, I will show them to you on the way."

They got into the car and Inspector Enderby handed Inspector McDonald the papers as they headed towards Argyle Castle.

"Och aye," said Inspector McDonald. "These will ensure that they come with ye tae London."

When they reached the castle, Inspector McDonald rang the doorbell. Nancy opened the door wearing a black dress, showing that she was still in mourning.

"Mrs. Nancy Maude Argyle?"

"How... how did ye know? What's this about?" she asked, taken aback.

"You and Lord Argyle are required tae accompany Inspector Enderby tae London. These documents signed by a judge in London behooves you tae comply without further delay."

— — —

That same evening, just before eight, a police car stopped in front of Fitzhugh Manor. Arthur Endecott got out of the car with a look of relief on his face. The murder charge against him had been dropped. He walked up the steps and rang the doorbell. Miss Carter was taken aback when she opened the door and expressed how nice it was to see him. He went to the living room where his mother and aunt were reading the newspaper. They were both astonished to see him.

Arthur explained that since Pippa and her accomplice had been arrested, the murder charge against him was dropped. However, he was still being charged for tampering with evidence and for the theft of the earrings. Arthur was just about to say something more when Alice came in and greeted him. She announced that dinner was ready and that she had set a plate for Arthur at the table. They went to the dining table and sat down, and Alice and Miss Carter started serving the soup from a tureen.

Arthur told them that the police had evidence that Bertram Kerr had found out about Pippa being an actress and informed Lady Fitzhugh during the party. Lady Fitzhugh privately told Pippa that she suspected her of being an actress and of having an affair with Francis Abernathy. She asked Richard and Pippa to meet her the day after the party. The police suspect that she wanted to give Pippa an ultimatum to marry Richard and give up being an actress and her lover or be disinherited. That is why Pippa murdered her and also then attempted to murder Hector for the estate. She knew the contents of both Lady Fitzhugh's and Lord Fitzhugh's wills.

"It was that actress thing, I tell you. Just as bad as what I thought she was when she came home with make-up on her face. That's what loose women get into and then they lose boundaries. I always knew that no good comes from being an actress. If Father or Allan were alive, they would've set Pippa straight," said Lilian.

Arthur tasted the soup. "Good to taste Mrs. Withers' cooking again. Too bad Pippa will never taste her cooking again after I give my statement to the police that I saw Pippa and her suitor in London and I saw her enter Aunt Doris' room that night. Oh, that's what I was going to tell you before Alice announced that dinner was ready. I've made a deal with the police to get the other two charges dropped in exchange for my statement."

"You mean that you actually saw her?" asked Lilian.

Arthur explained that he was not asleep the whole night, like he told the police. He woke up when he heard his bedroom door open. He saw Pippa enter and take something from his suitcase. After she left, Arthur opened his bedroom door a little and saw Pippa entering Lady Fitzhugh's room.

"What about this chap of hers?" enquired Flora.

"I didn't see him, but the police are sure that Pippa let him into the manor at some point. Pippa is also suspected of increasing the arsenic dosage in Hector's tonic. The police say that the station master saw Francis at the Meadowford Train Station on the days that Abigail and Kerr were murdered. He was acting very suspiciously. He probably killed Abigail because she was blackmailing Pippa for not seeing her in front of the library door at four-thirty and Mr. Kerr because he threatened to tell the police that they had a motive to commit the murders. Detective Carlyle speculates that Francis was the one who cut Hector's saddle strap and that Pippa summoned Charles through the indicator board so that Francis could enter the stables. She used the opportunity of Richard spilling the tea to carry out her plan."

"What about the diamond that the detective found in the room where Kerr was murdered?" asked Lilian.

"It seems that Kerr took those diamonds from Lady Argyle. You know how intimidating he could be. The police think that Francis took them after killing Kerr, although he's not admitting it."

"I'm not surprised, Mr. Kerr was a horrible beast," said Lilian.

"Why didn't you tell the police about Pippa after poor Doris' body was discovered?" asked Flora.

"I was afraid of what it would do to Cora. When Slattery was murdered, I knew that it was Pippa. However, I was afraid of a scandal. I knew that grandfather wouldn't want the family name dragged through the mud. He was all about keeping up appearances. After the indignity of Uncle Allan allegedly spying for Germany, we didn't need the family name tarnished again."

"Very good, Arthur. Father would've been proud of you for thinking of the family name," said Lilian.

"Where's Cora?" asked Arthur.

"She and Hector returned to the manor after Pippa was arrested. She's too upset to eat with us and so wanted to eat in her room. Hector is with her," said Flora.

"Poor Cora, the shock must be hard for her. She'll be upset when she learns that I've to make a statement to the police that will convict Pippa."

"Arthur, you mustn't feel guilty. If only Cora had taken some control over Pippa then she wouldn't have got involved with that awful man. Cora isn't strict enough and doesn't give a tuppence about how she raises either of them. Even as a child of six or seven, Hector would piddle all over the house..."

Flora snorted into her soup. "Lilian!"

"Don't worry," said Lilian, "he soon stopped when I gave him a walloping on his bum."

Flora picked up her napkin and then dabbed at the soup that she'd spilt on her chin. "I feel sorry for Richard," she said. "Pippa was using him while she was carrying on with that other chap. We all thought badly of him and we felt that he wasn't good enough for our Pippa, but it turns out it was the other way around."

"I have to be up early in the morning, Mother. Detective Carlyle will be picking me up at eight." Arthur looked at Miss Carter who was standing next to the table. "Miss Carter, can you please have a pot of chamomile tea sent to my room? It will help me sleep."

"Yes, Mr. Endecott. I will make it especially for you and place it right next to your bed."

"Thank you, Miss Carter. Aunt Doris was right; you are a wonderful housekeeper and we're glad to have you. She would be proud of how you've continued taking care of us."

Miss Carter thanked him and left.

After dinner, Arthur went to his bedroom and locked the door. After a bath, he poured himself a cup of chamomile tea and waited for it to cool.

— — —

As the clock struck eight, Dermot arrived and parked his car in front of the manor. He honked his horn and when nobody came out Dermot walked to the front door and knocked. Alice opened the door and greeted him. Dermot asked her about Arthur. She said that she hadn't seen him and that he had not yet had his coffee and toast that she had kept for him in the drawing room. Miss Carter appeared and she too found it strange that Arthur was not yet awake. Dermot suggested going to his bedroom to wake him. As they were about to go, Miss Carter sternly told Alice to go ahead with her chores. Alice paused to protest but then turned and walked away.

Dermot ran up the stairs, followed by Miss Carter. He knocked on Arthur's door, but there was no response. He tried the door, but it was locked. He asked Miss Carter to stand back and then he kicked the door open and entered. Miss Carter gave a muffled yell as she covered her mouth with her hand. Arthur's torso was hanging out of the bed, his head on the floor. His face was twisted in a grimace of agony.

Dermot went to the table where the teacup and pot of tea were kept. The cup had some traces of tea at the bottom. Miss Carter pointed to an envelope addressed to Dermot on the table. As Dermot read the note inside, his facial expression changed. "He has committed suicide. He has confessed everything and he has also named his accomplices."

"Ye Gods, this will devastate Mrs. Endecott. How will I tell her that her son has committed suicide?"

"...I don't know. But first, help me search for the bottle of poison."

They both began searching the room. A few minutes later, Miss Carter directed his attention to a bottle containing white powder in a drawer that she had just opened. Dermot came closer and looked. He asked her to call the ambulance and police. Miss Carter nodded and left the room. Dermot took out a handkerchief and wrapped the bottle in it.

The ambulance arrived; two hospital orderlies, along with Dr. Fielding, came in and examined the body. The orderlies shifted the corpse onto a stretcher, covered it with a sheet, and took it away.

—   —   —

A few hours later, Dermot was at the Meadowford Police Station. He and Inspector Enderby were waiting for the phone to ring. When it finally did,

Inspector Enderby picked it up. It was Scotland Yard. He motioned for Dermot to come closer and they both listened. When the call ended, they looked at each other and smiled.

"The stage is set and we have all the players. Time for the main act, Dermot," said Inspector Enderby.

Chapter 25: The First Act

Dermot arrived at Fitzhugh Manor with a few constables, along with Irene and Frida Shaw. The sky was dark and the wind tugged at their coats as they climbed the steps to the front door.

"Blimey! Looks like a storm's approaching," said Constable Blackwood.

Miss Carter opened the door with a quizzical look on her face. Dermot took her aside and told her in the strictest confidence that, because of the suicide note found in Arthur's room, they knew who the killers were and would shortly be apprehending them. He asked her to send the staff to the library and also to make tea for everyone gathered there. Miss Carter nodded and said that she would also bring some freshly baked scones.

"Would you like Indian, Chinese or Ceylon tea?" she asked.

"Indian," Dermot said. "I'm sure everyone would like it too."

Dermot asked everyone gathered in the library to sit down, against the protestations of Lilian who didn't see the point of having a meeting. Dermot placed his leather briefcase on the table and took out some of its contents. He went to the door and spoke to Constable Clarke, who closed the door and put his huge frame in front of it as if daring anyone to try to make him move.

"Where's Hector?" asked Cora.

"Two of our female constables are with him in the servants' dining room. He's in good hands, Mrs. Fitzhugh."

Dermot held up his hand. "Ladies and Gentlemen, I apologise for the short notice, but this meeting is of utmost importance... Now, let me begin... This case has been very puzzling from the start. Many clues didn't make sense or even add up..."

There was a knock on the door and Dermot nodded to Constable Clarke to get the door. Richard Seymour came in and scanned the crowd in the room. He asked for Pippa and said that Inspector Enderby had telephoned him, telling him that Pippa had been cleared of all charges and had been released.

"Ahhh, please come in, Mr. Seymour," said Dermot. "We've been expecting you."

"Have we?" asked Lilian in surprise.

"Yes, we have. Now please sit on that chair, Mr. Seymour, and I will continue."

Richard looked sideways and saw the burly constable standing behind him. He acquiesced and sat on the chair.

"Now, as I was saying, many clues in this case..."

At that moment, there was another knock and Miss Carter, followed by Alice, came in bringing in tea and scones.

"Let's wait until we are all served tea," said Dermot.

Once the tea was poured, Dermot requested that Alice and Miss Carter sit down. They both looked at the elderly sisters and Flora nodded, giving her consent.

As Alice was about to sit next to Miss Carter, Dermot insisted that Alice sit across the room, next to Constable Barnaby. Alice looked perplexed but complied.

"Now," Dermot continued. "Many people had motives for murdering Lady Fitzhugh. Arthur Endecott, because he needed money; Mrs. Fitzhugh, because then she could control the estate until Hector turned twenty-one; and Pippa, because she was next in line to inherit the estate after Hector."

Cora almost dropped her teacup when she heard she was still a suspect.

"What was strange was that the wills of Lady Fitzhugh and her father went missing for some time when the solicitor came to visit. Then, mysteriously, these two wills reappeared in Mr. Kerr's briefcase after he left the manor. Why were these wills stolen and then returned? The missing wills are the key in this case. They were stolen because the murderer needed to know the contents of Lady Fitzhugh's will and, most importantly, the order of inheritance.

"Mr. Kerr was here with the wills because Lady Fitzhugh wanted to add someone to her will. She had discovered that Irene Shaw was the illegitimate daughter of Lord Fitzhugh."

There were murmurs throughout the room. "Do you mean to say that Irene is our half-sister?" asked Lilian.

"Yes," said Dermot. "Mrs. Ainsworth told me that her father was a philanderer. Even his son, Allan, had nicknamed him Henry VIII. A few months after Lord Fitzhugh went to South Africa, a baby was born in St. Crispin's Village and was named Adele Irene Wilson. The mother, Frida Wilson, had worked here as a maid and was dismissed by Doris Fitzhugh when she learnt of the pregnancy. After Lord Fitzhugh returned from South Africa, Frida – who had moved to London – wrote to him about the baby. He secretly acknowledged his illegitimate child and supported her through a bank account in the name of Portia Hartford, to avoid a scandal. When he died, Frida closed the account and obtained a job as a secretary.

"Adele was now named Irene Shaw – as Frida had married when she moved back to St. Crispin's – and came to work here as a lady's maid. When Irene got close to Lady Fitzhugh, she revealed her true identity. Being remorseful for the way she treated Frida Wilson, Lady Fitzhugh decided to include Irene in her will and to leave her a legacy, but on one condition: that she never reveal her true identity. That never happened, however, because Irene was dismissed for stealing the emerald necklace."

Dermot paused and sipped his tea.

"Although Irene was dismissed, there was still one person here looking out for her interest."

Everyone looked around the room.

"I'm talking about you, Charles," Dermot said.

"What are you saying?" asked Charles, startled.

"Irene and you were in love. On the night that Mr. Seymour first visited the manor, he overheard you telling Irene in the stables that she would get her inheritance sooner if her Ladyship were to die suddenly."

"Yes, I heard Charles say that when Irene told him that Lady Fitzhugh was going to add her to her will," said Richard.

Charles and Irene were surprised at the accusation. "We didn't mean we wanted her dead soon," said Charles.

"Once she was dismissed, Irene told you that Mr. Endecott also needed money and so you two collaborated with Mr. Endecott to kill her Ladyship and Master Hector and to frame Pippa for the murders. Mr. Endecott wrote this suicide note confessing everything. You two had the motive and the opportunities to carry out your plans, but, unfortunately, they didn't go as planned." Dermot held the suicide note up for everyone to see.

"That's not true," said Irene. "Mr. Endecott, Charles and I never collaborated to murder anyone. I never really knew Mr. Endecott because I was dismissed a few days after he arrived."

"True, but you had another motive besides being fired for stealing the necklace. You were born on the wrong side of the blanket and your mother was thrown out when she was pregnant with you, you wanted to get even with her Ladyship…"

"Stop, Detective," interrupted Charles. "You're upsetting Irene. She'd never hurt anyone. The note ain't telling the truth."

"Only you, Charles, had the opportunity to cut the strap on Hector's saddle."

"Fine, but if Master Hector had died then Miss Fitzhugh would've got everything because she weren't hurt. And you can't blame me for killing Abigail and Mr. Kerr as I have alibis. Besides, why would Irene or I steal the wills when Irene knew that she was going to be added to them. You just said that the whole idea for the murders started when those wills were stolen."

"By Jove, you make some relevant points," Dermot said. "You had the opportunity and motive to kill Lady Fitzhugh and also the opportunity to try and kill Master Hector, but you couldn't have killed Bertram Kerr, Abigail, and Sister Claudette Fleming. All of them were killed by the same murderers. So, there were others involved. I admire the tenacity of the killers. Even though it took many years, they waited for the opportune moment and struck when least expected."

"Who's Sister Claudette Fleming?" asked Cora.

"She was a hospital worker from St. Cuthbert's Hospital who died after she was pushed in front of a car. She was bringing me a photograph of the killers of Allan Fitzhugh," said Dermot.

The family members looked at each other in disbelief.

"These two people killed Allan Fitzhugh because he suspected them of being moles after he had found out that certain intelligence was being compromised. He set a trap for them to steal the plans for the submarine that the Royal Navy had given to the intelligence service for safe keeping."

"So he wasn't a traitor?" asked Lilian.

"No, he wasn't. He was actually a hero. But before I get to that, let me first explain about these murders..." Dermot took a sip from his cup. "The murders were planned so that one person could inherit this estate and the wealth that comes with it. Three people needed to be eliminated in order for that plan to work. Lady Fitzhugh and Master Hector needed to die and Arthur Endecott needed to be framed for their murders so that he would eventually be tried and executed..."

"Arthur? You just said that he confessed to everything in that note," said Flora, confused.

"Yes, you heard me correctly. It was Arthur who needed to be framed and not Pippa, because he was the only one who could contest the will if Pippa gave the Fitzhugh wealth to a non-family member. That was what was stated in Lord Fitzhugh's will. At the time of his death, Hector hadn't been born and Pippa was just a child. Lord Fitzhugh knew that Lady Fitzhugh would eventually will the entire estate to Allan and, of course, Allan to Pippa in due course. Mrs. Ainsworth told me that Lord Fitzhugh was very possessive of this estate and he only wanted it to go to a family member... So, once all three were gone, the murderers could then go ahead with their plan to eliminate another innocent victim. I should tell you now that the suicide note is a forgery."

"Detective, are you suggesting that the murderers are amongst us now? Are they from the family?" asked Flora.

"I suspect one of them is... Now, before I reveal who they are, let me explain what I did. We arrested Pippa so that one of the murderers would play into our plan and that's how we now know who the real murderers are."

"Detective, my son is dead. Why are you torturing us with this charade?" asked Lilian tearfully.

Dermot looked at her sympathetically. "No, he isn't dead." Raising his voice, he then turned to the door. "Inspector Enderby, please come in."

Constable Clarke opened the door and Inspector Enderby came in with Arthur Endecott.

"Arthur, you're alive?" Lilian was aghast and almost spilled her tea.

"Yes, Mother, I'm alive. My suicide was part of an ingenious plan to catch the murderers."

"Detective, what the blazes is going on?" said Flora with anger. "We've been through enough and we even saw the hospital orderlies take Arthur's body out."

"That's true. Mrs. Ainsworth, Arthur agreed to take part in our plan so that the charges against him in India would be dropped. Arthur never heard anything when Lady Fitzhugh was murdered, even though his room was right next to hers. He told me that he had drunk Miss Carter's chamomile tea before going to bed. I suspect that the tea had been drugged with one of the two sleeping powders that were stolen from Mrs. Withers' room, so he slept soundly. The other sleeping powder was used to drug Slattery and he lied about doing his nightly rounds that night.

"While Arthur was sleeping, the murderer slipped in and took the dagger from Arthur's suitcase. The murderer had probably seen it earlier when dusting the room. That dagger had to be used to kill Lady Fitzhugh because Arthur's fingerprints would be on it and that would be enough proof to convict him of murder. As part of our plan, I told Arthur to say that he'd seen Pippa come into his room and take the dagger and then go into Lady Fitzhugh's room. I also told him to say that he had seen Pippa with Francis Abernathy in London. He was to make sure that he said all of this at the dinner table, because only the killer would know that what Arthur was saying was untrue. It worked, and when he asked for a pot of chamomile tea before going to bed, the arsenic was slipped into it. He didn't drink it, but pretended to be dead just as we had planned. He played his part well and the real murderer was exposed."

"Who is this person?" demanded Lilian.

"I am talking about your housekeeper, Miss Carter."

"What are you talking about?" said Miss Carter sharply. "I never poisoned Mr. Endecott's chamomile tea."

"Yes, you did. You even increased the arsenic dose in Hector's tonic to try to kill him. The gardener, Mr. Lacey, told me that he was missing half of the tin of arsenic that he bought to get rid of pests. Only you could've taken it."

Everyone looked at each other, startled, and then put down their teacups.

"No need to worry. The tea isn't poisoned; even Miss Carter drank hers." Dermot took another sip from his cup.

"I was with you when we found the suicide note and the bottle containing the poison," said Miss Carter.

"Correction. You found the suicide note and the bottle. You played into our plan very well. You had to get into Arthur's room with me. When I came asking for him, you pretended to show concern and came along with me. When we discovered the body, you placed the note – which you had in your pocket – on the writing desk while I pretended to examine the body. You took the stationery last night when you took the chamomile tea to Arthur's room.

"You forged the note cleverly, and you named Irene Shaw and Charles as his accomplices. You also named Francis Abernathy as an accomplice, stating that Arthur promised to give him money for his theatre if he helped Arthur get rid of Lady Fitzhugh, Hector, and Pippa. You heard Arthur say at dinner that we suspected Francis of cutting the saddle strap and also of killing Abigail and Mr. Kerr.

"Miss Carter, you fell for what Arthur said hook, line, and sinker. It's my guess that you would've later identified Francis as the person coming out of the stables while you were talking to Constable Barnaby and as the person who attacked you and killed Abigail. You wrote in the note that Francis killed Kerr because Kerr was blackmailing Arthur about being wanted by the police in Delhi. You knew about it because you overheard Inspector Enderby mention it to Mrs. Endecott.

"By the way, we also know that you sent this note many years ago." Dermot pulled an envelope out of his pocket and removed the note inside.

"That's the note that Father received just before he died," said Flora.

"Correct, and I'm glad that you allowed me to take it. The handwriting on this note was compared to Arthur's suicide note that Miss Carter forged. Even though the handwriting appears to be different on the two notes, the handwriting expert at Scotland Yard swears that they were written by the same person. Fortunately, Lady Fitzhugh kept the note and we now know that you sent it, Miss Carter."

Dermot continued before Miss Carter could speak. "When I asked you to search for the bottle containing the poison, Miss Carter, you opened the drawer and carefully placed the bottle inside, and then you pretended to find it in there. However, in your haste, you made a grave error."

"Tell me, Detective, I'm all ears," said Miss Carter sarcastically.

"You wiped the bottle clean, probably with your apron, before placing it into the drawer. You told me that you did not touch it. If you didn't, then the only fingerprints on it should've been Arthur Endecott's. I carefully wrapped the bottle with my handkerchief so as to not smudge any fingerprints if they existed and the lab confirmed that there were no fingerprints on the bottle. Inspector Enderby and I had searched Arthur's room a few days earlier and we found no such bottle then. The only person who could've placed the bottle there was you."

"Why would I want to frame and kill Mr. Endecott and also frame Irene and Charles?" retorted Miss Carter in anger.

"When you stole the wills from Mr. Kerr's briefcase, you read the clause in Lord Fitzhugh's will. You realised that Arthur could contest the will later and so you had to frame him for the murders of Lady Fitzhugh and Hector. You were also the one to tell me about Arthur's Indian dagger, but you later told me that you hadn't seen the dagger when you entered Lady Fitzhugh's room.

"That Irene was the illegitimate daughter of Lord Fitzhugh was known only to two other people besides Lady Fitzhugh. One is Charles and the other, by his own admission, is Richard Seymour – your accomplice. Richard carefully avoided mentioning it when he told me about the conversation he had overheard in the stables. I suspect that Lady Fitzhugh also requested that Slattery and you be witnesses when she mentioned that Kerr would be bringing her will and you knew the reason why."

"That's poppycock," said Richard. "I'd never met Miss Carter until I started courting Pippa."

"That's not true. You pretended not to know her and she played her part of not liking and disapproving of you very well. It was part of the plan and it would have been easier for Lady Fitzhugh to talk to Miss Carter about you. Some ladies confide in their housekeepers, especially if they trust them and have something in common."

"You mean to say that Pippa's innocent after all?" asked Cora.

"Yes, Mrs. Fitzhugh. It was necessary to arrest her as part of our plan to flush out the real murderers and that's exactly what happened. Once Pippa was accused and in prison, the real murderers had to act since she was vital to their plans."

"How could Pippa be vital to their plans?" asked Cora.

"If you remember, when I arrested Pippa I said that she was trying to kill Hector because if he died before her then she would inherit everything."

Cora and the elderly sisters nodded.

"Well, that was how these murders were planned. After Miss Carter read the wills, she put them back in Kerr's briefcase while she was serving Lady Fitzhugh tea in the living room. Lady Fitzhugh and Hector definitely needed to be eliminated. Therefore, Miss Carter added extra arsenic, which she stole from the shed, into Hector's tonic. Since arsenic is an ingredient in Fowler's solution, the coroner would conclude that Hector died due to the chemist accidentally adding an extra dose of it. After Hector's death, Richard would propose marriage to Pippa and would then convince her to make a will in his name as he had Pippa under his power."

"So Hector ruined their plans?" asked Cora, stunned.

"Correct! Hector's disobedience is what saved him. He pretended to take a spoonful of the tonic and spat it out into the sink when you were not looking. He was actually getting better by not taking the toxic tonic. Therefore, they decided that they had to get rid of him another way, and that opportunity came when Hector wanted to go riding with them."

"What do you mean that Richard had Pippa under his power?" asked Cora.

"Hector told me that when Pippa was comforting him after his fall, he heard Richard telling Pippa to fetch help. Pippa was about to leave when Hector, who was in a semi-conscious state, gripped her hand, forcing her to stay. Richard was then forced to ride back and get help. What bothered me was why would any man ask a lady who was comforting a wounded child to go get help? Hector, being an astute child, told me that Richard was the only man who had showed interest in Pippa and that she always obeyed him because she was afraid of losing him."

"You're right about Hector, Detective. He's very observant," said Cora proudly.

"If Pippa had left Hector, Richard would've suffocated the boy. When help arrived, it would've been too late. Everyone would've been convinced that Hector had died due to his injuries from the accident. Once I worked that out, I eliminated Pippa from my list of suspects. If Pippa had then married Richard and made a will in his name, she would have been signing her own death warrant. Having murdered before, Richard would not have hesitated to murder Pippa in order to inherit the estate and, after inheriting, he would then have made a will making his daughter the beneficiary."

"His daughter?" asked Cora.

"Yes, his daughter who was born in the Kimberley Concentration Camp during the Boer War."

"Detective Carlyle, it seems to me that you have a talent for making up intriguing stories," said Richard. "I suppose you missed your calling to be a writer of detective stories. I'm not listening to these silly accusations; I'm leaving."

Dermot shouted as Richard got up to leave. "Constable Lyons, please bring in Mrs. Argyle and her husband."

The door opened and Constable Lyons came in with Nancy and Gerard Argyle.

"This is Gerard Argyle and his wife, Nancy, the daughter of Richard Seymour."

Nancy looked at Miss Carter and Richard. "Alister, Jane, what are you doing here?" The two were silent; the look of surprise and defeat were evident on their faces.

"Nancy is the main reason why all this has happened," Dermot continued. "This estate would've been hers one day if their plan had succeeded."

"How did you find her?" asked Miss Carter.

"We discovered that Bertram Kerr had gone to Scotland because Lady Fitzhugh wanted Richard investigated. My theory is that when Slattery saw Richard he found him familiar. It was only when he was writing his memoirs that he suddenly realised who Richard resembled." Dermot held Slattery's memoirs up and turned to the page with the drawings. "Slattery had drawn pictures of men with and without facial hair, probably to while away time. However, it suddenly struck him that Richard had facial hair and that his hair was slightly longer than usual. He probably suspected that Richard wasn't who he said he was and that he was actually Peter De Villiers, the son of Lord Fitzhugh's business partner.

"Mrs. Ainsworth had told me that neither Lord Fitzhugh nor Slattery had met Peter. He'd been in Germany and had only returned to fight in the Boer War. Slattery told his suspicions to Lady Fitzhugh and, since she never liked Richard, she asked Mr. Kerr to go to Argyle Castle to find out if it were true. Kerr managed to gain Lady Argyle's trust and she showed him her engagement picture of her and a young Christiaan, who was her brother, with facial hair. Kerr, who had seen Pippa and Richard in London, found the resemblance of Christiaan to Richard striking. He forcibly took the picture and then threatened to expose Richard. A few hours before arriving back in Meadowford, Kerr made a trunk call to Lady Fitzhugh to explain that he was

Trevor D'Silva

bringing her the proof. That is why she told Pippa to invite Richard to the party so that they could be sure. At the party that evening, Kerr told Lady Fitzhugh who Richard really was when they went to the library. He showed her the picture as proof."

Dermot held up the picture of Lord Fitzhugh and Christiaan that he had found in the safety deposit box and a sketch of a man with facial hair.

"Here's proof that Richard and Peter are the same person. The man in the picture is Christiaan without facial hair. I remembered Mrs. Ainsworth telling me how different Slattery looked with a moustache when I saw this picture of Lord Fitzhugh and Slattery taken in South Africa. So I had Constable Beckett, the police artist, make a sketch of Christiaan with facial hair and slightly longer hair. The resemblance is uncanny.

"Once Lady Fitzhugh and Mr. Kerr had established who Richard really was, Lady Fitzhugh told Pippa and Richard to meet her the next day. She intended to reveal Richard's true identity to Pippa and then to threaten to disinherit her if she did not give him up."

"Will someone please explain to me what's going on," said Nancy in bewilderment.

"Mrs. Argyle, Alister – or Richard as he is known to us – is your father and Jane – Miss Carter is your grandmother. Her real name is Rowena Naude. Before they came to Argyle Castle, they were masquerading as Ethel and David Northam. They've been murdering members of the Fitzhugh family and any others who got in their way so that you could inherit this place."

Nancy looked horrified.

"What made you suspect that they were Alister and Jane?" asked Gerard.

"It was actually what you told me when I asked you why you didn't have a butler. You said that Alister and Jane came to work at Argyle Castle when the Somme battles were taking place. Your excellent memory for details helped me solve one part of the mystery that had stymied me as to what happened to Ethel and David Northam after they were presumed dead in a car crash."

Nancy sat on the chair next to her and covered her face.

"How did you know that she's my daughter?" asked Richard.

"When I saw her at Argyle Castle, I felt that I had seen her somewhere before. Later, I realised that she resembled the picture of your daughter, who you told me died in the Spanish flu epidemic."

"Who killed Bertram Kerr?" asked Gerard.

"It was Richard. Mr. Kerr used the picture he stole from Lady Argyle to blackmail Richard and to get the diamonds that once belonged to Richard's father. After killing Kerr, Richard took the train back to London and bought the engagement ring for Pippa, claiming that he had been shopping for the ring all day."

Richard looked stunned and Dermot continued saying that they had checked with the jewellers where he bought the ring and that he bought it after four p.m. After killing Kerr, he took the train leaving Meadowford Station at two p.m., giving him ample time to get there, buy the ring, and go to Selfridges when Pippa was about to leave work by five.

"Yes, Kerr was a greedy and unscrupulous man," said Richard. "He first sent me an anonymous letter telling me that he knew who I really was. He then disguised his voice when he telephoned asking me to meet him at the Carlton Inn. When we met at the inn, he told me how he had forced it out of my aunt that I had the diamonds and showed me the picture of my father. I gave him the diamonds, but he still wouldn't give me the photograph. When he turned to place the diamonds in his desk drawer, I took a thin rope from my pocket and strangled him. The diamonds fell on the floor, so I collected them and left," said Richard.

"He was a brute and liked to dominate people," Dermot said. "I personally witnessed that when I had lunch with him at the Meadowford Inn. You missed a diamond when you were collecting them from the floor, which gave me an inkling as to why he was murdered. I suspect that when Slattery told her Ladyship that you were probably Peter De Villiers, she went through her father's documents and saw the letter where Christiaan wrote about sending the diamonds to a safe place. She told Mr. Kerr about the diamonds and he forced it out of Lady Argyle about you having them."

"But Detective Carlyle, who killed Abigail and hurt Miss Carter?" asked Alice impatiently.

"That's another mystery that troubled me because we found no trace of the man, and the truth is that he never existed. When I attended Mrs. Howard's garden party at the vicarage, she was telling us about her classmate – Lily Anderson, who was also a student of Lady Fitzhugh – who had a habit of spinning a yarn just to get out of trouble. I realised that's what happened in this case. Miss Carter tried to kill Abigail by pushing her down the stairs to the laundry room, to make it look like Abigail had accidently fallen. However, Abigail dropped the basket, which rolled down the stairs, and fought back, pushing Miss Carter into the wall. That's how Miss Carter hurt her head. Despite her age, Miss Carter is a strong lady and may've tripped Abigail with her leg or Abigail must've lost her balance and fallen down the stairs, breaking her neck. Either way, Miss Carter's plan hadn't gone the way she intended. When Pippa and I arrived at the scene, she made up the story that an intruder attacked them and escaped through the laundry door."

Alice stood up with rage and like a wild tigress she ran across the room to Miss Carter and grabbed at her throat. "You witch," she screamed, "you killed our Abigail..."

The police constables sprang into action and pulled Alice away.

"Sit down, Alice, or you'll be sent to prison," said Inspector Enderby sternly. He then told Dermot to continue.

Dermot looked at Miss Carter. "Abigail was another person in your way and you had to get rid of her."

"But Abigail yelled that she was being attacked and asked me to help her," said Miss Carter.

"True, I admit that stymied me for some time. You heard her talking to me in the library when you arrived with Pippa and you questioned her later, while she was collecting the clothes to be laundered, about what she was telling me. When she disclosed what she had told me, you knew you had to get rid of her because if she said anything more it would arouse my suspicions. When she yelled 'Help... Miss Carter... Help me,' she was shouting for someone to help her and couldn't understand why you were attacking her."

Miss Carter sat stunned for a moment. "That stupid girl. When I questioned her, she told me about hearing the clock chime twice at four-thirty and how she didn't see Pippa in front of the library door. She wanted to talk to you again and I couldn't allow her to do that."

"You're very cold hearted, Miss Carter. You treated Abigail's life like a piece of crockery that's easily discarded. You also had no qualms about blaming Francis Abernathy for cutting the saddle strap and for killing Abigail in the suicide note. When I suggested that you must've been the intended victim and not Abigail, you lied about seeing someone leaving the stables while talking to Constable Barnaby. You knew from Richard that Francis was in love with Pippa and that he used to follow them at times. You used the information we gave Arthur about Francis being seen at the train station when Kerr and Abigail were killed to your own advantage."

"I don't understand, why kill her?" asked Alice, exasperated.

"Because of whom she didn't see and what she heard while airing the laundry," said Dermot. "While talking to me in the living room, Abigail refused to say anything more when she saw Miss Carter and Pippa standing at the library door. She was mistaken about Pippa being responsible for Hector's accident. When I was interviewing Pippa after Hector's accident, I remember Abigail came in with the tea and she heard Pippa telling me that she was outside the door at four-thirty.

"I do not contest what Pippa told me. However, I do believe that Abigail didn't see Pippa at that time. How is that possible? One of them must have been lying, right? No! They were both telling the truth. Why would Miss Carter want Abigail to give Constable Jenkins lemonade just as she was going to air the laundry? It's because she had to get Abigail away from the laundry yard so that she wouldn't see Richard emerge from the woods and enter the stables to cut the saddle strap after Charles had left. It was Miss Carter who summoned Charles through the indicator board.

"Since the clock chimes every half hour, Richard moved the hands on the clock forward by nearly fifteen minutes. So when he and Constable Barnaby heard the clock chime it was actually four-fifteen. Later, I found out from Alice that Abigail had found it odd when she heard the clock in the library chime four-thirty again through the open library window while she was in the laundry yard."

"Why would Richard do that?" asked Flora.

"To have an alibi so he could leave the manor and cut the saddle strap."

"That's impossible. Constable Jenkins was guarding the front door and he didn't see anybody leave or enter," said Cora.

"That's true, but the reason Richard was at the window was to see when Charles left the stables. He could act only after that. You're right that he never left the manor from the front door. However, there's another way he left without being seen."

Dermot walked to the statue of Queen Elizabeth and pushed it hard to the right. The statue moved to reveal a low tunnel. Everyone gasped.

"The entrance is low, but the tunnel behind is high enough for people to walk normally. Richard used this tunnel, which leads to an opening in the woods, close to the stables, hidden by a slab and bushes. He cut the leather saddle strap with the knife that Miss Carter had kept on the tray for the apples. No wonder it became blunt, Alice told me that Mrs. Withers was grumbling about it later. Miss Carter deliberately suggested that Pippa and Richard have tea in the library so that Richard could then use this tunnel to go to the stables without being seen when he was alone in the library.

"Richard also used this tunnel on the night that Lady Fitzhugh was murdered. Miss Carter let him in because it can only be opened from inside. I found some oil stains from a car on a dirt road near the tunnel's opening in the woods. Richard had parked his car there when he pretended to go back to London after the party. He also brought the rope that was used to tie Lady Fitzhugh. Miss Carter, you signalled him with the candle from the library window, which was seen by Charles when he woke up hearing the horses agitated."

"My word! How did you find this tunnel, Detective?" asked Arthur.

"Charles told me about the horses being restless on the night of Lady Fitzhugh's murder and I went into the woods to investigate. Strangely, the cat that Abigail used to feed led me to it and I discovered the tunnel. It was an escape route for priests when the Catholics were being persecuted during Queen Elizabeth's reign. Mrs. Ainsworth told me that the library used to be a Catholic Chapel and that this statue was placed to fool the Queen's soldiers that she had been accepted as the head of the new church. The tunnel was forgotten after the manor was renovated by Lord Cecil Fitzhugh in the early 1800s."

"How did you know that the statue had to be pushed?" asked Flora.

"Because of the way the mechanism behind it is positioned. I suspected the statue covered the entrance to the tunnel because a part of the wall behind the statue looked ancient and the rest looked like it had been renovated in the previous century. I noticed that difference when I first came into the library," said Dermot pointing to the spot where the difference was noticeable.

"How did you discover this tunnel, Miss Carter?" asked Lilian.

Miss Carter smiled. "When I first started working here, I was in the attic looking for books for the library and I found the diary of Lord Cecil Fitzhugh in a trunk. He wrote about the hidden tunnel and I knew it would be useful one day."

"What made me suspect Richard was a broken piece of glass that I found in the tunnel behind the statue," said Dermot. "I questioned Richard about the torch and he told me that he had put it in Hector's saddle bag and that it had probably fallen out when Hector had his accident. I went to the accident site and found the torch under a bush, the glass piece from the tunnel was part of the torch's lens."

Dermot produced the torch from his briefcase, pulled out a handkerchief from his coat pocket and unwrapped it to reveal a piece of glass. He placed the glass piece into the gap in the lens and it fitted perfectly.

"So if the torch was found where Hector fell, how could a piece of the lens then be inside the tunnel?" Dermot asked. "That led me to think of what happened after Richard cut the strap. He came running through the tunnel and that's why he was drenched with sweat, which Pippa noticed when he came out of the library. Due to the dampness in the tunnel, a little mud clung to his shoes and Alice found the mud on the floor when she was cleaning the library. She had also seen mud in the library the night after her Ladyship was murdered.

"Richard accidently dropped the torch when he was coming out of the tunnel and into the library, since the entrance is very low. Pippa heard the sound while she was knocking on the door and asked him what was wrong. Richard picked up the torch, hurriedly closed the tunnel by pushing the statue into place, and broke one of the teacups. That was the second sound that Pippa heard. Richard then moved the hands on the clock to four-thirty p.m. and Pippa heard the clock chime from outside the door. This was the same chime that Abigail heard while airing clothes in the laundry yard.

"In his haste, Richard didn't realise that a piece of the torch's lens was in the tunnel, but discovered it only after he had closed the tunnel. He had to get rid of the torch, so he put it in his pocket and told Pippa that they could explore the caves near the stream. While in the stables, Richard placed the torch in Hector's saddle knowing that it would come off when Hector fell."

"Detective, how did they communicate? Miss Carter disliked Richard and would always reprimand him for not keeping the books in place," said Flora.

"That's true, but the library books were the link to their communication. They first communicated through letters, which stopped after Richard was introduced to the family. Then, Miss Carter and Richard had to pretend that they had never met before. When I questioned Hector after his accident, he mentioned that on the night Richard first came to the manor he saw Richard in the library putting a note in one of the books. He thought it was a love note for Pippa, but it was a note informing Miss Carter about overhearing Irene telling Charles about being added to the will and why.

"Later, I discovered that when Richard visited the manor, he would frequently head to the library and pick a book that he then pretended to read. Whenever Richard or Miss Carter wanted to communicate with each other, to pass on information or instructions, one of them would put a note in a book and then tell the other that the book was out of place."

"Fascinating! But how did Miss Carter know that Hector was not taking his tonic?" asked Cora.

"I suspect that she saw the stain in Hector's bathroom sink, like I did. She then suggested that Hector go horse riding with Pippa and Richard. Once she knew Hector had your permission, she wrote her instructions and put them in *Moby Dick* and told Richard that *Moby Dick* was out of place."

"Who killed that hospital worker?" asked Flora. "Surely, you cannot blame Richard or Miss Carter."

"Yes, as a matter of fact, I can. Unfortunately, Miss Carter answered the phone when Sister Fleming called here to tell me that she had found the staff picture with Ethel and David Northam in it. Miss Carter recognised the voice and the name of her former co-worker. Sister Fleming disclosed to her the reason that she was calling. When I took the call, Miss Carter pretended to go down the staircase to the kitchen, but instead she stood behind the door and listened to me telling Sister Fleming where I would meet her.

"After I left to go to London, Miss Carter called Richard at his London flat. He then went to where I was meeting Sister Fleming and forcibly took her handbag containing the picture. Richard then pushed her in front of an oncoming car. I checked with the Meadowford telephone exchange and the telephone operator remembers that a call was placed to London around the time I headed to London; that confirmed my suspicions."

"I was painting Felicity on that day. She'll vouch for me," said Richard.

"We have already questioned Felicity and she said that you left after receiving the call. You told her that you had to run an errand and went away. When you returned, you were breathless and very brusque. You went into your room, then came back a while later and continued painting her."

"No, Felicity wouldn't lie," said Richard.

"No, she wouldn't... but she was upset with you. She tearfully told me that she overheard you comparing her to a common tart when she came back to get her purse. She was slighted by your comment and waited near the lift. I almost bumped into her after I left your flat and there was something bizarre about her manner, and now I know why. She was also annoyed with you for getting engaged to Pippa."

"Richard, you're a fiend. My sisters-in-law were right about you," said Cora with anger.

Richard looked defeated and hung his head in shame.

"You're forgetting that I was housekeeper to Mrs. Evans in Cumbria from 1902 to 1922 and not a hospital worker," asserted Miss Carter arrogantly.

"No, you were not," replied Dermot. "When I knew you made up the story of a man killing Abigail, I suspected that you were not honest about everything. Gerard Argyle told me that his grandmother subscribed to the *London Times* from 1916 to 1922. You joined here in September of 1922. In June, 1922, Lady Fitzhugh placed an advertisement for the position of a housekeeper at Fitzhugh Manor and that was exactly the opportunity you were waiting for. The advertisement asked not only for a housekeeper, but someone who would also be a companion to three older women. The reference letter was probably written by you or Lady Argyle.

"The expertise of Miss Cartwright from the London Library helped me. She discovered in the obituary column of the *London Times* in May, 1922, that a Mrs. Mable Evans had died of cancer in Silescroft village in Cumbria. Her housekeeper and companion was Miss Esmey Carter, who died a few days later in a gas leak from an apparent suicide because she was distraught over the death of her mistress. I went to Silescroft and verified everything, including the dates of employment of Miss Carter with Mrs. Evans' niece, Molly Stanwick, who has just returned from the Far East.

"In England, birth and death documents are public record. So, you went to the General Register Office for information on Esmey Carter and you found that she was the same age as you, unmarried, and had no relatives. It was convenient for you to exploit their deaths because they were from an obscure village."

Everyone looked at Miss Carter in disbelief and couldn't understand how this seemingly respectable older woman could be capable of such subterfuge.

Dermot turned to Richard, wagging a finger at him. "I suspect that you took the name of Ruiseart Seymour, the butler of Lady Argyle who was injured in the Somme. You thought it was convenient to use his name and also his war record for your new identity as Richard Seymour. Like Esmey Carter, Ruiseart lived in an obscure village where nobody outside knew him. He died in 1922 at Argyle Castle, supposedly of the effects of being gassed in the Somme but I suspect that he was poisoned by either you or Miss Carter. His death was never reported to the Office of the Paymaster General and so they have been sending you his cheques. Ruiseart Seymour's body was exhumed yesterday and his remains are being tested for arsenic poisoning.

"Miss Cartwright, from the London Library, also checked that Ruiseart is the Gaelic version of Richard. Just as Constable Andrew Barnaby told me that his name is actually Aindrea, which in Gaelic means Andrew... am I right?"

Constable Barnaby nodded.

Dermot signalled to Constable Clarke. He went out and brought Pippa and Francis into the room with him.

"Pippa, you're free!" said Cora. "Who's this man with you?"

"This is Francis, the owner of the theatre company where I work as an actress."

The two older sisters gasped in disbelief.

Pippa looked at Richard, tears in her eyes. "Is it true that you're not Richard Seymour? That you're only interested in marrying me for my inheritance and that you were also cheating on me with your model, Felicity?"

Richard suddenly stood up, drew a gun and aimed it at the crowd. "Very smart of you, Detective, but I've had enough. Constable, put your hands up and move away from the door."

Constable Clarke complied and Richard began walking towards the door.

Frida held her walking stick out, tripping him. The gun discharged as it fell from his hand, making the women scream. The bullet lodged into the wall above Cora's head. As Richard grabbed the gun, Charles lunged at him trying to wrestle the gun away. Lilian took the walking stick and hit Richard on his head and he released his grip on the gun.

"I always knew you were a scoundrel. My sisters and I were right about you."

Constable Barnaby took the gun away and aimed it at Richard. Charles made him stand up, while Constable Clarke handcuffed him. Then he was made to sit back down on his chair.

Chapter 26: The Final Act

As the people in the library settled down, the sky darkened and they heard a roll of thunder.

"Looks like Constable Blackwood was right when he said that a storm was approaching. Will somebody please turn on the lights?" said Dermot.

After the lights were switched on, Lilian turned to Dermot. "Detective, in what way have we harmed them for them to hate us so much that they want to kill us? These people are total strangers."

"Nothing. Your only crime was being related to Lord Fitzhugh. It's all about revenge, and he was responsible for this whole mess."

"But Father died many years before Miss Carter and Richard Seymour came here," said Flora.

"He didn't know them either, but they were related to his business partner, Christiaan De Villiers." Dermot put his hand into his breast pocket and removed a few telegrams. "These telegrams were sent to me by Mr. Griffin, a contact of my father in South Africa. His investigation revealed that a marriage had taken place between Peter De Villiers and Hermine Naude on the tenth of June, 1901, at the Dutch Reformed Church, close to where the family lived in Kimberley.

"Miss Carter, or Rowena Naude, was the bride's mother. Her husband, Johan Naude, died before the Boer War, but her son, David, survived the war and there's no record of him being married. A death certificate for Peter De Villiers was issued by the Boer Army but, Richard, you're really Peter De Villiers and Nancy is your daughter, am I right?"

Richard sat silently and refused to speak.

"Oh, what's the point of being silent when he already knows the facts? Yes, you're right, Detective," said Miss Carter in anger.

"Major Havelock, who was in Lord Fitzhugh's regiment during the Boer War, harboured a dreadful secret. He helped Lord Fitzhugh eliminate his business partner so that he could become the sole owner of the mine."

"Impossible... you must be raving mad," said Flora. "Father had his faults, but he wasn't a murderer."

"I'm sorry, but he did, and we have the sworn testimony of Major Havelock. He told me a few days ago that he rejoined his unit after convalescing in a British hospital in Pretoria on the tenth of September, 1901, but Slattery had written in his memoir that it was on the fifth of September.

"Mr. Griffin met Pastor Jan Louw of the Dutch Reformed Church where the family attended services. The pastor said that on the night of the seventh of September, 1901, a native servant of the De Villiers family came to the church and, before succumbing to his bullet wounds, he told Pastor Louw that the De Villiers family had been arrested and their property had been destroyed by Lord Fitzhugh. Incidentally, that was the same date that Slattery had mentioned that Lord Fitzhugh, Major Havelock – who was at that time a private – and a few men from the unit went hunting. Major Havelock confirmed that the hunting expedition was actually to the De Villiers' farm in Kimberley."

"Why would he have done such a thing?" asked Lilian.

"Because the mine produced hardly any diamonds; however, in 1901, Christiaan had discovered a huge deposit of diamonds, which was confirmed by a geologist from the Parr & Monroe Geology Company in Kimberley. Christiaan had trusted Lord Fitzhugh implicitly and sent him a letter – dated the twenty fifth of August, 1901 about the discovery. After reading the letter, Lord Fitzhugh decided to get rid of the De Villiers family so that he could get sole ownership of the mine.

"When Havelock returned from Pretoria after his recovery, Lord Fitzhugh promised to help him advance his career in the British Army if he helped to get rid of Christiaan and his family. So they arrested the family and sent them to the Kimberley Concentration Camp because the mortality rate there was high. Rowena Naude, who was staying with the De Villiers family, was also incarcerated, but she survived. She sits before us now as Miss Carter."

They all looked at Miss Carter whose face was ashen, but then she started talking in a very low voice that was filled with emotion. She explained how Lord Fitzhugh came with a few soldiers and arrested them. Christiaan had pleaded for his family to be spared and reminded Lord Fitzhugh of his promise to protect them. Lord Fitzhugh laughed however and asked Christiaan about the diamonds, but he had already sent them to his sister in Scotland. The whole family was sent to the Kimberley Concentration Camp, while the servants were either killed or driven away. The house and the farm were destroyed.

In the camp, conditions were squalid and food was in extremely short supply. Christiaan and his wife died of starvation after giving their rations to

Hermine who was pregnant at the time. Three days after giving birth in the camp, Hermine succumbed to septicaemia, but the baby survived. Peter found Rowena and his infant daughter at Pastor Louw's church after the end of the war and they decided to exact revenge on Lord Fitzhugh.

They first planned to kill Lord Fitzhugh at the mine. Peter signed up as a worker when the newspaper advertised for miners. On the day of the inauguration, he rigged some of the dynamite used to blast the rocks. He lit the fuse as Lord Fitzhugh and a group of British dignitaries approached the mine. However, it exploded too early and nobody was killed. After Lord Fitzhugh was cleared of insurance fraud and returned to England, Peter and Rowena decided to change their names to Ethel and David Northam and come to England to kill Lord Fitzhugh.

Peter and Rowena knew that Lord Fitzhugh visited St. Cuthbert's Hospital for treatment of his gall bladder problems, because he had once told Christiaan that Meadowford did not have a good hospital. They got employment at St Cuthbert's Hospital under their new identities, but Rowena couldn't doctor his medication because it would be traced to the dispensary where she worked. One day, Rowena pointed Lord Fitzhugh out to Peter. Peter followed him onto the street to kill him, but lost him in the crowd. Rowena chided him and cautioned him to be patient. Their chance for vengeance, she assured him, would eventually come. When Lord Fitzhugh came in for his surgery, they had their opportunity to take their revenge. Since Hermine had died of septicaemia, they decided to use the pus from the patient in the next room to infect bandages so that Lord Fitzhugh died of septicaemia too.

"So Father was also murdered by these people?" asked Lilian, stunned.

"Yes, and that's what Sister Fleming realised when she showed the staff photo to Dr. Butterworth and they were talking about Dr. Steward, who was Lord Fitzhugh's doctor. Thank heavens she told her suspicions to Eunice, her assistant, before she was killed by Richard. We'll have to now reclassify Lord Fitzhugh's death as murder."

"Detective, there's something I don't understand. You said that one of the murderers was part of the family. Miss Carter is our housekeeper and Richard is only engaged to Pippa," said Lilian.

Dermot looked at Miss Carter. "Oh, yes, there's just one more thing I need clarified, Miss Carter. Are you the daughter of Theo Fitzhugh?"

She looked at him dumbfounded. "How... how did you know?"

Dermot told her that two things got him suspicious. The first was when the two elderly sisters told him that when Miss Carter was interviewed for the job they felt that they had met her before. That was one of the reasons why she was hired. Another was when he questioned Miss Carter about the missing necklace after Abigail's murder and she looked directly at him saying that the necklace would never adorn the neck of another beautiful lady. Dermot had thought that she meant Lady Fitzhugh's neck, but only later realised that she'd actually been looking at the painting of Theo Fitzhugh and his family, which was behind him, and was talking about her mother, Rosalyn Fitzhugh. She was reminiscing about being a young girl and seeing her mother wearing the same emerald necklace. Irene had also mentioned that Miss Carter had shown unusual interest in the necklace when Lady Fitzhugh had first shown it to them.

"Detective, are you saying that she's our cousin, Eliza, who was killed during the Indian mutiny?" asked Flora. "That's impossible, because Father went to save them and came back wounded. Everyone else was killed, including the two scouts he took along with him."

"Your father was a liar and a killer. No doubt he must've inflicted the wounds on himself," retorted Miss Carter, seething with rage.

"There's no doubt about that," said Dermot. "Mrs. Ainsworth, you told me that at the lake your mother was pleading with your father to move on, but he kept delaying. I was wondering why the rebels only took your cousins as prisoners. Under normal circumstances, more prisoners would have increased their chances of successfully negotiating the release of their fellow rebels. In my opinion, your father was an accomplice to the plan to kidnap your cousins. He got the rebels to attack the garrison after the caravan left, so that his brother's family would all be killed and he would inherit the entire estate. Like the diamond mine, it was greed that motivated him to betray his brother."

"It's true, Detective," said Miss Carter. "That day still haunts me." Miss Carter then recounted what happened when William Fitzhugh, along with the two scouts, caught up with the rebels. They had expected to be rescued, but were shocked when William greeted them. Sitara pleaded with her husband to tell her what was going on and he told her that Chindi, one of William's native scouts, came to his brothel the previous night and passed on instructions to attack the garrison after the caravan had left and to target the weakened portions of the garrison's walls. After they had killed Theo and Rosalyn, they were then to kidnap Sitara and Theo's children. William would then pretend to come to their rescue.

"So, I was right!" said Dermot.

Miss Carter nodded and then cleared her throat and continued. Manu Lal told Sitara that Theo knew who had betrayed them and that he pleaded for the lives of his children before Manu Lal murdered Theo and Rosalyn. When

Manu Lal finished talking, William drew his gun and killed his two scouts. Then Manu Lal and William began shooting the others. The next thing that the young Miss Carter remembered was waking up and finding Sitara and Teddy dead on top of her. She had been wounded in the arm. Manu Lal lay dead, with a few gold coins next to him. William had shot him in the back. He had left no witnesses.

After wandering alone for hours, the young Miss Carter was found by a Dutch family escaping the mutiny. The husband, a doctor, extracted the bullet from her arm and she then travelled with them as they immigrated to South Africa. The family named her Rowena and brought her up as their daughter. She later married a Boer farmer and had two children: Hermine and David. David, who was Peter's friend, introduced Hermine to Peter and when Peter returned from Germany during the Boer War, he married Hermine and then left to join the same unit that David was in. Rowena was living with the De Villiers for the duration of the war because they thought it was safer.

Having blocked out the entire mutiny incident, Rowena found Lord Fitzhugh familiar when he came to arrest the De Villiers family in Kimberley. She continued seeing his face in her dreams during her incarceration in the camp and also when she came to England, but she couldn't understand why the people with him looked Indian rather than British.

"It is only when you read Lord Fitzhugh's account of his escape from the mutiny, at the London Library, that you realised who you really were. I have to thank Miss Cartwright's excellent memory for that piece of information," said Dermot.

"Yes, Detective," said Miss Carter. "Initially our intention was to kill Lord Fitzhugh. When he was dying, the newspapers mentioned that he had escaped the Indian mutiny and I went to the London Library to investigate. I read the account and knew that he had lied to make himself a brave hero. The dreams stopped after I realised that I was actually Eliza Fitzhugh. Richard knew about my dreams, and when I told him what I had discovered we decided that Nancy should get what was rightfully hers. Lady Argyle agreed to help us. We just had to wait for the right opportunity to infiltrate the manor and find out who needed to be eliminated in order for Nancy to inherit this place."

"Thank you, Miss Carter," said Dermot. He turned to Richard. "Who informed you about your family's arrest?"

"Pastor Jan Louw sent me a letter," Richard replied. "Unfortunately, the day after I received it we were ambushed in the veld by the British Army. I was badly injured, along with David who died a few days later in a makeshift hospital. Since we both had our faces bandaged, we agreed to switch identities because I knew that Lord Fitzhugh wanted to kill me for the mine. We exchanged beds and when David died I was recorded as one of the deceased. By the time I recovered, the war was over. When I met Rowena, we decided that I would continue masquerading as her son. After the war, many people were reinventing themselves to start a new life and we did the same."

"The commanding officer of your unit was Gerhard Von Schultz, a friend of your father. Did he help you to change your identities?"

Richard looked stunned. "Yes, but how did you know?"

"Mr. Griffin found that out." Dermot took a newspaper cutting from his briefcase and showed it to him. "Von Schultz published his memoirs about his time during the Boer War and explained how his hatred for the English made him spy for the Germans during the Great War. When the war began, he wrote you a letter from France asking you to help spy for him. It was to get back at England for starting the war in South Africa. Your former landlady, Sylvia Henderson, remembers you receiving that letter. He instructed you to be a double agent and pass him British military secrets, which he in turn would pass on to the Germans. Von Schultz was in France spying on the French at that time.

"That is why you were heading towards the coast to cross the English Channel. You were going there to give Gerhard the plans. When you realised that the coppers were gaining on you, you took the chance to destroy the plans and fake your own deaths when you were separated from the pursuing coppers by the flock of sheep. You then headed to Argyle Village in Scotland and established yourselves with new identities, as Alister and Jane."

"Yes, it was our only way to avenge what the British did to us, and we would gladly do it again," said Richard.

"You both met Allan Fitzhugh while working for the British Intelligence and saw an opportunity to humiliate or kill another member of the Fitzhugh family," said Dermot.

"We couldn't believe it when Allan told us who he was," said Miss Carter. "I remembered that when Lord Fitzhugh was dying I had read in the newspapers that he had a son born in England. Allan had mentioned that he had lived in Germany during his itinerant years. Allan suspected us and when he tricked us into stealing the submarine plans, we killed him and made it look like he had committed suicide to scapegoat him for our espionage activities and to humiliate the family by making him a traitor. We nearly got caught while escaping… well, you know the rest, Detective."

Dermot nodded, while Cora and Pippa stifled sobs.

"With regards to Slattery's murder, he tried to blackmail you, Miss Carter.

He realised that you were the one who had drugged his wine and Arthur's chamomile tea with Mrs. Withers' sleeping powders because you were the only one to handle the wine and the tea. He was also aware that only you and he knew that the wills were to be changed, disinheriting Pippa if she did not give up Richard, after Kerr told her Ladyship who Richard really was and she asked you both, in confidence, to be witnesses. Slattery also suspected you of stealing the wills from Kerr's briefcase and returning them later.

"When Charles told him about seeing the candle being waved from the library window, Slattery knew it was you signalling Richard. I think he also suspected that you two communicated using the library books. He probably heard you tell Richard that *The Count of Monte Cristo* was not in its proper place and then later saw Richard with the book in the library, as also witnessed by Pippa. You had written a note telling him that Lady Fitzhugh needed to die that night and why."

"Yes, Slattery slid a note under my bedroom door asking me to meet him near the pantry. When I met him, he told me that he knew I was involved in the murder," said Miss Carter.

"So he made a deal with you if you greased his palm."

"He was a greedy man. When he demanded more, I knew he had to be got rid of. On the second night, I waited for him in the dark in the library and when he turned after taking the money, I stabbed him in the chest."

There was stunned silence. "You killed so many," said Lilian sadly. "And for what? Revenge? Was this all necessary?"

Miss Carter looked at her with anger. "Don't you get it? Your father killed members of my family and other innocent people. So we were his nemesis. We executed him for the crimes he would have got away with had he died a natural death. It was only right that we corrected the wrongs he did to us. The others were only in the way.

"Doris didn't believe me and defended her father as an honourable gentleman. That enraged me and I sliced her throat with the dagger I had stolen from Arthur's suitcase."

The two sisters and Cora gasped in horror. Everyone in the room was stunned and speechless at the hard-heartedness of Miss Carter.

The library door opened slowly. A policewoman entered and signalled to Dermot. He waved her in. "After Miss Carter and Alice left the kitchen with the tea and scones, PWC Brent, under my strict orders, searched Miss Carter's room. Please tell us what you found."

"I found this necklace, a bottle of arsenic, the diary of Lord Cecil Fitzhugh, and some letters from Richard Seymour posted from London. They were all under some loose floor boards in Miss Carter's room."

"Good job, PWC Brent."

Dermot turned to Miss Carter. "After you murdered Lady Fitzhugh, you took the necklace because you were supposed to have inherited it from your mother. I knew it would be in your room," said Dermot.

PWC Brent gave the necklace to Dermot and he held it up for everyone to see. Richard looked angrily at Miss Carter. "You bloody stupid old cow, I told you not to take the necklace. If I knew you would send that note to William Fitzhugh, I would've stopped you."

Miss Carter hung her head in shame.

"I understand the reasoning behind your actions, but you will have to be held accountable," said Inspector Enderby. "We will have to take you both into custody."

Constables Barnaby and Jenkins made Richard and Miss Carter stand up and handcuffed them. As they passed by Nancy, who was wiping away tears, Miss Carter looked at her sadly. "Nancy, we did this for you," she said. "You were cheated out of your birthright and we needed to see that justice was done and that you got what was rightfully yours."

Nancy got up and embraced them. "I understand... but not this way."

"There was no other way," said Richard.

After Miss Carter and Richard were taken away, Lilian requested that the family be left to discuss Nancy and Irene getting a share of the estate. Dermot motioned for the remaining constables and staff to leave the room and allow the family to discuss in private.

As Dermot closed the library door, there was a flash of lightning and another roll of thunder. The darkened clouds, laden with moisture, finally burst open and it started raining heavily.

"Make sure that Miss Carter doesn't get wet," said Dermot.

"I'll cover her with my coat," replied Inspector Enderby.

As he watched the police get into the police van with their two prisoners, Dermot muttered to himself, "The bloody hot summer is finally over."

Chapter 27: The Detective Explains

Gerard Argyle came out of the library and walked up to Dermot. "How did ye ken that Nancy and I were married?"

"When you told me that you were both at the registrar's office that morning, I had my suspicions. Before we left Argyle Village, Inspector Enderby and I went to the registrar's office and the registrar who married the two of you, Mr. McDougal, told us that an irregular marriage had taken place between you and Nancy – in front of two witnesses who were sworn to secrecy – on the day that Mr. Kerr came to Argyle Castle... Lady Argyle didn't approve of your courtship with Nancy, am I right?"

"Och aye, she objected because Nancy was the maid's grandniece and she wouldn't make a suitable Lady of the castle. We grew up together and we have been in love for a long time."

"The real reason was because the two of you are second cousins and Lady Argyle couldn't reveal that fact to you or the whole plan would be out in the open. Did she plan on disinheriting you if you married Nancy?"

"Aye, she threatened tae give the property tae a distant cousin of mine. Her hostility towards Nancy was most strange. She said that she would state in her will that if I married anyone else, with the exception of Nancy, I could inherit what was rightfully mine. She even threatened tae change solicitors because hers was a long-term friend of the family and he didn't want tae draw up a will that would disinherit me."

"So when you saw Mr. Kerr's business card saying he was a will and probate solicitor, you assumed that he was there to talk to Lady Argyle about changing her will?"

"Aye, I thought that if I married Nancy that day then she would be forced tae accept us."

"I can only speculate that she was under the impression that if their plan had worked, then Nancy would inherit Fitzhugh Manor and its vast estate and then it would be hard for you to make a decision between staying at Argyle Castle and moving to Meadowford Village. She didn't want it coming to that."

"I didn't hae the opportunity tae tell her that we had got married because we found her completely shattered when we got back. She would've died of shock there and then if I had told her that we were married. We had absolutely no idea what she was up tae."

"Her desire for revenge was so great that she put aside her scruples to see that justice was done. Revenge can blind even the most virtuous of people," said Dermot.

"Tell me, Detective, how did ye ken that Ruiseart had been murdered?" asked Gerard.

"You told me that he suddenly died in agony before Alister and Jane left. When Miss Cartwright confirmed that Ruiseart is Gaelic for Richard, I remembered Pippa telling me that Richard was getting a pension cheque every month from the government for his service in the Great War. I asked Chief Inspector Gardner of Scotland Yard to check on this and the address listed in their files was Richard's flat in London. Lady Argyle hadn't notified the government about Ruiseart's death. Alister, or Richard as we know him, had taken his place to get the cheque every month. That's when I realised that the real Ruiseart had probably been poisoned with arsenic. No wonder Lady Argyle got sick after his death, her guilty conscience was gnawing at her."

Gerard sighed and shook his head in disbelief.

"Your telegram, informing me about the picture that Kerr stole, helped me to solve Richard's true identity," Dermot continued. "He had to grow his facial hair in order to change his appearance and to avoid being recognised if he ran into any of the people he knew in London. He didn't anticipate the artistic skills of Constable Beckett exposing who he really was."

"Thank ye for everythin', Detective," said Nancy, taking Gerard's hand in hers. "I'm happy wi' Gerard and would prefer tae stay in Argyle Village. Fitzhugh Manor and South Africa are buried in ma past and I want tae look forward tae the future wi' Gerard."

"Yes, but don't forget that the two elderly sisters would like you to be part of their lives and to make amends," said Dermot. "There's a happy ending to this sad story. Remember that you have family here too."

The rain had subsided a bit. Gerard and Nancy wished Dermot goodbye, walked out into the rain, and got into the taxi that was waiting to take them to Meadowford Train Station.

—   —   —

As Dermot passed by the drawing room, he noticed a figure standing in front of the window looking out at the rain. He walked into the dark room and slowly called out. Pippa turned; tears were streaming down her face.

"I'm very sorry, Pippa."

"All this seems like a bad dream." Pippa sighed. "He was so charming. I feel so guilty for bringing him here. Aunt Doris, Slattery, and Abigail would still be alive if it were not for me."

"Pippa, you mustn't feel guilty. He fooled a lot of people and he knew how to charm women."

"My aunts weren't fooled."

"No, but they were fooled by Miss Carter. It seems like everyone fell for the charms of these killers."

"It's not just that. I will never find anyone to marry me. Look at me… I'm not exactly a catch."

"I think you have, but you just don't know it yet."

Pippa looked at him in surprise. "Who are you talking about?"

"Francis. He loves you, but you didn't notice him because you were smitten by Richard's charm. Now that Richard is not here to toy with your affections, things will be clearer. Francis knew the risks involved, but he agreed to my plan to be arrested along with you because he loves you. He followed you and Richard several times because he knew that Richard was not being faithful to you after seeing him with Felicity."

"Thank you, Detective, but he'll not want me after all that has happened."

"Let's ask him, shall we?"

Pippa nodded and wiped her tears. Dermot walked out and called Francis, who was standing in front of the library door. Dermot whispered in Francis' ear. Francis nodded and went into the drawing room.

Dermot closed the drawing room door and then walked towards the front door where Alice was waiting for him.

"Thank you for everythin', Detective. Poor Abigail! I'm sure she's at peace now."

As he was about to speak, the cat appeared and stood in front of them. Alice picked it up and cradled it in her arms like a baby.

Dermot reached out and stroked the cat. "Abigail lives in this cat," he said as the cat purred loudly. "She led me to the tunnel and helped me solve a puzzling part of the case."

"I'll name her Abby after Abigail. It'll feel like she's back with me." The rain started coming down heavily again. "Oh, look at that rain. Do you want an umbrella, Detective?"

"No, thank you. After the heat of these past few weeks, the rain will feel good. Good day to you, Alice."

Dermot wrapped his briefcase in his coat and walked out of the front door, closing it behind him. He pulled his hat down lower and then walked towards his car.

—   —   —

Two days later...

Detective Duncan Newman Lloyd was in his office reading a report. A lit cigarette sat in the ashtray beside him, almost burnt to the filter. He was so engrossed in the report that he had hardly taken two puffs.

Dermot patiently sat opposite Detective Lloyd while he continued reading the report. He had learnt a lot from his superior and had the utmost respect for him. When Detective Lloyd finished reading the report, he looked at Dermot with pride. "Congratulations on solving your first solo case. I knew you could do it. Inspector Enderby is very impressed with your abilities and can't stop singing your praises."

"Thank you, sir. I have Miss Cartwright from the London Library and also the vicar's wife to thank for guiding me in the right direction."

Detective Lloyd laughed. "You're so right, Dermot. But there's something I do not understand. Why did Major Havelock lie about when he rejoined his unit? It was that lie which aroused your suspicions, right?" he asked as he caressed his neatly groomed moustache.

"Correct. But he wasn't aware that Slattery had written about him rejoining his unit on the fifth of September. Lord Fitzhugh had made them swear to never to speak of that incident and he knew that if I found out when the De Villiers were arrested then he would be in trouble. When I read that section of Slattery's memoir again, I knew that he was hiding something."

"What made you suspect that Miss Carter stole the dagger in order to frame Arthur?"

"When we first interviewed her, she brought it to our attention that Arthur had brought an antique dagger with him from India. However, when I asked her later if she had seen the murder weapon when she entered Lady Fitzhugh's bedroom after the murder, she said she hadn't. That got me suspicious that she was involved. Why had she mentioned the dagger to me if she hadn't seen the murder weapon? She didn't know that Arthur had taken the dagger when he entered Lady Fitzhugh's bedroom. When I realised that she was lying about who attacked Abigail and her, I was certain that she was involved."

"Miss Carter – or as we now know her to be, Eliza Fitzhugh – was brilliant at planning the murders and getting Richard or Peter De Villiers to execute some of them," said Detective Lloyd. "What is strange is that Eliza was at both places when Lord Fitzhugh committed his crimes due to his greed. The chances of that happening are very rare!"

"You're right, sir – one in a million! There are bizarre things that happen that have no explanation, but this was the way that Lord Fitzhugh's crimes would be exposed. Unfortunately, a lot of innocent people paid dearly. I'm sure that at some point they would've done away with Major Havelock for helping Lord Fitzhugh get rid of Christiaan and his family."

"I agree. What happened to the diamonds and the picture that Kerr stole?"

"We found the diamonds, the photograph that Kerr forcibly took from Lady Argyle, and also the photograph that Richard took from Sister Fleming; they were all in Richard's flat. They've been entered as evidence for the trial and, once that is over, they'll then be handed back to their rightful owners."

"This was all so unnecessary. Nancy Campbell – the new Lady Argyle – doesn't want any of the estate for which her father and grandmother murdered so many."

"Yes," said Dermot. "She must be feeling very guilty about the whole affair because they did it all for her. However, she's happy to connect with the Fitzhugh family. It's strange, Lord Fitzhugh's greed started this whole sordid affair, which affected his children, grandchildren, and strangers alike."

"Very true; the sins of the father always visit the children with tragic consequences. This case proves it," said Detective Lloyd, closing the file. He placed the file aside and smiled. "I have some good news for you. My superior has agreed that you should have two weeks of holiday after the trial is over. I think you've earned it."

Dermot smiled. "Thank you, sir. It means a great deal to me to have another break."

"Where will you go?"

"Definitely not to Meadowford Village; you can be sure of that, sir."

Detective Lloyd laughed heartily as Dermot bid him goodbye and left.

Epilogue

London – three weeks later...

The play, *A Mistress at Hand*, opened in London a week after the trial ended and was attended by all of Pippa's family, including her two elderly aunts. They liked Francis and approved of him courting Pippa, and they grudgingly gave their blessings for Pippa to pursue her dream of becoming an actress.

After the play ended, Dermot walked out of the theatre and stood outside the entrance. A few minutes later, he felt a tap on his shoulder. He turned around and saw the two elderly sisters.

"Detective, we're grateful that you brought Francis and Pippa together. They make such a delightful couple," said Lilian.

"How did you like her performance?" asked Dermot with a smile.

"She was wonderful," said Flora, "simply marvellous. Her French accent sounds so genuine. We didn't know she was so talented. Cora and Hector are with her in the dressing room, and the reporters want to interview her."

"Now that she's getting married, we hope she will settle down and be a good mother. People of our class don't become actresses," said Lilian with an air of superiority.

"And people of our class shouldn't be committing murder or cheating people. Remember what our father did, Lilian?" said Flora. "It's better that Pippa is an actress than what you assumed she was when she came home one day with make-up on her face."

Dermot looked puzzled. "What did you think she was working as, Mrs. Endecott?"

Lilian looked at Dermot. "A streetwalker," she said with a smile.

Dermot laughed. "She did play the part of a mistress in this play."

The two older sisters laughed along with him.

"With the trial now over, we can all get on with our lives," said Lilian.

"Yes, too bad that the judge didn't grant our appeal that their death sentences be commuted to life imprisonment," said Flora.

"They murdered so many and their families want justice. They are also guilty of blowing up the mine in South Africa, espionage against His Majesty's

Government, and defrauding the government. I'm afraid they have a lot to pay for. Makes you feel sorry for them, even though they are murderers. They are also victims of Lord Fitzhugh's greed," said Dermot.

"Father's greed ruined a lot of lives. He blamed poor Sitara – an innocent woman with a heart of gold – for betraying us, but he was actually the wicked one," said Lilian with sadness. "But whatever he was, he was still our father and that cannot be changed. Coming to know the truth has been very cathartic for me."

"Detective, our half-sister, Irene, will now be our secretary," said Flora. "She learnt to use the typewriter from her mother. After Irene marries Charles, he will help us manage the estate. He was very brave wrestling that gun away from Richard and that proves that he can be trusted. We are also paying for Frida's treatment. We gave the emerald necklace to Nancy. She was reluctant at first, but we insisted because we felt that she had a right to it since it belonged to her great-grandmother."

"And you will be happy to know that Cora has agreed to send Hector back to Harrow," said Lilian. "Now that Allan's good name has been restored, Hector will be looked upon as the son of a hero."

"Good news indeed! Hector needs to be around boys of his age, and the discipline at Harrow will make him a fine young man," said Dermot.

"Come on, Lilian, it's time we went home. Let's look to the future. Arthur's on his way to Kenya with his family. Pippa will soon be married and my two daughters and their families will be coming for the wedding. We have a guest list to make."

Lilian nodded. The two elderly sisters said goodbye to Dermot and asked him to visit them when he next came to Meadowford.

"Oh, Mrs. Endecott," Dermot said as the two sisters walked past him. "I just thought of something. Do you know who would also make a great actor?"

"Who, Detective?"

"Arthur. He played his part well and we caught the killers," said Dermot laughing.

"Don't you dare suggest that, Detective," Lilian said, amused. "Don't you dare!"

Dermot watched them leave. He looked at the sky and saw clouds gathering again. Ever since the heatwave had ended, it had kept raining on and off as if to compensate for the many weeks of extreme warmth. He pulled his coat around him and walked towards his car.

— — —

Two days later...

As Dermot drove down a secluded road, the heavy rain turned to a slight drizzle. His parents had been adamant that he remain in Meadowford until the storm passed, but he'd assured them that the weather reports predicted that the rain would soon stop. There was an important reason why he was on this road. Relieved that he could now see the street signs more clearly, he turned off the road and drove into the street he'd been looking for.

Dermot pulled up in front of a small house with a garden brimming with flowers. Dermot grabbed a book from the back of the car, opened his umbrella, and then walked through the small gate leading to the house. He knocked on the door and, a few seconds later, it was opened by a woman in her late thirties.

Dermot introduced himself and asked if she was Mrs. Geraldine Hudson. When she confirmed it, he held out the book. "I have something which belonged to your father. It helped me to solve the case, but it is only fair that you should now have it."

Geraldine took the book and flipped through the pages. "Father always talked about completing his memoirs that he began writing while in South Africa. He wanted to publish them. I didn't know that he had started writing again or that he had almost finished it." She looked up from the book at Dermot. "He was a good man," she said tearfully, "but his foolishness is what killed him."

Dermot comforted her and then handed her his card. "I know a publisher. Contact me when you are ready and I'll help you."

Geraldine thanked him and they said goodbye.

Dermot got into his car and drove off. After a few minutes, the sky began to clear and the sun shone. He could see the white cliffs of Dover and he began to hum 'The Grand Old Duke of York' as he drove towards the hotel.

Glossary

Anglo-Indians – Refers to at least two groups of people: those with mixed Indian and British ancestry, and those people of British descent born or living in the Indian subcontinent.

'A spot of' – A small amount of something (British English, informal).

Ayah – A native maid or nursemaid employed by Europeans in India.

Bai – In Hindi means 'lady' or 'ma'am'.

Bairn – A child (Scottish, Northern English).

Batman – An officer's personal servant (in the British Armed Forces).

Biscuit – Flour-based food product. American biscuits are soft and flaky and British biscuits are drier and crunchier, like an American cookie.

Blimey – Used to express one's surprise, excitement, or alarm (British English, informal).

Boer – A member of the Dutch and Huguenot population that settled in southern Africa in the late seventeenth century.

Bohemian – A socially unconventional person, especially one who is involved in the arts.

'Box his ears' – Slap someone on the side of the head as a punishment or in anger.

'Buck him up' – To be encouraged, reinvigorated, or cheerful.

Bum – Rear end or posterior.

By Jove (Jupiter) – An exclamation used to emphasise an accompanying remark or to express surprise, approval, etc.

Chap – A boy or a man.

Char (woman and girl) – A woman employed to clean houses or offices.

Chartered Accountant (CA) – An international accounting designation granted to accounting professionals in many countries around the world, aside from the United States. In the United States, the equivalent to the CA designation is Certified Public

Accountant (CPA).

Cheeky – Impudent or irreverent, typically in an endearing or amusing way.

Cheerio – Used as an expression of good wishes on parting; goodbye (British English, informal).

'Chit of a girl' – An impudent or arrogant young woman.

'Chock full' – Filled to overflowing.

Cupboard (British) – Closet (American English).

Dawdle – Waste time; be slow; move slowly and idly.

'Didn't give a tuppence' – To not care in the slightest (about something or someone).

Dish/dishy – A sexually attractive person of either sex.

'Donkey's years' – A long, long time.

Firangi – A foreigner, especially a British or a white person (India or Pakistan).

Garibaldi biscuit – Consists of currants squashed and baked between two thin oblongs of sweet biscuit dough.

'Grease his palm' – To bribe one discreetly, as by slipping money into their palm.

Grille – A door with bars to see who is on the other side.

'Hook, line and sinker' – Used to emphasise that someone has been completely deceived or tricked.

'I haven't the foggiest idea' – To not know or understand something at all.

IRA – Irish Republican Army.

Lift (British) – Elevator (American).

'Like a house on fire' – Getting on extremely well.

Lock-in – Between WWI and 2005, British pubs had to close at 11 p.m. A lock-in is a semi-legal way of holding a private party that landlords sometimes did to extend their hours. Technically it was not entirely allowed, but was often overlooked.

Marquee – A canopy projecting over the entrance to a theatre, hotel, or other building (North American). A large tent used for social or commercial functions (British).

'Mum's the word' – To keep silent or quiet about a secret.

'My eye' – rubbish; nonsense (British). An exclamation of contradiction, astonishment, etc (American).

'My God' – An exclamation of astonishment.

Nappy – A piece of absorbent material wrapped around a baby's bottom and between its legs to absorb and retain urine and faeces; a diaper.

Nautch girl – A professional dancing girl in India.

Nookie – Sexual activity or intercourse.

Official Secrets Act – First instituted in England in 1889. It is a term used in the United Kingdom for legislation that provides for the protection of state secrets and official information, mainly related to national security.

Piddle - 'Make water' or urinate.

Poppycock – Nonsense, rubbish.

Randy – Sexually aroused or excited.

Sassenach – Saxon born, an English person (Scottish).

Saucy – A good word for a person who really likes to flirt and be suggestive.

Sepoys – An Indian soldier serving under British or other European orders.

Shabash – A term used in the Indian subcontinent to signal commendation for an achievement, similar in meaning to bravo and kudos.

'Spun us a yarn' – Tell a story/lie, especially a long and drawn-out or totally fanciful one.

Stately pile – Mansion, stately home, hall, manor, big house, manor house, country house, castle, palace.

Sundowner – An alcoholic drink taken at sunset (British English, informal).

Suttee – A widow who committed sati (a former practice in India whereby a widow threw herself onto her husband's funeral pyre).

Tart – A female who is attractive and has the air of being promiscuous, even if she isn't.

Tartan – A woollen cloth woven in one of several patterns of plaid, especially of a design associated with a particular Scottish clan.

Trunk call – A long-distance telephone call for which the caller must pay an extra amount of money (British, old-fashioned).

Tureen – A deep covered dish from which soup is served.

Veld – Open, uncultivated country or grassland in Southern Africa. It is conventionally classified by altitude into highveld, middleveld, and lowveld.

Walloping – A beating.

'What the blazes' – Used in various expressions of anger, bewilderment, or surprise as a euphemism for 'what the hell' (informal).

'What the dickens' – Means 'what the devil'; expresses irritation or shock in a question.

'Ye Gods' – Used for showing that you are very surprised or annoyed (old-fashioned English). A less offensive way of saying 'Oh my God'.

Note from the Author

Word-of-mouth is crucial for any author to succeed. If you enjoyed the book, please leave a review online—anywhere you are able. Even if it's just a sentence or two. It would make all the difference and would be very much appreciated.

Thanks!
Trevor

About the Author

Trevor D'Silva has several degrees in engineering and accounting. He has lectured in mechanical engineering and environmental science subjects at various colleges. Trevor's debut novel, *Fateful Decisions*, a historical fiction, was released in October 2017. *A Bloody Hot Summer* is his second novel and first murder mystery. An avid anglophile, Trevor loves all things British and uses his free time to expand his knowledge in history and **reading** crime, thriller, and mystery novels.

Thank you so much for reading one of our **Crime Fiction** novels.
If you enjoyed the experience, please check out our recommended
title for your next great read!

Caught in a Web by Joseph Lewis

"This important, nail-biting crime thriller about MS-13 sets the
bar very high. One of the year's best thrillers."
-BEST THRILLERS

View other Black Rose Writing titles at
www.blackrosewriting.com/books and use promo code
PRINT to receive a **20% discount** when purchasing.

Lightning Source UK Ltd.
Milton Keynes UK
UKHW011126120121
376897UK00002B/26

9 781684 333714